THE GAME PLAN

MICALEA SMELTZER

Copyright 2022 Micalea Smeltzer

Copyright 2016 Micalea Smeltzer, originally released as The Game That Breaks Us

All rights reserved. This book or any portion thereof may not be reproduced or used in any manner whatsoever without the express written permission of the publisher.

This is a work of fiction. Names, characters, businesses, places, events and incidents are either the products of the author's imagination or used in a fictitious manner. Any resemblance to actual persons, living or dead, or actual events is purely coincidental.

Cover design: Emily Wittig Designs

Formatting: Micalea Smeltzer

Editing: Ready, Set, Edit

THE GAME PLAN

TRACE & OLIVIA SERIES FAMILY TREE

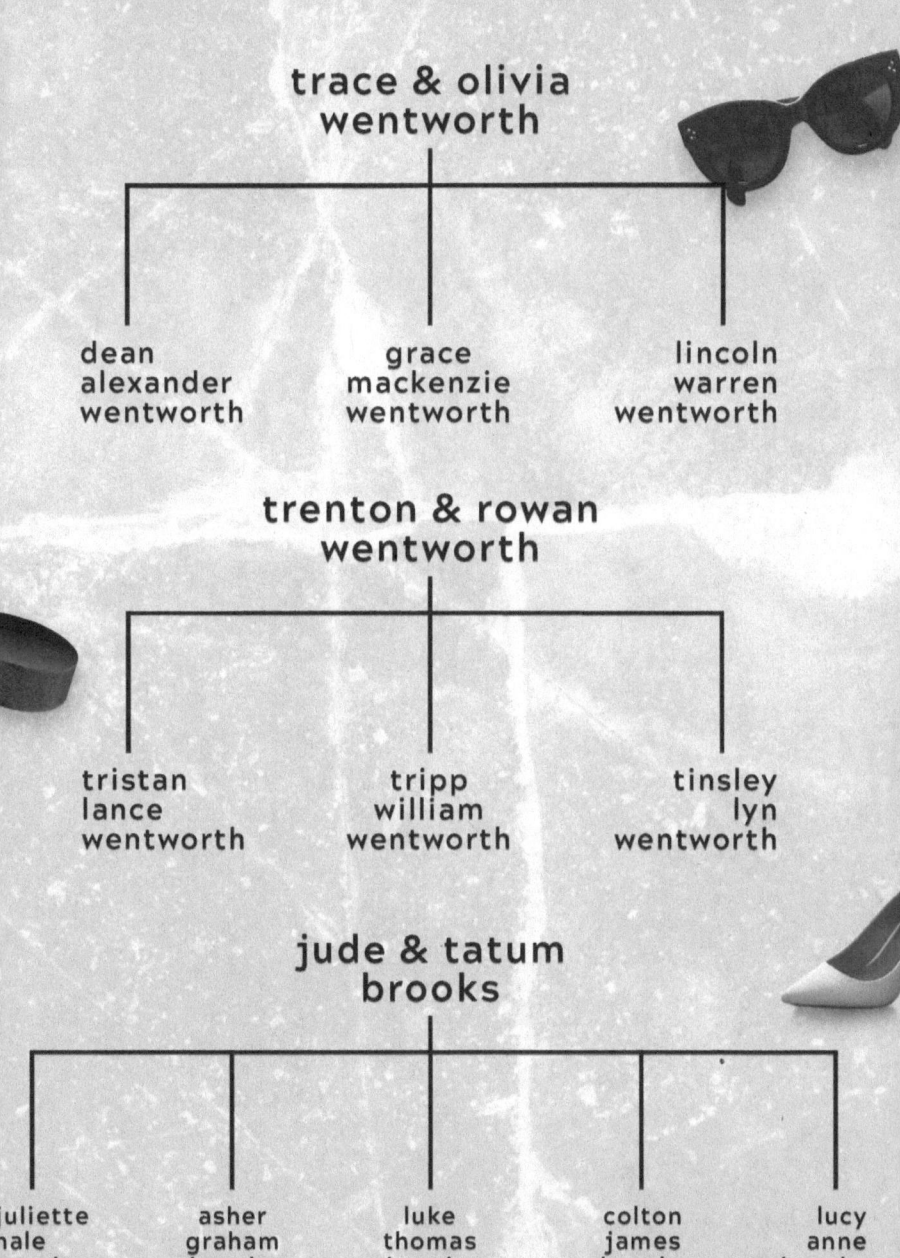

trace & olivia wentworth
- dean alexander wentworth
- grace mackenzie wentworth
- lincoln warren wentworth

trenton & rowan wentworth
- tristan lance wentworth
- tripp william wentworth
- tinsley lyn wentworth

jude & tatum brooks
- juliette hale brooks
- asher graham brooks
- luke thomas brooks
- colton james brooks
- lucy anne brooks

WILLOW CREEK FAMILY TREE PART ONE

maddox & emma wade

- willow elise wade
- mascen zane wade
- lylah rose wade

mathias & remy wade

- hope wade
- liam maxwell wade

WILLOW CREEK FAMILY TREE PART TWO

joshua & arden hayes

- mia lee hayes
- adalyn marie hayes
- noah carson hayes

ezra & sadie collins

- everett torrance collins
- everly mae collins

PROLOGUE

BENNETT

"You've got to get your act together."

I glare at my manager, wishing I could set the fucker on fire with my gaze alone. Bernard Wright might be one of the best sports managers in the business, but he's also an asshole. I've come to learn most people are.

"Tell me something I don't know."

"This—" he shoves a finger onto the front cover of some tabloid "—is unacceptable."

The photo shows me making out with some random puck bunny at a bar. The picture is nothing new. Photographers follow me just about everywhere nowadays, so they're always catching me doing something they deem *scandalous*. I call it normal. I'm aware that makes me as much of an asshole as Bernard, but in a different way.

"It was just a kiss," I say. "It's not like I fucked her right there on the bar. Give me a break. I don't even remember her name."

Bernard snaps his fingers together. "Exactly, you don't even know her name. You're not new to this business, and I know that there're plenty of other guys out there just like you, but most of them aren't in your predicament." He glances down at my casted leg. I try to pretend the cast isn't there and him drawing attention to it only sours my mood even more. "You're about five seconds away from losing your career between this injury and your personal life. Hockey should be more important than chasing tail. Figure out your priorities and clean up your act, Bennett, or I won't be able to help you." He raises his hands, signaling that he's done.

I sigh and pinch the bridge of my nose.

Hockey is my life. I can't lose that—I *won't* lose it.

"What do you propose I do then?"

He shrugs. "You figure it out, Bennett. I've cleaned up

too many of your messes, made it easy for you, and I'm not doing it anymore. You need to do what you can to get back out on the ice, and while you're at it, you need to change the media's perception of you. Think you can do that?"

I grin. "Fake it till you make it, right?"

He smiles and leans back in his plush leather chair. "Right. I have faith in you. You're a good player, so don't throw away your career."

I sigh and stand up. "Are we done here?"

"Yes." He nods and stands to shake my hand.

I leave, already knowing what I have to do to get back on track.

CHAPTER ONE

GRACE

"Fucking hell, of course they'd give me an uppity bitch for a roommate."

I pause in the doorway to my dorm. "*Excuse me?*" I gasp. I haven't set one foot into my dorm room and my roommate already appears to hate me.

The girl—Elle, according to the information packet I got—has long, wavy, dark-brown hair that looks like it hasn't ever seen a brush. Her eyes are slightly slanted, giving her an exotic look, and her top lip is slightly larger than her bottom. On someone else it might look odd, but it suits her. Freckles are sprinkled across her nose and she's dressed in a thin black tank top, black skinny jeans, and black boots.

She points to my outfit. "Who dresses like that? It must take you all day to get ready."

I look down at my black tights, light-gray skirt, pink blouse, and black heels. I look like a preppy beauty queen next to her simple outfit, which I guess is what I am, but I'm definitely *not* a bitch. My hair is curled to perfection and I know my makeup looks flawless. I spend enough time watching YouTube tutorials that I know my way around makeup brushes.

"Not really," I say, wheeling my suitcase and duffle bag into the room and over to the empty bed. "When you know what you're doing it doesn't take time."

She huffs in disbelief.

I hike my suitcase onto the bed that will be mine for the remainder of the school year.

My parents begged me to go to school near home, but I wanted to get away. Growing up the middle child, surrounded by two annoying—but awesome—brothers and an overprotective dad, I just needed to get away. I ended up picking a school in Massachusetts—Addams University sits about three hours away from Boston—which means I'm still close enough to my parents in Northern Virginia to see them for holidays, but far enough away to avoid random visits.

"I'm Elle, by the way, but I guess you knew that." She turns her head to the side, appraising me. I feel like a bug under a microscope.

"Grace." I glance at her over my shoulder and give her a smile. It doesn't seem to be appreciated.

"Not Grac*ie*?" she asks with a little smirk.

My brows narrow in irritation and I whip around. "You really think you're something, don't you?" I snap, my patience having reached its limit with her snark. I point to her all black ensemble. "You think you're some kind of rebel, but you're exactly like everyone else, whereas I—" I point to myself "—dare to be myself. I guess originality is under appreciated where you come from."

Her face remains neutral, and then little by little her lips begin to lift into a smile. She claps. "I underestimated you."

"You don't even know me."

"True." Her lips twist. "But I guess we'll be getting to know each other pretty well considering we're *roomies*." She says the word like it's dirty. She bounces on her bed, which is covered in an old quilt in colors of purples and reds. She already has a tapestry hung on the wall beside her bed, and so far, that seems to be as far as her decorations go—unless the clothes strewn across the bed and on the floor count as decorations.

She crosses her legs and flips through a magazine.

I turn my back on her and open my duffle bag. My bedspread is stuffed in there, and when I pull it out it's all wrinkled, which irks me, but I try to pretend like it doesn't because it would only give her more ammunition against me. We don't have to like each other, but it would make things easier. I don't want to have to be worried about her slipping blue hair dye into my shampoo or something.

I make my bed with the clean white sheets and spread out the teal-and-white printed comforter. I'll need to buy some throw pillows since I didn't have room to pack any and I can't stand a bare bed. My bed at home was so full of pillows you could barely see the bed itself. My older brother, Dean, used to joke that I liked so many pillows because I could get lost and never found in them.

When I finish with my bed, I start to unpack my things. Elle and I each have a tiny closet that will barely hold anything. Thankfully, we're also provided with a dresser. It's small, but it'll help with the storage problem. We have two oak desks with two rickety chairs that were provided along with a small refrigerator tucked into the corner. Our dorm room floor is in need of a rug to brighten up the place since the carpet is a drab gray color. Everything in this room is small, but at least I'm on my own for once. Well, kind of on my own since I have to share the room with *Elle*.

I get all my clothes unpacked and stuff my suitcase and duffle bag under the bed.

"I'm going shopping," I tell Elle, grabbing up my purse.

She glares at me over the top of her magazine. I don't

think she's even reading it, just using it as a shield. "Of *course* you are," she says.

I resist the urge to roll my eyes. "I need to get a few things for the room. Pillows and food and stuff." I don't know why I'm even explaining this to her. "You're welcome to come if you want." I smile, but it's forced. I'm *trying* to be nice, but she's making it damn near impossible and I haven't even been here two hours.

"No, thanks." She closes her magazine and lays it on the bed. "There's a party off campus tonight." She looks at her nails and I know she's baiting me.

I sigh. "Okay?"

"I'd invite you, but it probably wouldn't be your thing." Her eyes scale me from head to toe.

It wouldn't take an expert to figure out my clothes are expensive, but it's not something I necessarily flaunt. Yes, I came from a rich family but I wasn't spoiled. My parents made sure to raise my brothers and me with an understanding for the real world. Elle is judging me based on who she *thinks* I am, not who I *really* am, and that irks me.

"Maybe it *is* my thing," I counter, squaring my shoulders.

There's a challenging look in her amber eyes. "Then go."

I clench my fingers around my purse strap so she can't see them shake. "I told you, I'm going shopping."

"Go tomorrow," she challenges. "You have all weekend before classes to go shopping."

"I ..." I'm stuck and I see no way out. If I insist on going shopping, she'll think she's won and I'm never one to forfeit. "Fine, I'll go." I drop my purse back down on the bed.

Her eyes widen in surprise and her lips part. I've stunned her. *Good*.

"The party's not until tonight," she admits reluctantly, and I had figured as much, "so you have time to do your shopping."

I can't contain my smile as I grab my purse. "Don't leave without me," I chirp, closing the door behind me. "What a bitch," I mumble to myself out into the hall.

The hall is filled with girls; most of them shrieking in delight and excitedly talking about their summers. I envy them just slightly since it looks like I'm stuck with the devil incarnate for my roommate.

I call for a taxi as I head outside. My mom and dad wanted me to take my car to college, but I opted not to. Freedom to come and go as I liked would be nice, but this experience was all about pushing myself out of my boundaries. Riding the bus or taking a taxi was something new for me.

I hurry down the steps of my dorm and push open the door to the outside. The sun shines brightly above the bustling campus but I know it'll soon be going down. The campus buzzes with voices as people catch up with friends and say goodbye to family. There's a campus coffee shop not far from my dorm that I wanted to find, but I know if I'm to make it back in time to go to the party I can't linger.

I look around, trying to get my bearings, but it's impossible. As soon as I got here, I grabbed my information pack and headed straight into the dorm, not bothering to check things out. When I told the cab driver I went to Addams University he said he knew it well and he'd pick me up across from the fountain, only I don't know where the fountain is.

I look around blindly, panic building inside me.

I wanted to be on my own but it's only beginning to hit me how truly alone I am.

I turn to my left, where there seems to be more activity, and head that way. A normal person would probably stop and ask for directions, but I've always been a doer, and I hate asking for help even when it's necessary.

I can't believe how many people are on campus. I mean, I *knew* this was a big school, but knowing it and experiencing it are two different things. Besides, people only began arriving on campus yesterday and classes don't start until Monday so it's bound to get even more crowded.

I bumble my way around, looking every which way. I know I look like a chicken with its head cut off.

"Are you lost?"

The voice could belong to any number of people speaking to someone around me, but somehow, instinctively, I know they're speaking to me.

I turn toward the deep rumble, holding my breath.

My eyes collide with hazel ones and I look up at the massive wall—*man*—in front of me. He's tall, probably six-foot-four at least, with blondish-red hair that's shorter on the sides and slightly longer in the front. Not too long, but long enough that I could run my fingers through it if I wanted to ... which I don't want to. A white t-shirt stretches across his muscular chest and several tattoos adorn his arms. I want to look and see what they are, but I don't want to look like I'm checking him out so I don't.

"Um ... I'm looking for the fountain," I say.

He chuckles, and the sound washes over me like a summer breeze. "Which one?"

"There's more than one?" I frown. *Well, this isn't good.*

"Three, actually." He shrugs and his shirt rides up the smallest amount, showing off his smooth stomach.

"Is there a main one?" I ask.

"I guess you could say the one in the center of campus is the main one." He frowns.

"Would a taxi pick me up there?"

His brows furrow. "Uh, no. Sorry."

I sigh heavily. "The cab driver said he'd pick me up at the fountain, I assumed there was only one, but obviously I was wrong. He'll be gone by now anyway," I groan. There's no way the cabbie would've waited this long for me.

I turn to leave, not even bothering to thank the kind stranger.

"Wait," he calls. I stop and turn back around, tilting my head to the side as I regard him. "Where are you headed, maybe I can take you?"

"Um, I don't even know you."

He winces. "Right, *stranger danger*." He holds out his hand. "Bennett James—hockey player and Sour Patch addict."

I take his hand, stifling a laugh. "Grace Wentworth—aspiring stylist and chocoholic."

He lowers his hand. "Now that we thoroughly know each other, can I offer you a ride?" I eye him and he laughs. "Not *that* kind of ride. Although, maybe a different time and place." He winks. "I promise to be on my best behavior."

I bite my lip. "I appreciate the offer, but I really don't know you."

"You could get to know me on the car ride," he reasons, grinning from ear to ear. He's enjoying this, clearly.

I know the smart thing to do would be to turn around, go back to my dorm, and go shopping later, but for once, I don't want to do the smart thing.

I want to be daring and adventurous and not the stick in the mud my roommate already thinks I am—and she'd be right.

I square my shoulders and say, "Okay."

His mouth parts slightly. He didn't really expect me to say yes. "Let's go then." He turns to head back from the direction he was coming from.

"I'm not keeping you from anything, am I?"

He shakes his head. "It's not important."

"Are you sure?" I hesitate, not wanting to mess up his plans.

"Absolutely." He stuffs his hand in his pocket and pulls out his car keys.

I follow him around campus while he helpfully points out various buildings. We finally make it to the parking garage and he pushes a button to unlock his car.

"*That's* your car?" I ask when the headlights on a brand new red Camaro turn on. I know enough from my car junkie older brother that this is a top-of-the-line Camaro and doesn't run cheap. "Are you a student? Oh, God," I gasp. "Please tell me you're not a professor?"

I think I might die.

He laughs. "Neither."

I eye him with apprehension. "You're not about to drive me out to some remote location and kill me, are you?"

He laughs, keeled over in the middle like I've said the funniest thing he's ever heard. "You really don't trust me, do you?"

"Trust has to be earned," I tell him. "So earn it."

"O-o-h." He chuckles and opens the passenger door. "You're something, aren't you?"

"What's that supposed to mean?" I ask. My chest brushes his arm as I move around him to get in the car.

He pauses before closing the door. "Nothing bad. You're kind of testy, aren't you?"

"No," I defend, "but I'm not in the habit of getting in cars with guys I don't know." He smirks, just the slightest lift of his lips, and dimples pop out in his cheeks. It makes him look younger than he probably is. He doesn't say anything in response and closes the door. When he slides behind the steering wheel I ask, "So, if you're not a student or a professor, what are you?"

He shrugs. "I'm just visiting."

"Oh, do you have a sibling going here? Are you supposed to be with them right now? Oh, my God, I am so sorry. I can get out." I reach for the door, but before I can open it, he reaches across from me and holds it closed.

"No sibling," he says with a chuckle.

"Oh." I relax into the seat and he lets go.

"You're free to go if you want," he assures me. "But you're not keeping me from anyone. Promise." When I make no move to get out of the car, he asks, "Where to?"

"Is there a Target around here? I need to get some things for my room."

"Yeah, there's one about twenty minutes away." He starts the car and the engine purrs to life. "So," he says, driving around the garage toward the exit, "let's work on that trust thing."

"Huh?" I tear my gaze away from the car window.

"You said trust had to be earned, and doesn't that go along with getting to know someone?" I nod. "So I'm trying to get to know you."

He turns out of the parking lot and into traffic.

"Oh." I tuck a piece of brown hair behind my ear.

He chuckles. "Do I make you nervous?"

"No."

"Don't lie." He flashes straight, white teeth. "So you're

obviously a freshman," he says, "you want to be a stylist, and you like chocolate. What else should I know about you?"

"I have two brothers."

"In other words, they'll rough me up if I mess with you?" He glances over at me with a shit-eating grin.

I roll my eyes. "Not likely. Dean's too into his cars and girlfriend to notice and Lincoln is only in high school. What about you? Any siblings?"

"A sister. Sabrina."

"Older or younger?" I ask.

"Older."

"Ah." I smile. "So you're the spoiled youngest child."

He chuckles and flicks on the blinker, turning onto a main thoroughfare. "I guess you could say that. So where are you from, Grace?"

"Virginia," I answer. "What about you?"

"Mountains," he responds. "Nice. Born and raised right here in Massachusetts. What made you pick a school up here?"

I shrug and answer honestly. "Freedom."

He glances at me with raised brows. "That bad, huh?"

"No," I say quickly. "Not *bad*, just ... overwhelming. My dad's way overprotective. I know he means well, but it can be kind of stifling. I wanted the chance to figure out who I am."

He nods. "Seems reasonable."

"And so far, it's landed me in a car with a stranger."

He laughs, clearly amused. "Am I *still* a stranger to you?"

I look at the dashboard clock. "We've known each other approximately thirty-five minutes, so yes."

"What will it take for me to not be a stranger anymore?"

I twist my lips in thought. "A few days?"

He nods. "I'll take it."

He pulls into the Target parking lot and hops out, coming around to get my door before I can blink.

"Whoa," I say. "I guess manners aren't completely dead."

He shrugs with a crooked grin. "I try." He grabs a shopping cart from one of the return areas and wheels it over to me.

"Are you shopping too?" I ask, falling into step beside him.

"No, but aren't you going to need a cart?"

"Yes."

"Then it gives me something to do." He pushes it a bit faster and hops up onto it so he's gliding along. He nears the automatic doors and I fear he's going to crash into them. "I command you to open!" he yells, and they slide open just in time for him to roll inside. I breathe out a sigh of relief.

"You're like a big kid, aren't you?" I laugh.

"Eh, yeah, I guess so. I don't see the point in acting like a stuffy old fart. Might as well have some fun with life. You're only here once." He jumps off the cart and wheels it over to the dollar section. "Need any notepads?" he asks, picking up a handful of the kind with magnets on the back.

"No," I say, picking up some windmill type thing and flicking the ends with my finger.

"Too bad, you're getting some," he says and drops the notepads in the cart. I shake my head and move on. He pushes the cart behind me. "What are you here for? I'd say we should divide and conquer but I'm afraid of getting lost."

I look back at him and he winks. "I need pillows, lights, a corkboard, a rug—"

"Basically you need the whole store?" he cuts me off.

I sigh. "Yes."

"Okay, well, the home stuff is this way." He turns the cart down an aisle, cutting through the kid's clothes.

"How old are you?" I ask him.

"Grace—" he clucks his tongue "—don't you know you're never supposed to ask anyone their age? How scandalous of you." I eye him, and he sighs. "I'm twenty-three."

"Stop," I tell him, spotting a clearance end cap. I pick up a fluffy white pillow and drop it in the cart.

He eyes the pillow with distaste. "That looks like an animal."

I raise a brow. "Did I ask for your opinion?"

"Well, no."

"Exactly," I say, looking over the other clearance items. There are a few candles I'd love to grab, but they're a fire hazard so I have to refrain. Bennett follows behind me as I turn down the pillow aisle. I pick a few more.

"Do you really need so many?" he asks. I glare at him.

"Right." He raises his hands innocently. "You don't want my opinion. Zipping my lips."

I move on to the rug aisle and choose a plush white rug. I should probably ask Elle if she likes it before I buy it since it's our room, but since she's not here and she's too much of a bitch for me to care about her opinion, I go to put it in the cart anyway.

"Hey, let me help." Bennett jumps into action, grabbing the rug from my hands and stuffing it in the cart. There isn't much room now.

"Thanks," I say.

"No problem." He smiles.

"So," I say as we head further into the home décor, "you like sour patch kids. What else should I know about you?"

He grins. "My favorite color is red."

"The color of blood?" I laugh.

"No," he says with a wicked grin. "The color of love."

I laugh even harder. "Oh, you're good. But your favorite color isn't really anything earth-shattering. Give me the good stuff."

He chuckles and jumps up on the cart again, gliding on. "Like what, I lost my virginity at fourteen to an older woman and now I'm damaged goods?" I stop in my tracks and he laughs. "I'm *kidding*, Grace, but the look on your face is priceless."

I try to school my face into normalcy. "What look?" I mutter.

He simply grins and kicks off again like he's on a skateboard. "There's not much to tell, Grace."

I look at him closely. "You know that only makes me think there's a lot to tell."

He points. "Lights."

I head toward them but quickly do an about face. "Nice try," I say, crossing my arms over my chest. "You're avoiding."

He grins. "Maybe so."

"Come on," I plead. "Give me something."

"You first," he challenges.

"I've never done something like this," I admit. "Go off with a stranger, but, I kind of like it. Doing the wrong thing."

"I've done it a lot. The wrong thing, I mean," he says, his hazel eyes growing dark. "I'm trying to be a better person, though."

"And what is this?" I ask. "Us, right here, right now? Good or bad?"

He looks torn. "Bad," he finally admits.

"I'm keeping you from something, aren't I?" I ask forlornly.

He looks away. "Yes, but it can wait."

I sigh. "I don't want you to get in trouble on my behalf."

His eyes snap back to me, a fire shining in them. "I'm a big boy, don't worry about me."

"Bennett—"

"Hey," he cuts me off. "We're only killing more time

standing here talking about it. Let's get what you need and get back." He pinches the bridge of his nose. "Shit, I didn't mean for that to sound like that."

"Like you're an asshole?"

He winces. "Yeah. I mean, I guess I am. No, I *know* I am, but I didn't mean to snap at you like that."

"I don't think you're an asshole," I say softly. "An asshole wouldn't have bailed on whatever it was you needed to do to help me out."

He cringes. "I didn't have entirely selfless motivations."

"Oh, really?" I raise a brow.

"I thought you were hot." He grins. "Who wouldn't help out a hot damsel in distress?"

I laugh. "Well, thank you. No matter your motivation, thank you."

He laughs and tilts his head. "That wasn't the reaction I was expecting."

"What can I say?" I turn away from him and look back over my shoulder. "I'm full of surprises."

We head to the grocery section next, and I grab a few random items, like water and cereal bars.

"What's your favorite chocolate?" Bennett asks, flicking his fingers toward the candy aisle.

"Not any of those. I prefer my chocolate fix in the form of a cupcake. Are you going to make me some?" I joke.

He rubs his jaw. "Ah, probably not."

"I was kidding." I pick up a box of oatmeal and put it in the already overflowing cart.

He picks up the box and looks it over. "You actually *eat* this stuff?" He looks horrified.

I laugh and snatch the box from his hands. "*Yes*. Some people like it."

"Not me." He makes a face and pushes the cart forward. "This is more my speed." He grabs a box of Captain Crunch and shows me.

"A kid's cereal?"

He winks. "This is the good stuff." He puts it back on the shelf.

I look over everything I have in the cart. "I think I'm done here."

"Anywhere else?" He points to the various aisles surrounding us.

"Nope, I got it all."

Side by side, we head to the checkout. Bennett chooses the least busy checkout lane, which still has two people in front of us.

The man in front of us finishes putting his items on the conveyer belt and glances back. His dark brows furrow and he stares at Bennett. "Do I know you?" he asks.

I look between the man and Bennett. The man has to be in his fifties, so there's no way he's someone Bennett went to school with.

Bennett shrugs. "No, sorry. You must be mistaken." He seems unperturbed by the man's staring, but there's something in his eyes—a wariness that bothers me.

"Yeah, I guess so. Sorry." The man turns back around when the cashier begins to scan his items.

I don't ask Bennett about the encounter. We've only known each other two hours tops, so I don't feel like he owes me an explanation. Besides, after this, I doubt I'll see him again.

Bennett begins unloading my items onto the conveyer belt, and while his back is turned I grab a pack of Sour Patch Kids from the checkout candy rack and toss it onto the pile he has formed.

He laughs and turns to look at me. "For me?" He points at himself.

I smile. "Who else would they be for? *I'm* certainly not going to eat them."

I can tell the gesture pleases him. It's a small thing, sure, but the small things usually mean the most to someone. It's the little things that show you pay attention.

The cashier begins to scan and bag my items and Bennett immediately grabs them up, setting them in the cart.

"Leave those out," I tell the cashier, pointing at the Sour Patch Kids. She nods and scans those last and hands them to me. "Thanks," I say, and swipe my credit card. She hands me the receipt, and I stuff it in the bottomless pit that I call my purse.

I follow Bennett out to his car where he stuffs the rug in the back. It's a tight fit in his small car, but he makes it work. I hand him the bags and he fits them in beside the rug.

He closes the trunk and goes to return the cart while I get in the car.

When he gets inside, I hand him the Sour Patch Kids bag. His eyes immediately light up like a little kid and he rips the bag open, popping one in his mouth. "Here, have one." He holds the bag out to me.

I shake my head. "Sour's not my thing."

He shakes it. "Come on, just one? For me?" He literally pouts—I'm talking bottom lip curled under and puppy dog eyes, the whole shebang. So, of course, I cave.

"Fine." I grab one and bite into it. Immediately, my lips pucker and I spit it out, the red candy landing on the floor of his car in a blob. I glance over at him sheepishly. "Sorry."

He looks at me with a straight face, and I expect him to yell at me for spitting out a gob of gummy on his floor, but instead, he bursts into uncontrollable laughter. His laughter is contagious, and I can't help but join him. I pick up the red gummy and wrap it in a tissue from my purse.

"You weren't kidding about not liking sour things." He shakes his head, driving back toward campus.

I can still taste it on my tongue, the tangy flavor sticking to my taste buds. I wish I had some water.

"Here," Bennett says, almost as if he's read my thoughts, and hands me a half-empty water bottle. "I promise I don't have anything contagious."

I shake my head and take the bottle from him. I untwist

the cap and lift it to my lips. The water is slightly warm from sitting in the car, but it'll do. The tart flavor from the Sour Patch Kid finally leaves my tongue and I put the cap back on the bottle.

"Thank you so much for doing this."

He glances at me with a raised brow. "For making you spit out a Sour Patch Kid in my car?"

I laugh and shake my head. "No, for bringing me here to get my things. I'm sorry you had to ditch your plans."

He waves a hand dismissively. "It's okay." Something in his tone worries me, though, like maybe it's *not* okay.

We arrive back at campus and he parks in the garage in the same spot. I grab the bags from the back and he carries the rug. We walk side-by-side back to my dorm—at least I know where *that* is.

When the building approaches, I say, "I can get that," and try to take the rug from him.

"I've got it," he says, swiveling out of my way. The end of the rug nearly whacks my legs.

"Are you sure?" I ask. "I don't want to hold you up any longer."

"It's fine, Grace."

I shrug and start up the steps. I pull out my ID card from my purse and swipe it to so we can get inside. My dorm is on the third level, but thankfully, there's an elevator. The doors ding open and we step inside. I hate the awkward silence that's fallen between us. I've never been good at this —talking to guys I like and knowing the right thing to say. I wish I was one of those girls that always knew the right thing to say, or was confident enough in her sexuality to put herself out there, but that's just not me.

The doors slide open and show us an empty hallway. "It's this way," I say and he picks up the rug again. I lead him to my dorm room and he sets the rug down beside the door. "Well," I begin, shuffling my feet as my awkwardness grows even more profound, "I guess this is goodbye." I should probably ask for his number, but I don't want to seem desperate. Besides, he was only doing me a favor and probably doesn't want to see me beyond this.

He shrugs and steps back. "I don't think this is goodbye, Grace. Something tells me I'll see you again." He gives me a closed-mouth smile, ducks his head, and leaves.

I watch him get into the elevator and just before the doors close, he winks.

CHAPTER TWO

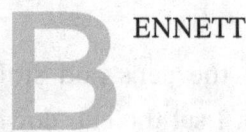ENNETT

"You're late."

I swallow thickly. I have no good excuse for being late, and even if I did, Coach Harrison wouldn't want to hear it. He doesn't like to hear "I'm sorrys", either.

"I'm here now," I say instead.

His shrewd green eyes narrow. They see everything and know too much.

"You smell like perfume." His voice is gruff and his finger taps restlessly against his desk—the same desk he had when I went to school here. It's old and worn, with scrapes and chunks of wood missing.

"I wasn't with a woman," I defend. "I mean, I was." I shrug, wincing. "But not like that."

"Dammit, Bennett." He slaps his hand against his desk so hard that his pen cup bounces and rolls to the floor. He glares at the cup and pens now littering the floor and then at me. "Pick them up, asshole," he says.

I sigh and bend down to pick them up. My hurt leg and knee protests with the movement and I wince. Coach notices but doesn't comment. The cast I've worn for *months* only came off a week ago and my leg is still stiff. It's not used to the freedom of mobility which is a damn shame considering the game I play. Getting out on the ice again is going to be brutal.

I make quick work of picking up the pens and stuff them back in the tin cup with a clatter. I set the cup down on his desk with a little more force than necessary and his lips lift just the slightest bit.

Coach Harrison is a hardass. It's why I've always liked him and why he's the right guy for this job—the job of getting me back to my team. Sure, my team has plenty of people who *could* help me, but they don't want to. All those assholes want is to see me fail. I'm determined to prove them wrong.

I called up Coach about a month ago, and after some persuasion on my part, he agreed to train me in his spare time—even going so far as to let me work with the university team. I've seen the guys on the team play and they're good—yeah, it's not the same as my NHL team, but I was one of these guys only a few years ago, so chances are, at least one of them will end up playing professionally. I know this is what I need to get back to my team, to go back to my roots. I've lost myself along the way, and it fucking sucks. I've always been cocky, according to everyone I know, but according to my manager, my head's gotten even more inflated. He's right, and I fucking hate that he's right. I needed a major reality check, and I hate that it came in the form of an injury—a near career-ending one at that.

Coach leans back in his chair, sizing me up. I have no idea what's going on in his head—his stoic expression sure doesn't give anything away. Finally, he sighs, his leather chair creaking when he adjusts his weight.

"You're not ready to get back on the ice," he says. "Hit the gym." He begins gathering his things.

"That's all you have to say?"

He pauses what he's doing and looks up at me with an expression like I'm the dumbest person he's ever encountered. "I saw that look on your face when you bent down. I'm not sending you out on the ice like that. Go do some fucking yoga and loosen up that leg."

"Yoga? Seriously?"

"I'm always serious," he says, standing and slinging his bag onto his shoulder. "I won't put you on the ice until you're ready. The last thing you need is another injury."

His words hit home, and my head falls in dejection. "Yeah, I understand, Coach."

He nods and slaps my arm as I pass. "See you tomorrow, Bennett."

"Mhm, thanks." I sigh heavily and press my fingers to my eyes, letting out a groan.

This is going to be harder than I thought.

CHAPTER THREE

GRACE

"You're not wearing that to the party, are you?" Elle crosses her thin arms over her chest and glares at me. Is it sad that in the short time I've been here I've already grown used to her glare?

I look down at my sequined skirt and white blousy top. "What's wrong with this?"

She rolls her eyes. "Everything." She taps a finger to her lips. "We're about the same size …" she muses. "Hang on."

She rifles through her drawers, making an even bigger mess of her already messy side of the dorm room. It makes me cringe. I like order.

"Here." She throws a pair of black jeans at me. I catch them and hold them out so I can look them over. The leg and knee area is ripped to shreds. She tosses something else at me and it covers my face. She snickers as I pull it off. It's a top that leaves nothing to the imagination. "Change," she demands. "We need to go before all the good beer is gone."

"Is there such a thing as good beer at a party like this?" I grumble, changing out of my clothes. She doesn't answer me, but I didn't expect her to. Her clothes are the slightest bit too short for my tall, thin frame, but it's not noticeable enough to be an issue. "How's this?" I turn around so she can appraise me. "Does this get your stamp of approval?"

"Almost." She steps forward and doesn't wait for permission before ruffling my hair. "That's better."

I grab my cellphone and some cash, stuffing both in my pocket, before following Elle out of the dorm.

The sky is dark, only a few stars and no moon, but the night is lit with the antique-looking lamps that dot campus.

"Should we call a cab?" I ask Elle.

"No," she snorts. "Cabs cost money and we're struggling college students." I almost open my mouth and tell her that

I have the money, but I quickly realize that would only make her hate me more. "Besides, the party's only a few blocks from campus."

"How do you even know about this?" I ask, shivering from the cool air. Goosebumps dot my flesh, and I wish I'd brought a jacket.

"I heard some guy talking about it and asked about it, then he invited me." She shrugs.

"Great."

The party turns out to be more than a few blocks away, and by the time we get there my feet are killing me, but there's no way I'm taking my shoes off and risking losing them—not to mention the hygiene hazard.

Beauty is pain, I remind myself.

Cars are parked all along the street and several houses are lit up so I assume they're occupied by people from the university. It would also explain why the cops haven't been called because of a noise complaint. The music is so loud that the ground beneath my feet vibrates.

Elle turns to me, and with the first genuine smile I've seen from her, asks, "Are you ready for this?"

"No," I answer honestly.

"Come on." She grabs my hand and pulls me inside. The front door of the house is open, inviting in anyone off the street.

The noise level only increases as we go inside and the place is packed with bodies. We have to force our way through to get anywhere. Someone elbows me in the side and my hand slips from Elle's as my breath leaves me. I try to push my way through on my own but I can't get through. Elle is gone and I'm on my own.

I turn and head the other way.

I immediately hate this. I hate the way people stare at me. I hate the smell of sweat and beer. I hate the too-loud music. I hate it all. I should've just stayed behind at the dorm and not given in to Elle.

I move through the foyer and finally end up in a family room. There's a large sectional couch covered in bodies. People talk, dance, and there's a couple on the couch that looks like they're ten seconds away from having sex right there in front of everyone. I stare, horrified, as the girl puts her hand down the guy's pants. Her shirt is off, lost somewhere in the room, and he sucks on her breasts.

I'm officially disgusted.

I run from the room, pushing my way past even more bodies. I end up in the kitchen and nearly slip on beer in my haste to find an exit.

A hand latches onto my arm, and I'm yanked into a hard body. "Hey, are you okay?" the male voice attached to the body asks.

I look up into warm brown eyes. Dark-brown hair tumbles over his forehead, and when he smiles, he has dimples.

"Yeah," I say, a little breathless. "Slipped on some beer."

"I noticed." He smiles again, and it seems like he's trying not to laugh at me. He lets go of me slowly and steps back as far as he can go since there's a kitchen counter behind him.

"Thanks for saving me." I start to leave.

"What's your name?" he calls.

I stop and turn back. "Grace."

"I'm Ryland." He smiles. He has an easy, relaxed smile. "Are you new here?"

"Freshman," I admit.

He nods. "I thought you must be since I've never seen you."

Since Ryland seems nice enough, I ask, "Which way to the outside?"

He steps away from the counter. "Follow me."

He pushes his way through the people crowding the kitchen—it seems to be the most packed room in the house, probably has something to do with the beer—and finally, we come to a door. He opens it, and cold air rushes inside. I run outside gratefully, plopping my butt on the last cement step. It's cracked with one lone dandelion growing up through it. Ryland sits down beside me, dangling his beer bottle between his fingers.

"Thanks for getting me out here," I tell him. "It was stifling in there."

"I know what you mean. One of my roommates is the one throwing the party. I wish he would've asked us first, but that's Trevor. He always does what he wants." Ryland shrugs and takes a swig of beer.

"My roommate is the one that dragged me here," I grumble.

"Ah." He nods. "Roommates are the worst."

"Tell me about it." I sigh. "It hasn't even been a whole day and she already hates my guts."

He laughs and stretches his legs out. The soles of his boots dig into the loose dirt. "I'm sorry."

I shrug. "That's life. I think that whole compatibility form they made me fill out when I requested my dorm is total bullshit. We're total opposites."

He drinks his beer. "I promise college isn't all bad."

"No, it's not," I agree, thinking of Bennett. "So, are you a senior?"

"Junior." He shrugs, leaning back with his elbows on the stair behind him.

"So you can give me all the details, right?" I joke. "Where to eat, what professors are a nightmare, who has the best coffee?"

His laughter echoes in the night. "Yeah, definitely. Maybe I could show you around campus tomorrow? This place is huge. I got lost like fifteen times my first day—went into the wrong class too, and sat through half the lecture before I realized I didn't belong in there, by that point, I was too scared to get up and leave."

"What?" I gasp. "No."

He nods. "Oh, yeah. It was so embarrassing. Luckily, I'm the only one who knew about it ... until now." He tips his beer at me. The action seems to make him realize I don't have one. "Do you want me to grab you a beer?" He starts to get up before I even answer him.

I shake my head. "No, thanks."

"Are you sure?" He starts to sit back down.

"Positive." I tuck my hair behind my ear. "And I'd be so grateful if you could show me around. I already got lost today and there's hardly anyone on campus. I don't know what I'm going to do on Monday if I don't know my way."

"I'll take care of you," he says with another one of those easy smiles.

Something about Ryland puts me at ease. I feel like I can trust him.

"What do you study?" I ask him.

"Sports medicine."

My eyes widen. "Impressive."

He grins. "What about you?"

"I want to be a stylist," I say. "So I'm studying business and marketing and taking a few fashion design courses."

He nods. "Can't say I've ever met anyone who wants to be a stylist."

"I like to be different." I stand and dust off my jeans—*Elle's* jeans. "I'm heading back in," I say.

Ryland follows me, and we push our way through the bodies again. The amount of people here is a bit ridiculous.

"Follow me," Ryland yells to be heard above the music. We end up in an empty room that's most likely meant to be the dining room. "You wanna dance?"

I don't, not really, but I find myself nodding yes anyway. He's nice, and frankly, I don't want to be left on my own.

Some super-fast electronic song plays, and I move my hips to the beat as best I can. Most people just sway or jump up and down, but that's not my style. Ryland dances with me, mimicking my moves. Soon people are staring at us as we dance and I find myself smiling. This isn't actually half bad. I end up wrapping my arms around Ryland's neck and he grasps my hips. We move together, speaking the same language with our bodies. I smile up at him, sweat dotting my skin, and he grins down, flicking his hair from his eyes.

The music changes and we keep dancing. We dance through at least five songs before I have to take a break and get some water.

Ryland drags me back through the house to the kitchen and gets himself and me a water. I drink it greedily, emptying the plastic bottle in seconds.

"That was fun," I yell above the din in the room so he can hear.

"Huh?" He bends down so my mouth is near his ear.

"That was fun," I say again.

"Oh, yeah." He nods and smiles before drinking more water. "Fun."

I glance at my watch, and I'm shocked to realize nearly two hours have passed and I haven't seen Elle.

I motion for him to bend down again. "I need to go find my roommate."

"What does she look like?" he asks.

"Long, dark hair, slanted eyes, always has a mean look on her face," I describe.

He laughs. "You described almost every girl I know. Besides you, of course." He winks.

I smile. "I seriously need to find her, though. We should head back to our dorm."

"Sure." He nods. "I understand. I'll help you look."

I push my way through the crowd again, searching every face I see for Elle. Ryland taps my shoulder and points that he's going the other way. I head down a narrow darkened hall where the line for the bathroom is. She's not there. Disgusted, I turn back the way I came. There's an upstairs, and something tells me I'm going to have to search there. *Yippee*. Based on the scene on the couch earlier I'm not thrilled at the possibilities of what lies upstairs.

As I go up the stairs, I use the vantage point to look down into the family room, but no one that I see is Elle.

I reach the top of the stairs and immediately spot her.

"Let me go," she says to the guy who has her pinned to the wall. His knee is in-between her legs, and he holds his hands firmly on her hips.

"Come on, baby," he says, lowering his head to her ear. Whatever he says I can't hear but it pisses off Elle.

"Fuck you," she snaps.

He leers at her. "That's exactly what I want. Fuck. Me. I want you to ride this cock so hard—"

I've heard enough. I tear off my pointed heeled shoes and run down the hall. "What the fuck?" the guy spits when he glances over and sees me running toward him. Before he can blink, I smack the pointed end of my heel against his face with a satisfying thump. He stumbles back, clutching his face, and I see a trickle of blood run down his cheek. "Bitch!" he screams, grabbing onto my arm and yanking me back. I stumble and fall into his chest. His fingers bruise my skin.

"Grace!" Elle cries, concern leaching into her voice as she blindly reaches for me.

"Must be my lucky night," the guy mocks, his breath reeking of booze. "A two for one deal."

"Let. Her. Go."

My eyes dart toward the stairwell to see Ryland standing there now, fists clenched at his sides. The muscle in his jaw ticked.

"You want in on the action?" the guy holding me asks. "I'm not really into sharing, but you can have them when I'm done."

"I said, let her go." Ryland stalks forward the smallest bit more.

"Or what?"

"Or this." Ryland runs forward in a crouched position, taking out the guy at the knees—they both fall to the ground and I am propelled forward into Elle. She holds onto me and keeps me from falling into the guys. Ryland and the guy throw punch after punch at each other. Ryland finally gains the upper-hand and ends up on top of the guy. He lands a solid punch to his face, and when the guy no longer hits back, he holds him by the collar of his shirt.

"You *never* treat a woman like that. You're the reason all men get a bad rep." He lets go of the guy and he falls back like a useless lump on the ground. Ryland stands up and wipes his bloodied knuckles on his shirt. "Are you okay?" he asks us.

"I am," I answer. "Elle?"

She shakes, and it's only then that I realize she's crying. "He-he ... I don't know what he might've done if you hadn't shown up," she tells him. "And then you." She turns her gaze to me. "I can't believe you defended me after what a bitch I was to you."

"Us girls have to stick together," I tell her.

She bites her lip and surprises me by saying, "I'm sorry. You're not so bad."

"Hey," Ryland says, interrupting us. "Why don't I drive you guys back to your dorm? I don't want you walking out there alone."

I look to Elle for her opinion. She nods.

"Thanks," I tell Ryland. "We'd appreciate it."

I wrap my arms around Elle and we start down the steps together. She's shaken after what just happened; I am too, but not as much as she is and I want her to know I'm here. I'm scared to think about what would've happened if I got there only a minute later.

Ryland leads us out to his car—a beat-up Toyota—and I help Elle into the back. Between her encounter with the guy and the alcohol in her system, her legs are barely holding her up. There's no way we could've walked back to campus. I would've had to call a cab.

I slide into the passenger seat, and Ryland starts the car. I shiver and he turns the heat on. I glance back at Elle. I don't like the glazed look in her eyes, and I'm worried something was slipped in her drink.

"Are you okay?" I ask her, worry leaking into my tone.

She nods woodenly, staring out the window as Ryland pulls away from the curb.

I don't believe her. *How could she be okay?* Anyone would be shaken up after something like that.

Heats blasts out of the vents, and I welcome it. It's late, nearly two in the morning, and all I want to do is go to sleep. I lean my head back and stare out the window at the passing houses. The houses soon give way to businesses and then we're back at campus.

I tell Ryland the best place to drop us off and I hop out, going around to get Elle who's passed out in the back now. I manage to get her awake enough that she gets out of the car and can rest against me.

"Thanks for this," I tell Ryland.

"What's your number?" he asks. He quickly adds, "So we can meet up and I can give you that tour tomorrow." He smiles shyly.

I rattle off my phone number, and he enters it into his phone. "I'll text you," he says.

I nod and lift my hand in goodbye.

Elle and I make our way back to the dorm. I have to basically drag her up the steps and into the building.

I finally get her inside our room and she collapses on her bed.

I do the same. I'm too tired to change, and for once, I'll have to commit the sin of sleeping in my makeup.

Before I fall asleep, I hear Elle whisper, "Welcome to college."

CHAPTER FOUR

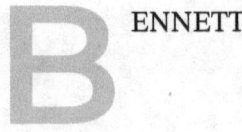ENNETT

MY FEET THUMP AGAINST THE GROUND AS I RUN.

I run hard, and I run fast.

I shouldn't. I *know* I shouldn't. The last thing I need to do is blow out my already compromised knee, but I have to run. It's the only thing that can clear my head.

My head's a mess lately. Between the injury and the negative media attention, my life has gone to shit. I had it all, and now I have nothing but grains of sand running through my fingers.

Thump.

Thump.

Thump.

I made matters worse by helping out Grace yesterday.

Fuck. *Grace.* Her looks were what first caught my eye, but it turns out I actually liked her. Spending the afternoon with her had been nice. I'd felt like the old me, the me before hockey and fame went to my head and ruined every-fucking-thing. I wasn't going to let it ruin things anymore. I could get my shit together, prove to the world that I was more than a playboy, that hockey really was my life—because it *was*. It was everything. Without hockey, I had nothing. I'd been playing basically since I could walk. My dad had played too—not professionally, but the sport had been everything to him and he'd wanted to share it with me. So, yeah, maybe he'd pushed me into it, but this was what I wanted to. The last year and a half or so I'd forgotten that, and let the money, the parties, the *lifestyle* get to me. With beautiful women throwing themselves at you, it was impossible not to indulge in the puck bunnies. Fuck, even some of the married guys were known to do it, so why was I targeted by the media so fucking much? I was pretty much always followed by the fuckers, and they rarely had anything good to say about me. It was like someone had it out for me.

Thump.

Thump.

Thump.

I needed to get back out on the ice. I needed to start training again.

But I knew Coach Harrison wasn't going to let me do that. He was going to stick to his word and wait until my leg had loosened up—so I'd make sure it got there as soon as possible.

Thump.

Thump.

Thump.

The sun began to rise above the tall gothic style buildings that dotted campus. Even I had to admit that Addams University was pretty damn nice. It was a beautiful location and only thirty minutes from where I grew up.

Speaking of, my mom would be wondering where I was. I promised to meet her and my dad for breakfast at a little diner halfway between campus and home. I turned back around and jogged toward the dorms—that was part of the condition Coach had for working with me; I had to stay in a dorm. My apartment in Boston was only two hours away, and I would've gladly made the drive every day, but he wouldn't have it. He said something about, "That shiny apartment of yours will only inflate your already inflated head, Bennett. It's time to come back down to Earth."

So here I was, back on campus, living in the fucking dorms.

I'd say it was the fucking Circle of Life, but I'm pretty sure that's not how that works.

Thump.

Thump.

Thump.

The dorm is in sight so I slow to a walk. With the sun only beginning to rise, the campus is dead. I'm the only one crazy enough to be up at this time. Once upon a time, I would've never even been to bed yet.

I lift my formerly-injured leg onto the stairs and use them to stretch the stiff muscle.

Playing right wing, I was constantly getting hit and doing the hitting. Hockey is a fucking aggressive sport. My injury, though, hadn't happened on the fucking ice. Oh, no, this idiot fell down a mountain because I was trying to save my fucking beer. I'm never drinking again.

I stand with my hands on my hips, breathing in and out deeply trying to catch my breath.

I like this time of morning.

The peace.

It is one of the only times I ever feel that wholly calm feeling. I know all too soon campus will be packed and soon word would spread that I am here. There will be the ones who revere me and the ones who hate me. I'm not ready for all the attention. The questions. The speculation as to why I am here. The only people who know I am on campus at this moment are the dean, Coach, and Grace—and she obviously doesn't know who I am. Most of the freshman arriving yesterday haven't noticed me, either, since they are too busy finding their way around campus. That will all be a different story soon.

I finish stretching and head inside the building.

When I attended school here, I'd had a shared dorm, but this time, Coach had mercy on me and made sure I got a single since I wasn't actually a student. The room is small, barely enough room to turn around in. It's definitely nothing like my apartment in Boston. I swing the door open to my room and inhale the stale air. It smells like disinfectant.

My tennis shoes squeak on the linoleum floor and I take a seat on the lumpy mattress. I kick off my shoes and flop back on the bed. I know I need to get in the shower. My mom will be calling if I'm late for our eight o' clock breakfast, and the last thing I want is to upset her—especially with all the shit I've put her through.

I rub my hands over my face. I have to make things better. Not just with my mom, but with everyone. I have to be the person everyone expects me to be.

I have to become respectable and not the laughing stock of the NHL.

Fuck. My. Life.

I grab my clothes from the dresser and smell them—yeah, they're clean—and head into the small-attached bathroom. It's so small that it makes my room look like a fucking mansion.

The water in the shower is either scalding or too cold, with no in-between, and I seem to have no way to control it. It's Russian roulette as to what I'll get.

I step inside and am pelted with shards of ice.

I shower as quickly as I can and get out, drying off my hair and getting dressed before I catch frostbite.

I check my phone, and sure enough, there's a missed call from my mom. She worries about me more than she should—scratch that, I've given her every reason in the world to worry about me.

I stuff my phone in my pocket. I'll call her back once I'm in the car. I grab my wallet and check the room to make sure I'm not forgetting anything and spot my gym bag. Yeah, I'll need that. As soon as I get back to campus, I'm hitting the gym.

I head out of my room, keeping my head low in the off chance that there's someone in the hall. I doubt anyone is in this building but me. It usually only houses upperclassmen, and they probably won't arrive until Sunday.

It takes me ten minutes to get from the dorm to the garage where I park my car. My mom's going to be standing on her head by the time I call her back.

I start my car and my phone hooks up to the Bluetooth.

"Call Mom," I say.

"Calling Mona."

"No. Call *Mom*," I yell at the stupid piece of shit.

"Calling Papa John's."

"Why the fuck is Papa John's in my phone?" I mutter as it starts ringing. "Shit," I curse and quickly end the call. I end up dialing my mom myself.

"Hello? Bennett? Where are you?"

"I'm on my way, Mom," I tell her, speeding down the highway.

"Don't speed."

I eye my speedometer and back it off. "I'm not."

"Don't you know you can't lie to your mother, Bennett?"

I rub the back of my hand. "Yeah, I know."

She laughs on the end. "We'll see you soon. Sabrina's coming too."

"Great," I say, sarcasm leaking into my tone.

"Be nice," she warns.

"I'm always nice."

"Mmhmm," she hums. "We'll see you soon."

I love my sister, don't get me wrong, but sometimes she can be a judgmental thorn in my side and with the shit storm that's my life right now I don't need to hear it from her too. Right now, what I need is my family on my side.

There's barely any traffic since it's so early, and a Saturday at that, so I make it to the diner only two minutes late.

I head inside and back to the booth that my mom always chooses. I spot her and my dad on one side and she waves, bouncing in her seat. She's always so happy to see me, and it makes me feel like an ass for not visiting more when I live so close.

"Where's Bina?" I ask, sliding in the booth.

When I was little, I couldn't say Sabrina to save myself and called her Bina. The name has stuck through the years. She says she hates it, but I know she secretly loves it.

"She's coming," my mom says, picking up her menu.

I don't know why she even bothers looking at the thing; she always ends up getting the same breakfast every time. The Denver Omelet with hash browns on the side. If my mom's anything, it's predictable.

"Well, if it isn't my favorite family," the waitress, Jolene, says cheerily. She's older, probably in her sixties, and has been working here since I was a little boy. She always waits on us when we come here and knows our order by heart. "The usual?"

"You know it." I slide my menu over to the edge of the table, and she picks it up.

My mom and dad hand over their menus as well when the bell above the door chimes.

"I'm here!" Sabrina waves enthusiastically, pushing her sunglasses up into her hair. Sabrina and I look a lot alike, although her hair has more blonde while mine has just a bit more red. We both have freckles covering our arms and noses and the same hazel eyes. There is no mistaking us as siblings, that's for sure.

"Bina!" I call, throwing my arms out.

She rolls her eyes and I laugh. "Hey, *Bennie*," she retorts.

I smirk as she takes the empty seat beside me in the booth. "Still excellent with the comebacks, I see."

"Stop it, you two," my mom scolds.

"Hey, Jo, you know what I want, right?" Sabrina calls over.

Jolene nods. "I've got your orders memorized." She winks and comes over with a tray of drinks. Like a little boy, I grin when I see the root beer float. She sets the glasses down and leaves us alone.

I take a sip of my drink. *Ah, that's good.*

Sabrina turns back into the booth and glances at me. "So, some magazine is saying they have a picture of your dick."

I spit out my drink all over the table and my mom and dad.

I glance over at them sheepishly. "Sorry."

My dad wipes the droplets from his face, his expression stoic. He doesn't say much anymore. He had a stroke a few years ago and hasn't been able to talk right since.

My mom dabs at her purple shirt with a napkin, wiping away the moisture. "Oh, Bennett," she groans.

I turn to my sister. "Where the fuck did you hear that?"

She shrugs. "One of my friends texted me about it last night. I think she thought *I* had them, which is so wrong on so many levels." She gags. "Please tell me you weren't dumb enough to take a dick pic and send it to someone?" I look away. "*Bennett!*" she cries and slaps the back of my head.

"Ow!" I grab my head and glare at her. "I could've done without that, thankyouverymuch," I slur.

My mom pinches the bridge of her nose. "The last thing you need is another scandal."

I roll my eyes. I love how no one will refer to the *first* scandal.

"I'm sure nothing will come of it," I reason. "Plus, I'm not the first athlete to send a dick pic." I glare at my sister. "And I'm certainly not the only guy to do it."

She rolls her eyes and plays with the paper of her straw. "I don't know why you guys think we want to see your dick so bad anyway. Trust me, we don't." She lifts her gaze to me. "Do you not care about anything other than sex?"

I bristle. "Hockey is the most important thing to me. Period."

"Then prove it," she challenges. "Because so far, all you've done is prove to me and everyone else that it's *not*. You're going to end up kicked off the team." Her voice softens at the end and she bites her lip. There are tears in her eyes. Bina is truly worried about me.

"Don't worry about me," I tell her.

She glares at me. "Shut the fuck up. You're my little brother, of course I'm going to worry about you."

"Guys," my mom intervenes, "I wanted us to have a nice family breakfast, can we please let this go?"

"Already dropped." Sabrina raises her hand in surrender.

"Ditto," I agree.

"How's Coach Harrison?" my mom asks, changing the subject.

I shrug. "Same old Coach, riding my ass."

"It's what you need," Sabrina and my mom say simultaneously and then laugh.

I sigh. "I know. He's good. Without him, I probably wouldn't have made it to the pro level."

My dad grunts, and I know it's his way of disagreeing with my statement.

My mom shakes her eyes. "I'm sure Coach Harrison helped sculpt you into the amazing player that you are, but you underestimate your raw talent."

I slurp at my root beer. "He won't let me out on the ice," I grumble.

I need to be out there. To have my skates glide against the ice and feel the hockey stick in my hands as I slap it against the puck.

"He must have a good reason for keeping you off the ice," my mom reasons.

"He says my leg isn't ready," I mumble, looking into the depths of my empty glass like it holds all the answers to the world.

"Then it isn't ready," she says.

I sigh. There's no point in explaining my need to her. People don't understand even if they have their own obsessions.

Jolene brings out our food, and my stomach comes to life.

I'd forgotten how good the food was here.

I look down at my plateful of scrambled eggs, sausage, and toast, and lick my lips.

"You're so weird," Bina says, having seen my reaction.

"So are you." I bump her elbow with mine and she glares.

My mom sighs heavily. "You guys are old enough not to act like children anymore and yet..." she trails off.

I take a bite of sausage and smile through the food. "Get used to it, Mom, you're going to be stuck with us acting like two big kids for the rest of your life."

She cuts into her omelet. "Trust me, I'm very aware."

"So what's new with you, Bina?" I ask, *trying* to be nice. It's rare but it happens

"Work, work, and more work."

Sabrina works for a newspaper as a reporter. Luckily, she's not a sports reporter, or I'd be fucked.

"I hope you're doing your finger work outs." I flick my fingers through the air.

She rolls her eyes. "You're such an ass. At least I don't party for a living."

I wince. "Touché."

Her face softens. "I think this will be good for you, though. Working with Coach Harrison again. He's a nice guy. There's something off about your new coach."

I look away. There *is* something off about my coach. He's a fucking prick.

Frank West is supposed to be one of the best coaches in

the league. He's been coaching my team, the Plymouth Hunters, for almost ten years, but he's crooked. A fucking bad guy in my opinion. He wants me off the team and fuck, if I was in a position to be traded, I'd fucking take it just to get away from him, but with my recent media firestorms *no one wants me,* and the Hunters are stuck with me until my contract is up next season. I have one year. One fucking chance to make this right.

We finish breakfast and I pay; everyone protests that fact, but fuck it. I have the money and I want to treat my family.

Out in the parking lot, I hug Sabrina goodbye, and she leaves, having to get home to finish an article.

"Come by the house soon," my mom says as she hugs me. "We miss you."

"I miss you too." I let her go and hug my dad, holding on a little tighter. I thought we were going to lose him after his stroke and I don't know what I'd do without him. This man has always been my rock, someone I can admire and look up to. "I love you, Dad."

He nods against my shoulder. "L-Love y-y-you." His hands shake against my back.

I clap him on the shoulder and step back so my mom can get him in the car.

"I'll see you soon." I wave and climb behind the wheel of my car.

Gym time.

CHAPTER FIVE

RACE

I OPEN THE DOOR TO MY DORM, BALANCING TWO coffees carefully in my arms.

Elle sits up in bed and rubs her eyes. Her dark hair is wild around her head and her eyes are bloodshot and puffy from crying. My heart breaks for her. She might've been a bitch to me but I would never wish for anyone to experience the situation she was put in last night.

"Hey," she says softly. She looks down at her bed covers, biting her lip.

"I got you coffee." I stride over and hold out the peace offering. She takes it.

I take a seat on my bed and she looks over at me. "Thank you, for last night. For stepping in and getting me home."

"You're welcome. I hope you would've done the same for me."

She looks away, shame flashing across her face. "I don't know if I would have," she admits quietly. "I know that's really shitty of me, but I think before last night I would've let it happen. Said it was karma." She shrugs.

"I hope you know better now?" I raise a brow and take a sip of my coffee and cringe. It's way too watery and weak. Looks like I'll be checking out another coffee cart before classes tomorrow.

"Oh, yeah." She nods quickly. "I'm sorry for misjudging you," she whispers. "I won't make that mistake again." She tucks her wild hair behind her ears. "Friends?"

I smile. "Are you sure you want to be friends with a priss like me?"

She laughs. "Yeah, I'm sure. You're cool."

"Friends then," I agree. My phone buzzes in my purse and I fish it out, finding a text from Ryland asking if I can meet him at ten. "Hey, Elle?" She looks up. "Ryland is going to give me a tour of campus, you want to go?"

"Who's Ryland?" Her dark brows furrow.

"He's the guy that drove us back to campus."

"Oh." She nods. "He was nice."

"Yeah, he was," I agree. "So, are you in?"

She taps her fingers against the side of her coffee cup. "Yeah, sure."

"Get ready then," I tell her. "He wants to meet at ten and it's already nine-thirty."

She sets her coffee aside. "Since we're besties now, I have to say, that's the shittiest coffee I've ever drank."

I laugh. "I have to agree with you."

She stands and stretches. "I'm going to take the quickest shower of my life, promise. I feel dirty." She shivers. I know her feeling comes from the encounter with the guy in the hall at the party and not with sleeping in her clothes.

"I'll let Ryland know we might be a little bit late."

"Thanks." She gathers up her things and heads out into the hall to the shared bathroom.

I've never had to share a bathroom before, and I can't say I like it. It'd be one thing if it was only Elle and me sharing a bathroom, but instead, one bathroom is allotted to half the floor. Community showers are *not* my thing.

Since Elle is gone, I spend my time tidying her side of the room. I just can't help myself. The mess is about to give me a panic attack. I don't know how someone can make so many messes in less than twenty-four hours. That has to be a record or something.

Elle comes back into the room with damp hair and dressed in a pair of jeans, a loose t-shirt, and red Converse. She takes one look at her side of the room and raises a brow.

"Sorry." I back away. "I couldn't help it."

She shakes her head and laughs. "My sister is the same way. She hates messes."

"You have a sister?"

"Yeah, and a brother. What about you?"

"Two brothers."

"Bless you." She laughs, drying the ends of her hair with the towel. She drops the damp towel onto her bed and pulls her hair back in a messy topknot.

My phone buzzes again and I look down. "Ryland says he's outside our dorm and he has coffee."

"Tell him I love him," she deadpans.

I shake my head and respond back. "Are you ready to go?" I ask.

She nods and picks up a jean jacket. "Ready."

We head down the hall—which is nothing but bare cinderblock walls painted a drab yellow color—and to the elevator since we're too lazy to take the stairs.

The elevator door opens, and I can already see Ryland sitting on the front steps with his back to us.

When the door whooshes open, he looks back and

smiles when he sees us. "Hey." He stands and holds out the two cups of coffee.

"Thank you, you're a saint." I take one from him and slurp greedily at it. I nearly moan in ecstasy. Now *this* is coffee. "Please tell me a stop at the coffee shop that makes this is on your tour."

He laughs, his eyes shining. "Sure." He looks at Elle. "I don't think we were properly introduced last night. I'm Ryland."

"Elle." She does this shy little dip with her legs. I press my lips together so I don't laugh. *Elle, shy? Oh, this is interesting.*

"Nice to meet you, Elle." Ryland smiles, and the dimples in his cheeks pop out. He's kind of adorable in a dorky way, not ruggedly handsome like Bennett.

Bennett.

Why am I even thinking about him? We didn't exchange numbers and the chances of me running into him again on a campus this size are slim to none. Plus, he said he's not a student, so whatever reason he was here yesterday might not apply today. I hate that I feel forlorn at the thought of never seeing him again. I barely even know him.

"I thought we could head this way first." Ryland nods to our left.

"Sure," I say. "You're the one that knows your way around, not us."

He laughs. "Right." He glances at Elle again with a slight smile, and I swear I think she bats her eyes. "Those are dorms and those are dorms too." He points as he begins his tour. "Administrative building there. That's the astronomy building. They have a tower on top with telescopes that anyone can use. Cool, huh?"

"Very." I nod, impressed.

"Gym is there. Coffee shop—that one sucks, FYI. Football stadium is over that way." He points, and I can see the shape of it in the distance. "The hockey arena is in that building, and let me tell you, Addams University loves their hockey."

"So does the whole state." Elle snorts.

Ryland continues on, unaffected. By the end of his tour, my head is spinning. There are so many buildings that I barely remember any of the ones he pointed out.

Enough time has passed that we're all hungry and stop off for lunch at one of the cafés that dot campus.

"This is one of my favorites," Ryland says as we get in line. "They have some of the best sandwiches and they're fast so that's always a plus when you're in a hurry in between classes."

We each place our order and they give us a card with a number. We choose a table in the back corner. There's one other guy sitting at a table, typing away on his laptop.

"Do you have a girlfriend?" Elle asks Ryland.

I laugh and shake my head.

"No," he says, fighting a smile.

"Good." She sits back in her chair and says no more as she looks around the room.

Ryland looks at me for an explanation and I shrug. There is no explaining Elle. That much I know.

Our food arrives, and I have to admit, my B.L.T. looks pretty good.

"So—" I munch on a chip "—where are you guys from?"

"Nebrask*a*," Elle says, enunciating the end of the word.

"Maine," Ryland answers. "You?"

"Virginia."

Ryland smiles. "A lot of us from different states end up here for some reason. Most of my friends are from out of state."

"It's a good school," I reason.

"And most of us want freedom." Elle raises her glass of water in cheers.

I clink my glass to hers and Ryland does the same. "To a new year," he says.

"And new friends."

My alarm goes off and my eyes shoot open.

"Shut it off," Elle groans, covering her ears. When it continues to trill, she turns over and screams into her pillow.

I fumble for my phone and finally grab it, shutting off the annoying alarm.

My first official day of college—I'm not ready. I've never

felt more unprepared in my whole life. I know I have everything I need, but mentally, I'm just not ready.

I get out of bed and gather up my things for the shower. I purposely set my alarm for five in the morning so I could have the bathroom to myself. I didn't want to deal with the chaos of everyone getting ready at the same time and the overabundance of first day nerves.

Like I predicted, the bathroom is empty. I pad in my shower shoes across the room and get into the shower at the very end.

I don't know why I'm so nervous. It's not like I'm about to get up in front of a stadium full of people and sing.

I shower quickly, too hyped up to enjoy it, and shut the water off. I wrap the towel around my body and go to the sink and brush my teeth. I gather up my stuff in my arms and leave, heading back to my room. I can hear other girls on our floor moving around now, and I thank my forethought that I decided to get up early.

The door clicks shut behind me, and Elle groans.

"You better go grab a shower," I tell her.

"No."

"It's going to get too busy in there soon," I warn her.

"Ugh." She presses her face into the pillow.

I lift my foot and kick her bed. "Come on. You'll thank me later. We'll go get breakfast when you get back."

She reluctantly pushes her body up and grumbles the whole time she grabs her things and leaves the room.

Once she's gone, I dress in a pair of ripped skinny jeans,

a loose, off-the-shoulder, gray sweater, and choose a pair of nude-colored pumps. I slip my large gold watch onto my wrist. It was a graduation gift from my parents and they engraved it on the back.

I lean over my dresser to see into the mirror above it so I can put on my makeup. I apply a gray smoky eye look and put a nude color on my lips.

Elle comes back with wet hair hanging down her back and goes over to her closet. She shoves back the garments roughly, looking for something to wear.

I plug in my hair dryer and turn it on. She glares at me.

"That's loud enough to wake the dead," she yells.

When my hair is dry, I opt to curl it. I finish and flip my head upside down, shaking them out so they're not so tight.

I stand back up and find Elle sitting on her bed, pulling on a pair of purple boots.

"Beauty Queen," she jokes.

"Goth," I shoot back with a laugh.

She stands. "What? You don't like it?"

I look at her black jeans and black t-shirt. "You're making a statement, that's for sure."

"And what statement would that be?" she asks with a challenging look in her eyes.

"That you don't give a fuck," I say.

She smiles. "Exactly."

I grab my mint-colored backpack and look inside to make sure I have my laptop packed and ample pens and pencils.

Elle coats her lashes with mascara and adds a little black eyeliner.

"Ready," she announces.

"Where's your backpack?"

"Oh, shit. Right." She drops to her knees and looks under her bed. "I forgot I kicked it under here." She pulls out the black backpack and I roll my eyes.

"You need some color in your life."

"That's what you're for." She waves her hand at me. "Come on, let's go. I'm starving."

I check one last time to make sure I have everything and then we're out the door.

"Oh, wow," I gasp at all the bodies in the hall. Girls linger in the hall in all kinds of stages of undress, chatting excitedly.

"Whoa," Elle says, rearing back. We push our way through and manage to get to the elevator. When the doors close, she looks at me. "I thought I'd escaped the crowded halls of high school. Looks like I was wrong."

I look down at her with a raised brow. "Now you're *living* at high school."

She rolls her eyes. "Oh, fuck."

I laugh. "Maybe it won't be that bad."

"Or maybe it'll be worse," she counters.

I shrug as the elevator doors open and we walk the few feet to the main doors. I push open the door and Elle sulks behind me.

It's a nice sunny day in Massachusetts, albeit chilly for

August—at least for me, I'm used to warmer weather and it must only be sixty degrees.

Elle and I make our way across campus to one of the café's. There are several all across campus so that no matter where you are, you can grab a bite—or coffee, and I definitely need coffee at the moment.

Elle and I place our order and grab our coffee before finding a table to sit at.

The café is already getting crowded, and I expect in the next hour for it to be a packed house with barely any standing room.

Elle flips her dark hair over her shoulder, and I try not to cringe at the rat's nest forming in the thick dark strands since she neglected to brush it. "So, do you like Ryland?"

My eyes widen with shock. I hadn't been expecting that. "Um, what?"

"Do you like Ryland?" she asks again.

"I mean, I *like* him, but not how you're implying," I explain.

She wraps her slender fingers around her coffee cup, and I notice a tattoo of a skull on the middle finger of her right hand. "You wouldn't mind if I ..." she trails off, letting me fill in the blanks.

"Do whatever you want," I say, raising my hands in surrender. "I don't care."

She smiles. "He's cute and nice—not the kind of guy I normally go for, but the fucktards I normally date only screw me over. I think it's time to try something different."

I nod. "Different can be good."

Our food is brought out and they swipe the number card from our table. My egg sandwich smells amazing and reminds me of the one my mom always made. She insisted on making us breakfast every morning before school, and if she was sick, she always made my dad do it. I'm suddenly hit with a severe case of homesickness and my need to get away seems so silly now. *What was I running from?*

I dismiss my thoughts from my mind and eat my breakfast, chatting with Elle. She tells me all about her hockey obsession when one of the players comes into the café. She knows everything about the university team and it's a bit shocking, but I'm learning Elle is full of surprises.

"Let's meet back here for lunch," Elle says, since we both have a break in the middle of the day at the same time.

"Sounds good." I ball up my napkin and get up to throw away my trash.

I grab my backpack and slide my arms through the loops. My first class is a few buildings to the right and back so it shouldn't take me long to get there—if I don't get lost, that is.

Elle trails behind me as we head for the exit, pushing our way through the growing crowd of people. A guy sees us coming out and moves to open the door for us.

A breeze hits my face as I look up and say, "Thank you." I gasp. "Bennett?"

Elle slams into me. "Bennett?" Her head whips from me

to where I'm staring. "Holy shit, Bennett James! I'm a huge fan!"

"Hi, Grace," he says with a lopsided smile. He tips his head at Elle and looks back at me with a twinkle in his hazel eyes like he's silently laughing. "See you around."

He steps back into the building, and the door clamors closed.

Elle grabs my arm and holds on so tight that I yelp. "Ow, let go." I shake her off.

She steps back, looking at me with a shocked expression. "How do you know Bennett James?"

"He took me to Target on Saturday," I say.

She stares at me. "You've never met him before?"

"*No*," I say, wishing she'd get to the point.

"*Grace*," she cries, jumping up and down. "He's only the hottest NHL player *ever*. He's got this whole cocky bad boy thing going for him, and on the ice, the guy is a beast. I'm telling you, it's something to see."

"Wait ..." I pause. "You're telling me that guy—" I point at the café where Bennett stands "—is a professional hockey player?"

"Yes, that's exactly what I'm saying. Why is that so hard to comprehend?"

I shake my head. "He didn't tell me."

"He probably figured you knew," she reasons.

I shake my head, biting my lip. "No."

"I'd heard rumors," she continues like I haven't spoken, "that he was on campus to train with his old coach—our team's coach—but I figured it was just that. Rumors." She shrugs. "He was injured really bad," she explains. "Broke his leg or something. He missed out on half of last season, and I heard that the Plymouth Hunters might be dropping him after this season regardless of whether or not his leg is okay." She nods, her lips pressed together. "Lots of drama in hockey. It's delicious."

I can't help but laugh as we start down the cobblestone path to our classes. "Elle, you know, you're nothing like what I thought."

She bumps my hip with hers. "Neither are you, Miss Priss." We start to part ways when she calls out, "If you think the conversation about Bennett is over, you're mistaken. I need details. All of them." She waggles her brows suggestively and then turns completely away.

I'm sure she's imagining things to be much juicier than they are, and I'll have to crush her dreams later.

I take a deep breath and step into the building that houses my English class. I think it's so stupid that I have to spend the majority of my first two years at college studying the basics before I can delve into my major. It's a necessary evil, though, so I suck it up and search for the correct lecture hall. I know I look like a major dweeb searching the building, but hey, better that than sitting through the wrong class like Ryland.

I finally locate the room and startle at the amount of people already in the room. I thought I was early.

"Excuse me," I say softly, shuffling past a girl setting up

her laptop and a guy texting. He's not paying attention and I trip over his feet falling right in his lap.

"Oomph," he breathes out on impact.

I'm practically sprawled across the poor guy's lap and I quickly jump up like I'm on fire.

"I am *so* sorry," I apologize quickly, my cheeks flaming red. I avoid looking at him and sprint down to the other end of the aisle, dropping into one of the chairs. I can feel him staring at me, and my mortification grows. All I want is for a huge gaping hole to open up and swallow me whole. That'd be lovely.

I keep waiting for him to say something and embarrass me further, but by some miracle, he doesn't say anything.

The class fills up steadily while I pull out my laptop so I'll be ready to take notes. A few people fill in the seats between me and the guy I fell on. Thank God. I couldn't take his staring any longer.

The professor comes in and introduces himself. He's tall with graying hair and black glasses. He's dressed in a suit and tie with shiny black shoes. There's something regal about him—like he came from royalty and knows he's better than you.

"I'm Professor Hanagen. I take my classes seriously and I expect you to do the same. Conduct yourselves in a professional manner or I'll ask you to leave and drop my class." He crosses his hands together. "I'm going to pass out the roll sheet. Check off your name from the list—you will be required to do this every class. Whatever seat you've chosen will be yours until the end of the semester so I hope you like it." He grabs a sheet of paper, clipboard, and pen, and hands it to the student nearest him.

"Is this guy for real?" the girl beside me hisses under her breath.

Professor Hanagen immediately launches into his lecture and I scramble to type fast enough. All around me, the clacking of keyboards fills the air.

Forty-five minutes later, class ends and my fingers ache. I pack up my stuff as the room empties out.

"Hey."

Oh, shit.

I know, without even looking up, that it's the guy I fell on.

Lovely.

"Hi," I say reluctantly, looking up into impossibly-blue eyes. His blond hair is shaggy and his skin is tanned like he spends a lot of time outside.

"I thought I should introduce myself after that whole ... incident." He points over his shoulder to his chair. "I'm Tanner."

I want to say that he most certainly didn't need to introduce himself, but considering *I'm* the one that sat in his lap, I kind of owe the guy. "Grace," I say, giving him a small smile. "I'm really sorry about that."

He shrugs. "S'okay."

I stand and grab my backpack. "Well, it was nice to meet

you," I say rather fast, trying to get past him. "I need to get to my next class."

"Oh, yeah, right," he mumbles. "I guess I'll see you around?"

"Yeah, sure," I say quickly, scurrying down the aisle and out the door.

Once outside in the daylight, I shake my head like I'm trying to shake away the memories of the embarrassing incident.

But it sticks like putty to my brain.

I look up to the sky and sigh.

It's going to be a long day.

CHAPTER SIX

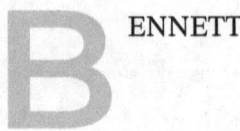ENNETT

THIS HAD BEEN ONE LONG ASS FUCKING WEEK.

"Coach," I plead, hands on my hips. "I *need* to get on the ice."

Coach Harrison narrows his shrewd eyes on me. He hates begging, but I'm desperate at this point. "Get in the gym with the rest of the guys. Now." The tone in his voice allows no argument.

The old me would punch something and spout off, but the new me takes a deep breath and lets it out.

This Zen shit is harder than I thought it would be.

I stalk off toward the training facility with Coach hot on my heels.

The team is already there, lifting weights and running on the treadmills. It's easy to pick out the senior members and the newbies. They automatically segregate themselves. The older players hover around the weights, cheering on one guy. The freshmen are on the opposite side of the room, using some of the other strength training equipment and watching the guys with awe in their eyes.

When I step into the room, everyone stops.

Up until this moment, I've been working out on my own when they're not around. To be honest, with my weakened leg and knee, I was embarrassed to work around them. They're all athletes in their prime and I might be only a few years older than them but I feel like an elder.

Coach claps me on the shoulder and bellows, "A'ight, fellas, I'm sure by now you've heard the rumors that Bennett was on campus. Those rumors are true. He's here to train with you guys until he's ready to rejoin his team. This is a unique situation, and I hope you'll be mindful of that." He glares at each and every one of them. I know he's warning them off from blabbing their mouths about everything I do and say. I appreciate his effort, but I doubt it'll do any good. When people want to talk, they do. "Get back to it," he orders. In a lower voice says to me, "You too."

I sigh and move over to one of the weight-lifting machines by the freshmen.

"Dude, what's the NHL like?"

I turn to look at the freshman on my right. "Like this but harder," I answer, increasing the weight on the machine before taking a seat.

"Why'd you get kicked off the team?" another one asks.

I push up on the machine, my arms straining. "I didn't get kicked off the team."

"But you're on probation. Isn't that the same thing?"

I glare at the guy. "No, it's not."

One guy hits them in the arm and they move off to the treadmills. The two other guys beside me seem uninterested in talking to me, which is fine by me. Besides, they seem to be having a conversation of their own.

The blond guy says, "Dude, this girl in my English class fell in my lap on the first day. It was hilarious."

"Was she hot?" the other one asks.

"Oh, yeah. Legs for days and long brown hair."

I perk up at that. *Could it be? No ...*

"Have you talked to her?"

"A few times. We also have economy together so I purposely took the seat beside her," he chortles. "She's pretty embarrassed around me after the lap incident, but I think I'm wearing her down."

"What's her name?"

"Grace."

Fuck. Can he be talking about Grace?

I quickly tune out what the guys are saying. It's none of my business anyway.

I push myself harder. Sweat courses down the side of my face, but I keep pushing harder, trying to quiet my mind, but I can't let go of that conversation and I hate that it bothers me. I spent *one* afternoon with Grace—the brief run-in with her at the coffee shop on Monday doesn't count—and all we did was go to fucking Target. How can she possibly be under my skin this deep?

"You're gonna regret that in the morning," one of the senior guys says, coming over to stand beside me and crossing his arms over his chest.

"Don't worry about me," I say.

"Here," the guy says, holding out a towel. "It's clean. Promise."

I take the towel from him and mumble a quick, "Thanks." I wipe the sweat off my face, cursing myself for leaving my bag back at Coach's office. It has all my stuff in it, including my water.

"Michael Thomas," the guy holds out his hand. "I just want to say, I really admire what you do on the ice. I don't think you get enough credit."

I look up at the guy. He's tall, slightly taller than me, and wide like a wall. He has close-cut brown hair and brown eyes, and he sports a near-beard.

"Thanks," I say. "Are you a senior?"

"Junior," he answers. My eyes widen, the guy is huge so I just figured he was already in his final year. "Hoping to get drafted this year."

I nod. "Good luck." I start to leave.

"Maybe you could train me?" he calls out questioningly.

My feet falter. "Uh..." I pause, not knowing what to say. I laugh lightly. "There's not much I can teach you that you don't already know."

"Yeah, but you *made* it. You've been there—on the big stage. That counts for something." Michael's eyes light up.

I sigh and lean against one of the pieces of equipment. "I'll be out on the ice with you, practicing like I'm one of the team—I'm sure you guys are going to teach me more than I can you, but yeah, I'll do what I can." I shrug. It would feel good to give back in a way. I *was* these guys only a few years ago with stars in my eyes—dreaming of being drafted. I would've shit my pants to work with a pro—even one as fucked up as me.

"Thanks, man." Michael holds out his fist for me to bump mine against.

"I'm going to hit the showers," I tell him. "See you tomorrow."

He nods, lifting two of his fingers to his forehead and saluting me.

I go to Coach's office to grab my bag and stop when I hear my name. "Are you fucking crazy? Letting Bennett James train with us? What were you thinking?"

"I will not be reprimanded by *you*," Coach says in a

steely-calm voice. "You might be the team captain, but I'm the coach and you *never* address me that way ever again or you're off the team."

"But, Coach—"

"No buts."

I grab my bag and haul ass down the hall to the showers before Coach or the team captain spots me. I knew some of the players were bound to not want me here, but to have the team captain be the main one isn't going to be good, and something tells me he's going to set out to make my life a living hell. After all, you never really leave high school.

I HEAD OUT OF THE GYM AND TOWARD THE GARAGES. I need to get out of here. It's late and I need a fucking drink. The last thing I need to do is get drunk at a bar and have it show up in a magazine, but fuck it.

I shove my hands in the pockets of my jeans, hunching my shoulders as I power across campus.

I become distracted when I notice a girl standing at one of the coffee carts. She's dressed in a blue skirt and white blousy thing with long dark hair.

My gut tells me it's Grace even if I can't see her.

I should keep going, ignore the urge to speak to her, but I can't, and the conversation the guys were having back at the gym comes flooding back to me.

I hesitate for one second—warring with myself—before

I veer to my left and over to where she stands in line. I settle into line right beside her. "You have a thing for hockey players, don't you?"

She looks up at me, jumping back a bit. "Jesus, Bennett, you scared the crap out of me." She raises a hand to her heart. "And what do you mean?" Her nose crinkles in confusion.

"The guy you fell on is a hockey player."

Her mouth pops open and pink blooms across her cheeks. "How do you know about that?" She hisses, looking around like she's afraid someone's going to overhear.

"The prick was talking about it in the gym," I answer, unable to keep the sneer from my voice.

Her eyes widen in horror. "I'm going to kill him," she hisses under her breath. Raising her voice, and her chin, she says, "I didn't know he was a hockey player. I'm not one of those fuck bunnies if that's what you're thinking."

My lips twitch ever so slightly with the urge to laugh. "They're called *puck* bunnies."

She wrinkles her nose again and we move forward in line. "I like my term better. It's more accurate."

She's got that right.

"I'm going to the bar, you wanna come?" I find myself asking before I even thought about what I was going to say. *What the fuck is the matter with me?*

"Um ..." She looks up at me with wide, doe-like eyes. "Bars aren't really my thing."

"Come on," I find myself coaxing. "It'll be fun. You'll be with me."

She bites her lip. "I'm supposed to meet Elle and Ryland," she hedges.

The monster named Jealousy rears up inside me when I hear the name Ryland, but I quickly douse it. I have no right to feel jealous. "Tell them to come."

She bites her lip and I know she's caving. "Let me text Elle."

We step out of line so that other people can get their caffeine fix. I shuffle beside her as she texts her friend. I've never been so awkward around a girl before. It's kind of alarming. I lean against a lamppost and stare down at the ground; it's riddled with splotches of gum and pebbles and dirt.

"Elle says they're in." Grace puts her phone away and looks up at me. Her hair blows slightly in the wind, a stray piece getting caught in her lip gloss. Before I can stop myself, I reach out and grab the strand of hair, plucking it away.

I swallow thickly; the way my heart's beating in my chest is something I've never felt before. My gut tells me to run, run far and fast, away from this girl, and yet my feet are planted firmly to the ground. I'm frozen, locked in her gaze. We stare at each other, neither of us saying a word. I wish I could read her mind, to know if she's as confused by this as I am, but I'm scared if I open my mouth I'll discover I'm the only one with these thoughts, and for some reason, I can't bear the thought of that.

"Cool," I finally say in response to what she said. "Shall we go?" I point over my shoulder in the direction I'd originally been headed.

She looks away and then back up at me with uncertainty in her gaze. "Just tell me the place. Ryland has a car; he'll make sure we get there."

I've never hated a person I've never met before the way I hate this Ryland guy. It's a bit—no, a lot—ridiculous. I don't want to argue with her. I mean, I *do* but I don't want to wave my asshole flag, so I sigh and say, "Yeah it's Costello's down on the corner of 5th and Main. You can't miss it."

She nods. "I'll see you in an hour then?" She starts to move away and her backpack strap starts to slip. She quickly hikes it back up before it falls.

"Yeah, see you then," I say.

She smiles one last time and hurries down the cobblestone walkway to her dorm.

I watch her go. When I can no longer see her, I finally force my legs to move back to my dorm—still sounds fucking ridiculous to say *dorm*—so I can change. If Grace isn't going to be there for another hour, there's no point to rush.

It doesn't take me long to change, and I spend the rest of my time trying to figure out what's so different about Grace and why I can't get her out of my head.

CHAPTER SEVEN

Grace

The bar is packed with college kids and what looks like a few professionals enjoying an after work drink.

"Do you know if Bennett is here?" Elle asks, shouting to be heard above the noise. "I still can't believe you know Bennett James."

I shake my head. "I don't have his number."

"Girl, you have to get his number," she says with a look like I'm crazy.

"I think he's back there." Ryland points to a horseshoe-shaped booth in the back where someone has an arm raised, waving. I can't see them, but I head that way, dragging Elle along by her arm with me. Ryland moves behind her, paving his own way with his wider body.

I've only been at school for a week, but in that time, Ryland and Elle have become my friends. I'm beyond shocked by how much Elle and I actually have in common, considering she probably wanted to slit my throat when she first saw me. I'm learning that's just *Elle*, though. She's like that with everyone until she gets to know you—except Ryland: she let him right on through her fortress, but I think that's in part to him saving her that first night and the crush she has on him which she won't admit to.

I finally break through the crowd, and sure enough, Bennett occupies the booth. I slide in beside him with Elle on my other side and Ryland beside her.

"Hey," I say in greeting to Bennett. A glass of beer sits in front of him, half-empty.

He gives me a close-lipped smile back. "Hi." He lifts his fingers in greeting at Elle and Ryland.

"Oh, this is my roommate Elle, and my friend Ryland," I introduce.

"Hey, man." Ryland holds his fist out for a bump, and

Bennett reluctantly returns it, giving Ryland a disgruntled look.

"I'm a huge fan," Elle chimes in, lighting up. Her obsession with hockey cracks me up considering her dark princess persona she insists on wearing. "That one play you did in your last game was *ah-mazing*. I've never seen anything like it. You're a rock star on ice."

Bennett chuckles and lifts his glass of beer to his lips. "Thanks." He signals for a waitress. "Order whatever you want. It's on me," he says.

Elle and Ryland both order beers, and I'm shocked when the waitress doesn't card Elle. I've drank before, at parties, sure, but never in a bar like this. "Water for me," I say. "And some food. What do you guys want?" I ask.

"We'll take an order of cheesy fries and nachos," Bennett tells her.

"Sure thing. I'll be right back with your drinks." She smiles up at Bennett, and I swear she bats her long, obviously fake lashes. It shouldn't bother me—it *doesn't* bother me. Bennett's not mine, and we barely even know each other. Women are free to check him out, and he's allowed to return the favor. Although, at this particular moment, he's not returning it. Instead, he's staring at me.

"You don't want a beer?" he asks, twirling a coaster between his fingers.

I shrug and trace my fingernail over the word DICK carved into the top of the table. People are so amusingly base. "Beer's not my thing."

His lips twitch. "Maybe you'd prefer one of those girly fruit drinks with the little umbrellas."

I suppress the urge to laugh. "Yeah, that's probably more my speed," I agree.

Beside me, Ryland and Elle chat, and for the moment it feels like Bennett and I are alone, when in reality that's the farthest thing from the truth.

Bennett's brows draw together, and he seems to be mulling over what he wants to say. I don't pester him, knowing he'll speak when he's ready. "You really didn't know who I was, did you?" he asks.

"Honestly? No," I admit. "My dad and older brother are into cars, not sports, and the only sport my little brother likes is football, so I hate to disappoint you, but I don't think I've ever seen any hockey games ever in my life."

Bennett grins—I get the feeling he doesn't smile like that very often. At least around me it seems like he's always trying *not* to smile. Like he has to keep up some bravado of the big bag hockey player that's going to hurt you. My gut tells me that's not the *real* Bennett.

"We're going to have to change that," he says.

I raise a brow. "Oh, are *we*?" I emphasize the word.

He lifts his beer to his lips. "Yes, *we* are."

Elle punches my arm. "I have to go pee."

I snap my head in her direction. "What does that have to do with me?"

"*Girl code*," she hisses under her breath.

I roll my eyes and glance at Bennett. "We'll be right back."

Ryland slides out of the booth so Elle and I can pass. She takes my hand and pulls me into the bathroom. The noise from the bar dulls and only one stall is in use so we're relatively alone.

"I think Ryland likes me," she states.

"You dragged me into the bathroom for this?"

"Grace," she whines. "What do I do? I'm not good at this kind of thing. I mean, you saw what happened at the party—the kinds of guys I tend to go after. Ryland is ... He's sweet and he makes me laugh. I *like* him."

I lift my hands at my sides. "I don't know what to tell you other than to just be yourself."

She rolls her eyes. "You sound like a damn fortune cookie."

I sigh. "It's the truth, though. You are your own most unique quality about yourself. Embrace it."

She heads over to the sink, gripping the white porcelain between her fingers. "That's hard for me," she says softly.

"It's hard for everybody," I agree. "We think if we can't love ourselves for who we are that nobody else can. We rarely see the beauty in who we are and just the ugliness. We all focus too much on what's *wrong* and not what's *right*. I promise you, even if you can't see it, you're pretty amazing."

"Really?" she asks with wide puppy dog eyes.

"Really," I concur.

"How can you even say that, though? I was such a bitch to you that first day."

"And that's not who you really are, is it?" I counter. "Just like I'm not the uppity rich girl you thought I was." Well, technically, I *am* rich but I certainly am *not* uppity. In fact, in high school, I was noted for letting people walk all over me. I just wanted to be liked, but something I learned is you can't roll over and expect people to love you—they'll only use you.

The girl in the stall comes out, washes her hands, and leaves all without sparing us a single glance.

Elle inhales a deep breath, looking at her reflection in the mirror. "I'm overthinking this, aren't I? I've only known the guy a week."

"Yeah, you are. Just let things play out."

"Okay." She nods and takes a step back. "Now I really do have to pee."

I laugh as she scurries into the stall. I figure since I'm in the bathroom, I might as well do the same.

When we head back to the table, Bennett looks at us with a knowing smile. Ryland stands, and I slide back into my original spot. Bennett now has his arm stretched along the back of the booth and his fingers dangle dangerously close my shoulder when I settle.

"It doesn't really take girls *that* long to pee." His lips graze my ear when he speaks, and I can't stop the shiver that runs down my spine. He notices and grins, his hazel eyes twinkling.

"Sure it does," I say. I hate how breathless I sound, like he's stolen all the air from my body. Our drinks now sit on the table, and I reach for my water, stick the straw in, and slurp down half of it. My throat feels as dry as the Sahara with him staring at me like that.

"Mmhmm," he hums, and I swear his eyes flick down to my lips.

I feel like I'm in the same predicament as Elle—liking a guy I just met. It seems wrong to like someone so quickly, but I think sometimes there are people you meet and there's just this immediate connection. Good *or* bad.

"Cheese fries and nachos," the waitress announces loudly above the din in the bar. I have to admit both look delicious and my stomach rumbles. I've barely eaten anything all day. All I had was a muffin for breakfast, and I didn't have time for lunch so I'm running on fumes. "I'll be right back with some plates for you guys," she says, speaking only to Bennett.

"Bring some napkins too," he tells her, already picking up a nacho and shoving it in his mouth. I guess I should feel sorry for her, since he's paying more attention to the nachos than her.

"Anything else?"

He lifts his empty beer glass. "Of course." She curtsies.

I'm the only one that notices and I snort. She realizes what she's done and her whole face turns as red as a tomato.

"Day made," I whisper under my breath.

"What's that?" Bennett asks, grabbing another nacho.

"Nothing," I say quickly. I might've not liked the waitress checking him out, but I wouldn't make fun of her for making a bluff. That just wasn't me.

As my mom likes to say, I am nice to a fault.

I tell her it runs in the family.

"Here, have some food." He shoves the plate with the cheese fries on it over to me. "They have the best food here, trust me."

I pick up a fry and take a bite. "Mmm, you're right."

The waitress comes back with the plates, napkins, and Bennett's second beer and quickly leaves the table.

I grab a plate and pile some cheese fries on it and pour out a little of the ranch.

"Have some nachos too," Bennett says, forking over a bunch onto my plate. "You guys want some?" he asks Elle and Ryland.

"We're good with these," Ryland says, picking up a fry and popping it in his mouth.

"Cool, more for me." Bennett shrugs and shovels more nachos into his mouth. "Eat." He points at me.

I laugh. I hadn't realized I was staring at him. I take a bite of the nachos and swear my stomach sighs with happiness. I really have to get better about taking the time to eat between classes. It's hard when a class is on one side of campus and the next is all the way on the other. Since I'm an overachiever—according to my brothers, at least—I loaded up on as many classes as I could possibly take. I'm regretting that decision now.

"So," Bennett begins, "how are you liking college life so far?"

I shrug. "It's more adultier than I expected."

He chuckles. "Adultier, is that even a word?"

"I just made it one." I shrug, dipping a fry in ranch.

"How is it more *adultier* than you thought?" He takes a sip of beer to hide his smile.

"Well, for starters, I have to do my own laundry."

He laughs. "Laundry?"

"I hate doing laundry," I reason. "It's just time consuming, and when I went yesterday, the room was full so I had to wait for someone to finish before I could even start. It took my whole afternoon. Luckily, I brought my laptop with me so I could work on my paper."

"You already have homework?" He raises a brow.

I laugh. "*Yes*, this is college, you know? Oh, wait," I whisper under my breath, "I bet you had one of your fuck bunnies do yours."

His lips quirk up slightly on side. "Touché."

Now it's my turn to question him. "I've heard rumors, but I want to hear it straight from you. Why are you on campus? I don't know much about hockey, but it seems odd that you'd be doing your rehabilitation with your college coach. Isn't that what the coach on your professional team is for? And if not, surely they could've hired someone to get you back into shape? Frankly, I'm not buying what I'm hearing."

Shutters come down over his eyes. "Whatever you've heard is true," he says.

"Why don't I believe you?"

"Believe me if you want or don't want. It doesn't matter to me." He looks away and finishes his beer. He immediately signals for another.

I've struck a nerve, and now I'm desperate to uncover the truth.

One way or the other, Bennett will tell me.

Maybe not tonight, but someday.

CHAPTER EIGHT

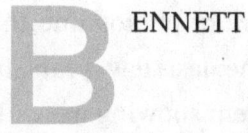ENNETT

"Fucking hell," I curse and crumble up the magazine in the grocery store checkout line.

"You're going to have pay for that," the clerk informs me.

I give the pimple-faced teenager the middle finger salute.

I grab up all of the magazines showing Grace and me in the bar and throw them on the conveyer belt with my snacks and water. I came to the store to stock up on healthy things to eat and then ended up having this stupid magazine shoved in my face. It's been a week since that night, and I hadn't even given it any thought that a photo of us might end up in some gossip magazine. After all, we were there with two other people. But the photo, obviously taken on some punk asses phone, has Elle and Ryland cropped out. It's zoomed in on Grace and me, and I'm leaning close to her just as she is to me. Her hair hides most of her face, but the angle from which the photo is taken makes it look like we're kissing. There's another photo too, smaller than the first that shows our faces clearly.

The headline reads: ***Is Bennett back to his old antics?***

I grab one of the magazines off the conveyer belt and flip through until I find the article. More photos line the pages—this time, ones taken over the last few years in various bars and nightclubs, most of them showing me with a different woman.

"Fuck, fuck, *fuck*," I yell in the middle on the grocery store and slam the magazine in front of the checker so he can ring it up. I know I look like a psycho, but I'm beyond pissed that Grace of all people has been dragged into this mess. I know enough about her to know that she's a good girl. The kind of girl you wouldn't think twice about bringing home to your parents. And now the media has portrayed her as just another notch on my bedpost. It's *not* okay with me.

The checker reluctantly gives me my total—I think he's terrified of me after the performance I've put on—and I slide my card through the slot. My receipt prints, and I snatch it out his hands, shoving it into one of the plastic bags. I grab all my stuff and haul ass out of there to my car. I'm tempted to go back and buy every single one of those blasphemous magazines that are bound to line the other checkouts. But I know that's only the tip of the iceberg. There are hundreds of thousands of those out in the world, all across the United States, and I can't hunt down each and every one.

I might be crazy, but I'm not mad—there's a difference, trust me.

I throw the groceries in my car and head back to campus, driving at speeds I shouldn't. I'm so fucking mad, and I need to do something to release the tension.

I shouldn't let this get to me. After all, it's commonplace, the media spinning the truth, but the fact of the matter is, they're usually right when it comes to me. This time they're not and Grace has gotten dragged into this clusterfuck.

My phone rings and I curse. I press a button on my steering wheel, answering the call. "Hello?"

"What the fuck is this, Bennett?" Bernard yells over the phone. "I thought we talked about this? You need to clean up your image and all you're doing is throwing it down the fucking toilet. How the fuck do you expect me to help you if you can't even help yourself?"

I pinch the bridge of my nose. "Dammit, Bernie, it's different this time. We were at a bar with two other people. I didn't even kiss her. Give me a break."

"It sure as hell looks like you kissed her in this photo!" I hear something slam, and my gut says he's thrown the magazine at the wall. "Luckily, these photos aren't as incriminating as some of your others, but I'm done, Bennett. Clean up this mess, I'm not doing it this time. You're not worth the headache."

I wince. That was harsh. "I'll fix this," I say. "I have a plan."

"Sure you do," he says sarcastically, and the phone clicks off a second later.

I sigh and mutter to myself, "What the fuck am I going to do?"

Think, Bennett, think.

CHAPTER NINE

GRACE

"Dammit," I curse when my purse falls from my hands in my haste to grab my phone. I hadn't been going to answer the call, but after someone's third repeated attempt to reach me, I feared something bad happened.

I drop to the ground and pick up my bag and the lip

gloss, pens, and other various items that had spilled out, shoving them back inside.

Breathless, I pick up the phone, seeing that it says DAD, and just before it stops ringing, I answer. "Hello? Dad? Is something wrong?"

"Yeah, *yeah*, something is *wrong*." He sounds *pissed* and anyone that knows my dad knows he doesn't get mad often. He's the most carefree person on the planet. Protective, yes, but never angry.

"Is it Mom? Lincoln?" I worry, taking a seat on one of the benches dotting the picturesque campus.

"No, no," he stutters, "this has to do with you."

"With *me?*" I squeak. "What could I have possibly done?" My tone of voice grows slightly defensive.

"I'm standing in line to checkout at Wal-Mart and I look over, and what do you know, there's my daughter on the cover of a magazine kissing some guy. I thought I was paying for you to go to college, not to do *this*," he hisses.

"What are you talking about?" My brows furrow in confusion. "Dad, I'm sorry, but I think you're mistaken."

"I'm not *mistaken*," he throws the word back. "It's obviously you with some Bennett guy."

"Bennett?" I question. "I know him but I certainly haven't kissed him." *Not that I haven't thought about it or anything.*

"Some hockey player prick," he rants. "Do you know what hockey players do, Grace? Huh, do you? They shove their stick in every puck they can find."

I pinch the bridge of my nose, fighting the urge to laugh—if I laugh, it'll only make matters worse for me.

"Dad." I sigh. "I didn't kiss him, and even if I did, there'd be nothing wrong with that," I say softly. "I'm grown up now. You have to realize that eventually. You're not this hard on Dean or Lincoln."

He's quiet, and then in a small voice that breaks my heart, he says, "But, Gracie, you're my little girl—my *princess*. I know you're grown up now, but all I see is a little girl that still needs her daddy."

I bite my lip. "Dad, I still *need* you. I'll always need you. You just ... have to take a step back and let me explore the world on my own. I'll always come back."

"I know." He takes a deep breath. "I love you. We all miss you."

"Love you too, Dad. Tell Mom and Linc I love them too."

"I will."

"Bye," I say and hang up, just in time, too.

"Grace!"

I look up from my phone and see Bennett running toward me.

I wave and stay seated. He comes to a stop in front of me, and I glare at him. He winces. "You already know about the magazine, don't you?"

"My dad just called and chewed me out," I explain.

"Shit." He sits down beside me. "I'm sorry."

I shrug. "It's okay."

"I have a plan, though. One I need your help with."

I give him a speculative look. "What could you possibly need my help for?"

He looks around at the various people strolling along campus. Several people look at us and whisper. I'm learning that Bennett draws attention wherever he goes.

"Come to my dorm. We can talk in private."

"You're staying in a dorm?"

He shrugs. "It was part of the deal."

"If I go with you to your dorm aren't people only going to talk *more?*" I argue.

"People will always talk, but I don't want anyone overhearing what I have to say."

I wrinkle my nose. "This sounds dangerous. You're not going to cut me up into a million pieces in your bathtub, are you?"

He cracks a smile and holds up a finger. "One, I don't have a bathtub." He lifts another finger. "Two, I thought we'd established that I'm not a killer. What's your obsession with that anyway?"

"Better safe than sorry," I argue.

"True." He stands. "So, my dorm?"

I sigh and look around. I know I should tell him no and head to the food court like I'd originally been doing before my dad called, but I know the curiosity will kill me if I don't go.

"Sure." I finally agree. "Lead the way." I swish my arm through the air.

Bennett grins, pleased to have finally worn me down.

"It's this way." He nods with his head to the right, shoving his hands into the pockets of his worn jeans. He's probably loaded with money—at least, with my understanding of professional athletes—but he dresses like a bum. I'd love to get ahold of him and show him that there's more in the world to wear than ripped jeans and old t-shirts that have been washed so many times they're practically see-through. Although, those shirts give an excellent view of his muscular chest and stomach, so maybe I'm jumping the gun.

Bennett leads me up the steps of the dorm and swipes his keycard.

"Please tell me you have a single," I whisper-hiss as I follow him to the elevator. He chuckles, his eyes twinkling, and I smack his arm. "That's *not* why I was asking. Get your head out of the gutter. Pig," I groan as we step into the elevator.

He laughs, shaking his head, and pushes the button for the fourth floor. "You're amusing."

"No, I'm not," I argue.

"You're *different*," he amends.

I shrug. "You're probably right."

"Oh, I know I am. Most girls drop to their knees when they meet me, but not you." My mouth pops open. He grins crookedly. "Yeah, they usually open their mouth just like that too." He uses his index finger to push my jaw up and closed.

"You're ... you're ... *Ugh*."

He laughs. "I didn't say I *asked* them to do it. I was just being honest."

The doors slide open to an empty hall and I follow Bennett to his room. He opens the door and lets me in first.

"Ew, it's so *plain*," I groan. I've spent the last two weeks making my dorm my *home*. Heck, even Elle's side of the room is decorated. But Bennett has done nothing except put sheets on his bed. There's not even a comforter or quilt. The walls are bare, the floors are bare, everything is just ... blank. There's no personality, nothing that says this is Bennett's space except for the hockey gear piled at the foot of the bed on the floor. That's *it*.

He chuckles and closes the door, pulling the chair at the provided desk out for me to sit on. "Sorry it's not up to your standards, Princess."

I cringe. When my dad calls me Princess it's sweet, but Bennett says it like it's a bad thing. "It's just boring," I explain. "Nothing in here is personal."

"It's only temporary," he reasons, sitting on the edge of the bed across from me.

"Still," I say, looking around. "I'd think you'd want it to feel homey. Now, what was it that we needed to talk about in private?"

"I need your help," he starts.

"My help?" I laugh. "What could you possibly need my help with?"

He bites his lip, and for a moment, he looks adorably boyish. "My manager is beyond pissed with me," he explains, gesturing with his hands, "and he said that this time it's up to me to fix it."

"And how exactly am I supposed to do that?" My eyes narrow.

He raises his hands innocently in front of his chest, like he's surrendering. "I want you to be my girlfriend." I laugh. "My *fake* girlfriend." He looks at me pleadingly with puppy dog eyes.

I glare at him, my mouth popping open. "Oh, my God, you're serious?"

"As a heart attack." He presses his hands together like he's praying. "I *need* you."

"Why me?" I ask, sitting on the edge of the rickety wooden chair. "You could've asked any girl on campus and I'm sure she would've jumped at the chance."

"For starters, we've already been pictured together," he reasons. "It's the perfect setup. Secondly, you're a good girl, Grace. That whole goody two-shoes vibe you have going on is exactly what I need." I glare at him, conveying with my eyes that I'm about two seconds away from strangling him. "Fuck, Grace, I don't mean it in a *bad* way. It's cute that you're so ... *girly*."

I roll my eyes. "Why should I help you?"

He appears thoughtful, pressing his lips together. "Because hockey means the world to me, and I'm going to lose it if you don't do this. I have to prove to the media, to my manager, to my coach, to *everyone* that I'm not up to all my old antics."

"And what do I get in exchange?" I tilt my head to the side.

He sits up straighter, brightening now that I'm contemplating this. "Anything you want. Money?"

I glare at him. "I don't need your money."

"Sorry," he says sheepishly. "Whatever you want, name it, and it's yours if you do this."

I bite my lip. "I'll have to think about it." His shoulders sag. "About what you'll *owe* me," I amend.

He grins, his eyes lighting up. "You'll do it?"

"Yes," I say on a sigh, "but you better not make me regret this."

"Never," he vows.

I stand up. "I better go, *boyfriend*."

He grins. "See you later, *girlfriend*."

CHAPTER TEN

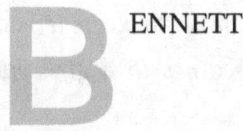ENNETT

I haven't seen Grace all weekend, and I'm sweating bullets that she's changed her mind. I stupidly didn't even get her fucking phone number.

Good one, Bennett.

So now, I stand outside her dorm at the ass crack of

dawn with coffee and cupcakes—because that's what a good boyfriend would do, right?

I've only ever had one serious girlfriend, and that was in high school. It lasted two years and ended badly—bad enough that it left a sour taste in my mouth when it came to relationships.

I see Grace through the glass door, but she hasn't spotted me yet. Elle has, though, and her mouth pops open. She smacks Grace in the arm and points. Grace turns and looks, her perfectly-curled hair swishing against her shoulders. She looks surprised but quickly schools her features and says something to Elle before they head out the door.

"Hey." I step up onto the stairs and hold out the coffee and cupcakes—I purposely got enough for Elle too. It would've been rude to leave her out. "I got you this," I add unnecessarily and immediately want to smack myself in the forehead.

Brilliant, Bennett. You really know how to keep it cool under pressure on the ice, but when it comes to a girl, you completely lose your marbles.

"Thanks." She takes a coffee.

"For you, too." I indicate the other coffee for Elle.

"Thank you," she takes it and I hold onto the holder, letting my hand fall to my side.

"There are cupcakes too." I indicate the other box I hold.

Grace takes it. "Thank you. What's the occasion?"

"A guy can't surprise his girlfriend?" I grin crookedly,

tilting my head to the side. I said it purposely, to see if she'd freak out.

"I guess it's okay," she reasons, shrugging. A smile tugs on her lips.

"I can't believe you *just* told me you guys were dating. How long has this been going on? Since the bar?"

"Yes," I say at the same time Grace says, "No."

She glares at me.

"Officially it just happened," I amend. "But there's always been something between us, right, Grace?"

"Right?" she says, lifting the coffee cup to her lips.

Elle looks between as if she's not quite buying our story. I don't blame her: Grace and I are terrible actors.

"Well," Elle begins. "I better head to class before I'm late. Professor Bend is a bitch with a capital B." She rolls her eyes.

"I'll see you for lunch," Grace calls after her.

When Elle disappears, I whisper to Grace, "You're going to have to do better than that if you want people to think we're actually dating."

She takes a sip of her coffee and I know she's thinking through what she wants to say. Her eyes flick away and back to me. "Maybe you should pick someone else."

"I don't *want* to pick someone else," I argue as she starts toward her class. I fall into step beside her. "Besides, we've already been photographed together."

She sighs. "I know," she grumbles under her breath, her shoulders sagging.

"Hey," I say softly, grabbing her elbow to halt her. "If you don't want to do this, you don't have to. We can forget the whole thing."

She nibbles on her bottom lip nervously for a second and quickly releases it when she realizes what she's doing. "No, no," she stutters. "I want to help you." I smile. "This is just weird for me," she explains. "I've never actually *had* a boyfriend," she admits. My jaw drops. "Don't look at me like that," she hisses. "With an overprotective dad and two brothers, it was pretty impossible. I mean, I've been on dates with a few guys, but pretty much all of those ended in disaster," she admits, wrinkling her nose. "This one time my dad hid in the movie theater and threw popcorn at my date's head. My mom found out what he was up to when my brother spilled the beans, and she came storming into the middle of the movie—chased by ushers—grabbed my dad by the ear and hauled him out of there. It was mortifying. After a while, guys stopped asking me out." She shrugs.

I swallow thickly. "Their loss."

She gives me a small half-smile. "It is what it is."

We start walking again. "Grace," I say hesitantly.

"Yes?" She glances up at me when I don't continue.

"I'd understand if you didn't want to do this. I mean, this is like your chance to meet someone and have a real boyfriend, right? It's not fair of me to tie you up in this."

She shakes her head. "I don't mind, Bennett. Besides, I don't have the time to really date. My course load is packed so the chance for much of a social life is slim to none. I might as well help you out." She shrugs, adjusting the strap of her backpack.

"Are you sure?" I can tell Grace is the kind of person that goes out of her way to help people. I don't want her to do this because she feels like it's the right thing to do.

"Yes." She laughs. "I'm in, I promise."

"Okay. I won't pester you about it anymore." I nod, resolute.

She smiles up at me, and my lips quirk in response.

"This is me." She nods at the building we stand outside of. "Thanks again for the coffee and the cupcakes."

"You're welcome." She starts to leave, and I grab her hand, pulling her to me. She lets out a little sound of surprise and I duck my head, kissing her cheek—dangerously close to her lips because I like to live life on the edge.

"W-What was that for?" she stutters.

"Because you're my girlfriend." I wink.

"R-Right," she stutters again. "I-I have to go."

She practically runs into the building.

I laugh, shaking my head.

Grace Wentworth is highly amusing, and I'm thoroughly going to enjoy messing with her.

She might be my fake girlfriend, but that doesn't mean I can't have some fun.

———

I RUN.

I run, and I run, and I fucking *run*.

I lift weights. I even try some yoga shit. I do everything Coach tells me to do, and he still won't let me on the ice.

"Coach," I cry, clasping my hands together as I beg. "*Please*. I need to get out there." I point to the ice where the team glides around, doing warm ups.

Coach glares at me, hands on his hips. "You know I don't tolerate whininess. Get back in the gym and run another five miles."

My hands clench into fists at my sides. I would never admit this out loud but I'm close to tears. I need to get out there on the ice. I feel like a fucking drug addict needing their next hit. The passion I feel for hockey outweighs everything else, and to not be able to do it for *months* is torture. I lift my hands to my hair, pulling on the short strands.

"I'm losing my fucking mind, Coach."

His eyes narrow on me further. "Don't make me make it ten miles, James."

Oh, fuck. He called me by my last name. "I'm going, Coach," I grumble, heading back through the tunnel.

I make a beeline for the locker room and ram my fist into one of the metal lockers.

Again.

And again.

And again.

I collapse onto the floor, breathing heavily.

This is killing me. I know Coach has my best interests at

heart but *fuck* I really don't give a damn. I've worked so hard, he knows this, but he's still punishing me.

I know he's probably trying to teach me some powerful lesson here about self-control or some bullshit.

I pick myself up off the floor and go back into the gym. I know if I don't do the five miles Coach will somehow find out—he knows *everything*—and I'll only give him more ammunition against me.

I finish my run, shower, and go back to the arena so I can watch the end of the guys' practice. Even if I can't be on the ice, it feels good to be close to it.

Coach shouts orders at them, being particularly rough with the freshman. They're smaller and slower than the seasoned players. They'll get there, though, they always do.

Coach notices me but doesn't acknowledge my presence. I half expect him to yell at me to go run again or something, but he doesn't.

After another twenty or so minutes, he calls it a day and the guys head off the ice to shower.

Coach looks up at me from the bench and says one word. "Soon."

CHAPTER ELEVEN

RACE

ONE MONTH AT SCHOOL AND I HAVEN'T DIED YET, SO I guess that's good.

College is hard, though. So much harder than I expected. Books, TV, and movies make it out to be all fun and games, parties every night and no homework. Oh, boy, that couldn't be farther from the truth.

I barely get to see Elle or Ryland since I'm always cooped up in my room doing homework or pretending to be Bennett's girlfriend. It surprisingly hasn't been that bad. Bennett gets brownie points for being the best fake boyfriend ever. He makes sure I always have coffee and something to eat since he knows I forget when I'm busy studying. I don't much enjoy the times when we have to go out and put on a show for the world—Bennett makes sure to be extra gropey then and I know it's more to mess with me than to actually put on a show for the media—but I endure it because I know it's what I agreed to in the first place.

A knock sounds on the door, and I go to open it. Bennett grins.

"How fares the young maiden? I bring thee sustenance."

I roll my eyes. "You're ridiculous." I close the door behind me and he sits on my bed while I sit back down at my desk. Taking the to-go bag from him, I look inside.

"Turkey club with avocado and chips," he tells me before I can figure it out on my own.

I pull it out and spread the items on the little space I have on my desk.

He looks around. "Where's Elle?"

"No clue," I say. "She said she was going to study in the library, but I have a hard time picturing her actually doing that."

"So she'll be gone a while?" he asks.

I open the chip bag and pop one in my mouth. "Most likely."

He kicks off his shoes and lies back on my bed, making himself at home. "Should I put a sock on the door then?" He grins, wagging his brows.

"What?" I ask, and then a moment later it dawns on me. "Ugh! God! You're such a guy!" I throw a chip at him. It lands on his chest and he picks it up, shrugs, and eats it.

"You're so easy to rile up." He grins. "It amuses me."

"Well *stop*." I bite into my sandwich. "Thanks for the food, but if you're going to keep distracting me you can go. I have homework to do."

He clucks his tongue. "That's no way to talk to your boyfriend."

"*Fake* boyfriend," I remind him.

"Speaking of—" he sits up and grabs one of my many pillow, glaring at the ruffles "—have you decided what you want in exchange?"

I look away from him at my laptop screen. "I haven't decided yet."

I've thought of one thing, but voicing it scares me.

Bennett seems to sense this. "What is it, Grace?" He asks. "What do you *want*?"

My eyes slowly fall back to him. "It's stupid."

"Nothing's stupid," he argues. "Tell me."

"This really is stupid," I argue.

He levels me with a look. "Spit it out, Princess."

Princess. Again it sounds like an insult. "I want two things."

He raises a brow. "And they are?"

"I want you to let me shop for you—I can only handle seeing you in so many t-shirts and jeans. You need some variety."

He chuckles. "Okay, and the second thing?"

"The *main* thing," I emphasize, "is that I want ... I want you to teach me to be bad."

His eyes widen in surprise. "What do you mean?"

"You know what I mean. I just ..." I look away and take a breath before looking back at him. In a softer tone, I say, "I've always done the right thing. Never drinking too much or staying out past curfew. Like you said, I'm *the good girl*, but is that really me? I don't know, because I've never given myself the chance to be something else. *Help me*."

He stares at me for a moment. "But won't that be counter intuitive to the whole fake boyfriend and girlfriend thing? I mean, if you start acting bad, then ..." He trails off and shrugs.

"Bennett," I nearly beg. "I need this. We'll be careful, and I'll still look like the perfect little girlfriend in front of the media. Okay?"

He sighs and scrubs his hands down his face. "Okay. Don't make me regret this."

"Never," I say, grinning from ear to ear now that he agreed.

He stands up. "We might as well start lessons now."

"I have homework." I point at my computer screen.

"I thought you wanted to be bad?" he reminds me. "A bad girl would leave it."

I make a face. This is going to be harder than I thought.

"Change into something a little less ... covered up." He points to my shirt.

"So, in other words, I better borrow something of Elle's?"

"Precisely." He grins. "You catch on fast."

"Where exactly are we going?"

"Out."

"Thank you for the ambiguous answer. That really helps me, Bennett."

He strides over to Elle's closet and rifles through it. "Here, wear this." He thrusts a black garment at me. I hold the dress out, looking it over. It has a high collar—pretty much a turtleneck—but the modesty ends there. It's sleeveless with one of the highest slits I've ever seen.

"No. No way." I shake my head.

He holds out another dress. "It's this or that."

I gasp. The other dress he holds has a million cutouts all over it, like someone attacked it with scissors. Something tells me Elle's exactly the type to do just that.

"I'll go with this one," I squeak, clutching the first dress he gave me a little tighter for fear that he might snatch it out of my hands. "Leave so I can change." I wave my hand at the door.

He puts the other dress away and crosses his arms over

his chest. "We've technically been dating, what? A month now? I'm pretty sure everyone assumes we've seen each other naked. It'd be weird for me to wait outside."

I stare at him open-mouthed. Is he for real?

"We're fake dating," I remind him. "Now get out. Don't you need to change anyway?"

He looks down at what he wears. "Eh, you're probably right," he agrees. "I'll meet you on your dorm steps in thirty minutes."

"Make it an hour. I have to do my makeup and hair."

"*Right*. An hour. Don't flake on me, Wentworth."

"Don't make me regret this, *James*."

He grins at me over his shoulder, reaching for the door. "You're the one that wanted to be bad, remember?"

Before I can respond, he leaves.

I shake my head at the closed door. Something tells me I'm not ready for what he has planned.

An hour later, I meet Bennett outside. He sits on the stairs leading up to my dorm, speaking furiously into his phone.

"I *understand*," he hisses. "Fuck you, you insolent prick. I'm not the one in the wrong here. Don't forget what I know." He clicks the phone off and looks up to find me. He rubs tiredly at his eyes. "How much did you hear?"

"Not much," I whisper softly. "What was that about?"

"Nothing." He looks away from me, his jaw tense. I want to argue, because *something* is definitely going on here, but I keep my mouth shut. Bennett and I aren't really boyfriend and girlfriend, and I'm not even sure if we're really friends. I mean, I *think* we are, we spend enough time together, but ... He stands and smiles at me, but his eyes are still haunted. "You look nice. Beautiful."

"Thanks." I smile back. I'd spent a while on my makeup, getting the smoky eye just right—don't even get me started on winged eyeliner, that takes *for-freaking-ever*. On my lips I'd done a daring red—not my norm, but I figured I might as well—and for my hair, I straightened it and pulled it back into a sleek ponytail. "You don't look too bad yourself."

"I know." He winks.

Bennett's dressed nicer than I've ever seen him in a white button-down shirt with the sleeves rolled up and tucked into gray dress pants. The shirt and pants cling to his muscles, and I'd have to be dead not to notice. His reddish-blonde hair has grown longer since the first time I saw him and falls just the slightest bit over his forehead. He's hot —*really* hot—but unfortunately, he knows it and his cockiness grates on my nerves.

Bennett holds my hand as we walk over to the garage where he parks his car. It's all part of the ruse that we're really a couple. He does it every time we're in public. The disgusted looks I get from other girls are beyond annoying. They hate me because they think I bagged one of the most eligible bachelors in the state. They don't realize it's fake, but even if it wasn't, I don't know why women have to be so petty and jealous. We should have each other's backs, not be clawing at each other's throats. But it's the way things are, and I doubt they'll change.

We reach the garage, and Bennett unlocks his car, opening the passenger door for me. I bend, careful not to step on the longer part of the dress with my heels. That would end in disaster. When I'm inside, he closes the door and jogs around the front. He slides in and starts the car. The dashboard lights up, reminding me of the inside of a cockpit. Not that I really know what that looks like, but I imagine it would be similar to this.

Bennett pulls out of the garage and I look out the window at the setting sun—a promise that another day is soon to come.

I'm itching to ask Bennett where he's taking me, but I keep quiet because a large part of me is scared of what he might say. This whole pushing myself out of my element thing is harder than I thought it would be and I haven't even done anything yet.

The hour-long car ride is fairly silent between us, with only the sound of the radio filling the small space between us. Usually, Bennett never shuts up, or so I've come to learn.

He parks his car on the street and shuts it off. "We'll have to walk a few blocks," he tells me. "Are your feet going to hold up?" He eyes the heels I wear.

I roll my eyes. "Don't underestimate me."

He chuckles. "I never do, Princess."

"Don't call me that," I hiss.

He grins. "Does it bother you?"

"Yes," I say through clenched teeth.

He smiles wider, like the damn Cheshire cat. "All the more reason to call you it."

"Ugh," I groan. "Do you *want* me to stab you in the eye with my heel?"

He chuckles and opens the car door. "You're cute when you're trying to be threatening."

I sigh and get out of the car. How is it that guys always think girls are cute when we're trying to be menacing? Stupidest thing ever. It won't be so cute when I turn my heels into weapons.

Bennett comes around to my side and takes my hand. "No one's around," I tell him, trying to pull my hand from his.

He only holds on tighter and doesn't say a word. I groan, but let him have his way.

After three blocks or so, I can see the club, the line snaking out the door and wrapping around the building. A large sign on the side of the building declares it as VOLT and behind the name, the sign changes colors every few seconds. I can feel the pulse of the music inside and the people on the streets chatter as they wait.

Bennett completely bypasses the line, heading straight for the bouncer.

"Shouldn't we wait in line?" I point behind me at the outrageously long line. Like seriously, don't these people have anything better to do on a Friday night?

"They know me here," Bennett tells me, flashing a quick smile over his shoulder.

I sigh and mumble, "Of course they do," under my breath.

He stops in front of the bouncer. "Hey, Toby. Mind letting us in?"

Toby? Such an un-scary name for a guy as large and muscular as he is.

"Go on in," Toby says in the deepest voice I've ever heard. He undoes the rope and lets us pass.

"Ready?" Bennett asks, leading me to the door.

"Yes," I squeak, when the answer is really *no*.

He opens the door, and it's like I've been transported to another land. The inside is chaotic, but nicer than I expected. The floors are shiny, almost glittering and not covered in God knows what. The ceiling is a strange crinkly design that looks like foil or something, and it reflects the teal blue lights that strobe the entire place. The bar also glows with the same light. The bartenders run back and forth, taking orders and making them just as fast. The whole middle of the club is full of people dancing, but there are sections branching off of it where people can sit.

"So what's first on 'Bennett's Guide to Being Bad'?" I yell to be heard above the music.

He laughs. "Getting drunk. It's time for you to experience the glorious world of alcohol, Princess." He holds tightly to my hand and leads me up a narrow staircase.

"Really? Because it looks like we're headed *away* from the bar."

We reach the top of the stairs and he turns down a hall and opens a door.

The room is open to the club below, but there are dark curtains that can be drawn across if you don't want to be seen. There's a large round bed in the center, covered in numerous pillows, and directly in front of the balcony there's a high-top table with four chairs.

"What is this place?" I ask.

"The VIP section," he explains, flopping on the bed and making himself at home. "Ah, right on time. Hello, Danicka," he greets the perky blonde that enters the room with a tray of premade drinks. She looks like she's melted and poured into her teal dress and her face is covered in way too many layers of makeup—come on, girl, less *is* more. Her fake blonde hair is curled and hangs down to her butt—clearly extensions, and cheap ones from what I can tell. Her boobs nearly spill out of her dress and those are as fake as her blonde hair.

"I saw you come in," she says in this breathy porn star voice. She bends down to hand Bennett his drink, making sure he gets an eyeful of her cleavage, and of course, he looks. I can't help but look down at my own chest. It's a B cup at best—okay, so more like an A cup. It's never bothered me before, but suddenly I'm wondering what a guy like Bennett thinks of the little I have to offer.

Porn Star—that's what I'm calling her—bats her eyes at Bennett one last time before slowly making her way over to me. She makes sure to sway her hips in a way that Bennett can't keep his eyes off her ass. "Would you like a drink?" she asks. "I made several. I wasn't sure what you'd like."

"She'll take them all," Bennett says from his perch on the couch.

Porn Star smiles at me and removes the drinks from her tray, leaving them on the table.

"Let me know if you need *anything*," she tells Bennett before she leaves the room.

I shake my head at him and he blinks innocently. "What'd I do?"

"Her, I'm guessing," I say, picking up one of the drinks. I sniff it and nearly gag.

"You don't smell it, Princess. You drink it." He sits up and takes a sip of his own drink, something dark colored on ice. "And I've never fucked Danicka." His brows furrow and he stares into his glass. "That I can recall."

"Oh, my God, you're ridiculous." I take a seat on one of the chairs—no way in hell am I joining him in the bed. I lift the drink to my lips and start to take a sip.

"It's a shot. You don't sip it," he tells me.

I glare at him. "I'm beginning to think you talk incessantly because you like the sound of your own voice."

"I like everything about me. I'm one of a kind."

I shake my head. "Your ego must be the size of the Titanic."

"I actually think it's closer to the size of the ocean it sank in," he counters with a grin.

I take a deep breath then and gulp down the shot. It feels like fire on my throat and I cough. "What the hell was that?" My eyes water and I gag. I really hope I don't throw up, that would only be more ammunition for Bennett to use to make fun of me.

"I believe that was tequila. People usually follow it with a lime, but you took that like a champ."

"Hardly." I gasp for air. "That tasted like poison."

"I'm pretty sure alcohol *is* poison."

"I don't know if I can do this." I eye the five other drinks on the table.

Bennett stands and strides over to the table. He leans his elbows on the table, his glass dangling from his fingertips.

"This is what you wanted," he reminds me. "Let go. Be someone else for a night. Let your hair down."

"That's easier said than done."

He taps my forehead. "You need to get out of here. You spend too much time in your head overthinking things."

I look away from him and out on the dance floor. He's right, and I hate that.

He hands me another drink, and I take it reluctantly. "Bottoms up." He lifts his own glass in a silent cheers.

THE GAME PLAN

I take a deep breath and take the shot.
Then the next.
And another.

CHAPTER TWELVE

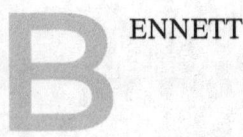ENNETT

THERE ARE ANGRY DRUNKS.
    Horny drunks.
    Loud drunks.
    Sad drunks.
    Silly drunks.

Happy drunks.

And reckless drunks.

Grace is a silly drunk.

"Another!" she declares, slamming her last glass on the table and hiccups, then giggles.

"Nah, I think you're good," I tell her, trying not laugh.

She pouts. "I want more."

I shake my head. "Maybe later." More like *never*, but I don't tell her that. The girl is a lightweight, and there's no way she'll be able to stomach anything else and still function.

"You're such a fun sucker."

I laugh. "I don't hear that one often."

She glances down at dance floor. "I'm going to dance." Before I can blink, she's up out of her chair, heading for the exit of the VIP room.

"Like hell you are," I mutter under my breath, storming after her.

When I get to the hall, she's already gone. I look left and then right so fast that my head probably blurs. How can someone in heels that high walk that fast? It can't be humanly possible.

"Fuck," I curse, tearing at my hair. I practically run down the stairs into the club and of-fucking-course she's disappeared yet again, swallowed whole by the crowd. The chances of me finding her are slim to none, like finding a needle in a haystack. But I never give up, and I'll burn down the damn haystack if that's what it takes to find the needle.

I shove my way through the crowd, my eyes searching every person I pass.

"Dammit, Grace. Where the fuck are you?"

Panic rises inside me and I *never* panic. But the thought that Grace is drunk off her ass and lost in here is killing me. If she gets hurt, or some guy gropes her, it's my fault.

"Hey, watch where you're going." Some beefy ass dude shoves me away. I'm tempted to punch the fucker in the face but I have more important matters at hand.

I spot a flash of glossy brown hair in a ponytail and grab the girl's shoulder. "Grace?" She looks up at me, her blue eyes pissed off. I immediately let go. "*Not* Grace."

I move along the dance floor, but she's nowhere to be found. I'm beginning to worry that she left, and the thought of her outside wandering the streets alone actually scares me.

I head toward the bar to find Danicka in the hope that maybe she's seen Grace.

That's when I finally spot her, leaning over the bar speaking to one of the male bartenders. The guy grins and she throws her head back and laughs.

Oh, hell no.

I storm forward. "What do you think you're doing, Princess?"

She nearly collapses in my arms. "Bennett, I was just talking to Peter here thanking him for the delicious drinks."

"Danicka made your drinks, remember?" I tell her, holding onto her waist so she doesn't fall.

"Ugh, Porn Star, that's right. I remember now." She taps her forehead.

"Come on, we're leaving." I start to drag her away.

"No," she cries, pulling out of my arms. "I want to dance. Dance with me, Bennett."

I lower my head, silently cursing Grace and this whole "Bennett's Guide to Being Bad" thing.

"Fine. One dance," I tell her, holding up one finger and wiggling it.

"Yay!" she cries, bouncing up and down. She all but tackles me, wrapping her thin arms around my neck and hugging me. "Your chest is so hard," she says in her alcohol-induced haze.

"I thought you wanted to dance," I remind her, pushing softly against her shoulders.

"Aren't we dancing?" Her words slur.

"Oh, yeah. Totally dancing."

"You're lying." She pulls away, her eyes glassy. Her pink lips pucker in a frown. "I'm going to go find someone who really wants to dance with me." She starts to flee into the crowd but I grab her arm and she ricochets back into my chest. She looks up at me with wide doe eyes. "That wasn't nice."

I lower my head, my lips skimming her ear. "You wanna dance, Princess? You dance with me."

Her breath catches, and I swear I can feel her pulse quicken where I grip her wrist. I lead her out onto the dance floor, telling myself that one dance won't hurt anything. As soon as the song's over, I'll haul her drunk ass out of here and call it a job well done.

She goes to put her arms around my neck, like we're about to sway like some awkward teenagers at prom. I shake my head and push her arms away. "That's not how you dance in a club," I tell her. "Turn around." She looks apprehensive. "Trust me."

She nods once and turns around, fitting her slender body into the space in front of me. She's so small, fitting perfectly into the curve of my body. I instantly feel protective of her, and I glare at all the guys around us in case they'd dare to try to come near her.

I put one of my hands on her waist, and the other on her stomach. She tilts her head back against my chest, her eyes closing with a wistful smile touching her lips. Something tugs in my chest—some emotion I can't even begin to understand.

We move to the beat of the song, our bodies automatically seeming to know what to do.

Grace winds her arms behind her and up around my neck. I don't stop her this time. She pushes her ass against me and I groan.

"You're playing with fire," I tell her. "You're going to get burned."

She opens her eyes and smiles lazily.

I clench my teeth.

Don't do anything stupid, Bennett. She's drunk and you're not. Besides, you need *her to make you look good. Don't fuck her and screw things up. Keep your dick in your pants for once.*

"We have to go," I tell Grace, dragging her off the dance floor and to the exit.

"What?" she protests. "I was having fun."

"We're leaving," I reiterate.

If I don't get out of here, I'll ruin everything, and I can't afford the fallout.

CHAPTER THIRTEEN

Grace

My eyes feel like they're sealed together with glue. And not like that glue you use as a kid, either. No, this is the heavy duty stuff, like Gorilla glue or something.

I slowly peel my eyes open and immediately shut them.

The light is too bright and my head pounds like someone beat me with a hammer.

This is the worst I think I've ever felt—and that's saying something considering the nasty flu I got two years ago.

I try again to open my eyes, but it's too much. "Elle," I groan. "Shut the blinds."

She laughs and I hear the sound of them being closed. "I have to say, coming home to you two snuggled in bed is hysterical. I was beginning to think you weren't a real couple. I mean, I don't think I've ever seen you kiss."

I open my eyes again, and this time I can leave them open. "Two of us?"

Elle nods at my bed, holding out a coffee from our favorite shop. I take the cup from her and look beside me in bed.

"You have to be kidding me," I mutter.

Bennett's stretched out beside me, fast asleep with his arm around my waist. I'm going to blame my raging hangover for my oversight in that little detail.

I can barely remember last night.

But I do remember all the alcohol ... and Porn Star.

I lower my head in shame. I hope to God I didn't do anything stupid while I was drunk, but knowing my luck, it's a very real possibility.

I set the coffee cup on the small table beside me bed and shake Bennett's shoulder roughly.

He stirs and tightens his hold on me. In fact, he pulls so

hard that I fall back on the bed as he snuggles me against his chest like some oversized teddy bear. His lips press to my neck. "Mornin'."

"Ugh," Elle groans, clutching at her chest. "You guys are too sickeningly cute."

I want to tell her it's all for show, but I'm not allowed.

"Bennett." I rock against him. "Wake up."

"Keep doing that. Feels good."

My pops open. "Ugh, you're so gross."

I yank my body from his octopus hold and fall to the floor. Oh, Jesus Christ, I'm only in my bra and panties—*did he undress me?*

The sound of me falling to the floor finally wakes him up and he peers at me over the edge of the bed with sleepy eyes and his hair ruffled around his head like a baby bird. I might think he looked cute if I wasn't so mad. "Why are you on the floor, Princess? That's dirty, and I thought princesses hated dirt."

"Ugh!" I stand up and stomp across the room, pulling on a pair of cotton shorts and a tank top so I don't feel so exposed. "You're so annoying."

"Good morning to you too, sweetheart." He grins and glances at Elle. "Morning."

She lifts her coffee cup to her. "Good morning, Bennett."

Bennett sits up and yawns, stretching his arms above his head.

"Can you put a shirt on?" I snap, looking around for his clothes. "And please, tell me you have pants on."

"I prefer to sleep in the buff." He grins crookedly.

I give him a horrified look. "We didn't have sex, did we?" I squeak. It's definitely the wrong thing to say in front of Elle, but I'm panicking. I can't even remember leaving the club so anything is a possibility.

"I was kidding, Grace," he sobers. "Jesus fuck, you were drunk off your ass—I wouldn't have taken advantage of you. You know that."

I inhale a deep breath, feeling the panic and fear leave my body.

He stands, and he is in his boxers so I feel infinitely better. He grabs his dress pants off the floor and slips into them.

"I'm sorry," I say. "I know you wouldn't have done that. It's just ... I can't remember much."

He nods in understanding. "It's okay. Want to go get breakfast?" He looks at his phone. "Or lunch, rather?"

I don't really want to. I'd rather lie in bed and sleep off the rest of this hangover, but I remind myself that I *am* his fake girlfriend, and I kind of have to save face after what just happened in front of Elle.

"Sure." I nod. "I need to eat," I lie. The thought of eating actually makes me want to throw up. I look down at the clothes I put on. "I better change. Meet me outside?"

Bennett grins and flops down on my bed. "Nah. I think I'll stay right here and enjoy the show. You don't have anything to hide from me, sweetheart." He winks.

I take a deep breath so that I don't yell at him or send him a death glare.

Bennett James is dancing across my last nerve and I haven't even been awake fifteen minutes.

"Fine." I give him an evil smile and shimmy out of my shorts. I don't even care that Elle is in the room and getting a show as well—living in a dorm together we've seen each other in all different stages of undress, it's just how it is.

I turn around and bend over, searching through one of my drawers, purposely wiggling my ass in the process. I hear Bennett hiss, and I smile with satisfaction. I grab a pair of jeans and put them on with my back turned to him. I glance over my shoulder and give him a coy smile.

I leave my tank top on and grab a loose, over-the-shoulder, purple sweater from my closet and tug it on. My hairbrush sits on my dresser and I grab it, swiping it through my hair before pulling it up into a messy bun.

"I'm ready. Where's your shirt?" I grin at him as he stares at me dumbfounded from the bed.

"Th-The floor."

I search the floor and find his white button-down, tossing it at him. "A little dressy for breakfast, don't you think?" I laugh.

He shakes his head, trying to clear his thoughts. "Yeah," he mumbles. "Better swing by my dorm and change." He glances at Elle as he stands and puts his shirt on. "Do you want to come get something to eat with us?"

She shakes her head and crosses her leg, her gaze focused on her phone. "Thanks, but I'm meeting some friends."

"What friends?" I ask, confused.

"Celine and Makenna. They live across the hall from us." She points like I don't know what across the hall means.

"Oh, right." I shake my head.

"You'd like them," she tells me. "If you didn't spend all your time studying and with lover boy." She nods her head at Bennett.

He chuckles. "I'm sorry for keeping her from you."

"You better be sorry," she chortles. To me she says, "We're in need of a girls' night. What do you think?"

"Sure." I grab my purse off my desk and sling it across my shoulder. "I'll see you later."

Bennett follows me out into the hall. I see a group of three girls standing by the elevator and I quickly veer in the other direction to the stairs. Bennett chuckles behind me.

"What are you so scared of?" He laughs behind me as I start down the stairs.

I halt and whip around. "You're wearing the same clothes from last night. You know what people would think."

He grips the banister and leans down to where I stand three steps below him. "So what? The entire campus already *knows* we're dating, so I'm pretty sure they assume we're having sex as well." My cheeks flame and his mouth parts in surprise. "Are you a virgin?" I look away and start down the steps then, embarrassment clinging to me like a second skin.

It's not like I *chose* to be a virgin. There was just never a guy I liked enough and my dad and brothers made it even more difficult on top of that.

We reach the last stairs and I sprint forward to push open the door but Bennett's faster. He comes up behind me and holds the door closed with his body pressed against the back of mine. My breath falters and I freeze.

"We're not done talking Grace."

I whip around. "There's nothing to talk about."

He peers down at me, his hazel eyes taking in more than I wish they would. "There's loads to talk about." He moves a little bit closer, which puts our bodies completely aligned. "Why didn't you tell me?"

"I didn't know I needed to. What's it to you?"

"Fuck, Grace. I just … I don't know. I feel like I should've known."

"I'm your *fake* girlfriend Bennett—so my virginity really isn't any of your business, and if I'd fucked half the student body that wouldn't be your business, either."

His jaw clenches and he shakes his head, his hair brushing my forehead in the process. "That's not why I feel like I should've known," he says softer. "If I'd known I wouldn't have …"

"You wouldn't have what?" I ask, my back flush against

the door. Every time I breathe, my chest rubs up against him and I *hate* that I like it.

"I don't know," he says gruffly. "I guess I wouldn't have made some of the shitty jokes and innuendos I have."

"Being a virgin doesn't make me a prude. You can say whatever you want. I promise I won't go running for the hills."

He smiles slightly. "Then what was that mini freak out in your room?"

I sigh. "I couldn't remember what happened last night, remember? Virgin or not, I'd think anyone sensible would be a little worried about what they'd done."

He nods. "Right."

He pulls away slightly—just enough for me to not feel like my personal space has been invaded anymore.

"I never want to talk about this again," I tell him, lifting my chin defiantly. "It's not important."

He nods and moves back completely so I'm finally able to open the door. "You're the boss."

I nod too. "Okay. Glad we're on the same page." I open the door and step out into the afternoon sunlight. "Ugh, kill me." I shield my eyes, barely able to keep them open. My head begins throbbing with a renewed force.

Bennett and I make the trek across campus, and as per usual, people stare and take photos. I don't understand it. Bennett's just a person—he's *normal*, even if his head is inflated to the size of Alaska.

Bennett reaches for my free hand and entwines our

fingers together. He smiles down at me and then brushes his lips against my cheek.

It's all a show, but no one but us knows that.

I just hate that it feels so real.

"Girls' night!" Elle screams shrilly, taking my hand and dragging me out of our room.

"Where are we going?" I ask.

"Makenna wants to go to the mall," she says, rapping her knuckles against the door to their dorm room.

While we wait, she picks up the marker for their dry erase board and begins doodling a little bird. Just as she finishes, the door opens and we're greeted by the two girls. I recognize them now from seeing them around the building but I've never spoken to them. I don't really speak to most people. The whole deal I have going with Bennett makes it hard to trust people—I've had a few people try to get close to me solely so they could meet him.

"This is Makenna." Elle points to the light-haired brunette with brilliant blue eyes. "And Celine." She points to the other girl—this one with dark-brown hair and unique gray-colored eyes.

"Hey," I wave awkwardly. "I'm Grace."

"We know." Celine speaks for both of them.

"Right." I nod. "Because of Bennett," I mumble under my breath.

The Makenna girl laughs and it's a light, twinkling sound. "No, silly. You live right across from us, of course we know who you are."

"Oh, yeah."

Someone give me the crown for Queen of Awkward.

I feel bad since the same goes for them and I had no idea what their names were until now.

"Should we get going?" I point over my shoulder. "Should I call us a cab or something?"

"I have a car," Celine says, shutting the door behind her. She's dressed in a pair of shiny black skinny jeans and a black sweater that falls over her shoulder. I then look at Elle and she's dressed similarly. I'm tempted to ask them if they're long lost sisters or something.

Celine's car isn't parked in the garage like Bennett's is. Instead, hers is in a lot all the way on the other side of campus.

"Inconvenient spot," she says, unlocking the doors to her beat-up Toyota. "But at least I have it, so I can't complain too much.

We all climb inside, and I swear to God the car *groans*—I'm afraid it's going to fall apart beneath us.

"Don't worry, it always makes that sound," Celine says from the driver's seat as if she read my mind.

I buckle my seatbelt and say a silent prayer that we make it to the mall and back to campus safe and sound.

It takes us thirty minutes to get to the mall, and when

we do, it takes us another twenty minutes of driving around to find a place to park.

"Everyone must have decided to go to the mall tonight." Makenna giggles from the front seat.

"Must have," I agree.

Once we're finally parked, we get out and the car groans again and *shakes*—I know, because some rust specks fall to the ground.

"She's got some more miles left in her." Celine taps the hood of the car and smiles at me.

I nod, even though I think the car belongs in a junkyard. I don't think I've ever seen a car falling apart the way this one is.

"Can we get something to eat first?" Elle grabs her stomach. "I'm *starving*."

"There's a really good Italian restaurant on the bottom level," Makenna says. "Is everyone good with that?"

"I am," I say.

"Good with me," Celine says, dropping her keys into her purse.

"Italian sounds like *heaven*." Elle licks her lips. "Lead the way." She motions her hand for Makenna to go first.

By some miracle, the restaurant is close to the area we parked, so we don't have to walk too far, but they're packed.

"It's going to be a thirty-minute wait." Makenna frowns, holding onto one of those vibrating things. "I put my name down on the waitlist, but we can go somewhere else if you want?"

I lean against the wall and look toward Elle since she's the one that's the hungriest.

"I've already smelled the food and it smells like heaven. We're staying. I'll live." She slides down the wall, plopping on the marble floor.

"I can wait here while you guys look around a bit." Makenna waves around the round device she holds. "I can text you when we're being seated."

"No." Elle shakes her head. "We'll wait with you."

We all end up sitting in a row outside the restaurant on the mall floor.

I learn that Celine is hoping to become a forensic scientist—I would've never guessed that—and Makenna doesn't know what she wants to major in. Makenna is also a cheerleader for the university team and she seems far more interested in that than school.

We're in the middle of chatting when we're interrupted by a male voice. "Hey."

I look up and my smile falls. *Tanner.* The guy I fell on my first day of classes. After that, he seemed to make it his own personal mission to get to know me. His flirtatious behavior was mildly annoying, but I did my best to brush it off. Once it became public knowledge that Bennett and I were a couple, he backed off ... somewhat. He was nice, I guess, but something about him made me feel dirty.

"Hi," I say.

He grins widely, and his eyes squint as he gives the girls

beside me a once-over. "Are you going to introduce me to your friends?"

I sigh. I wasn't planning on it. "This is Elle, Makenna, and Celine," I introduce blandly. Tanner never seems to pick up on my lack of interest. I can tell he's one of those guys that thinks he's God's gift to women. Bennett's cocky too, but not in that way—at least he has *some* humbleness about him.

"Nice to meet you." His eyes linger on Makenna, and I swear he licks his lips like she's a juicy steak he's about to devour.

Makenna blushes under his gaze, and I'm tempted to smack the back of her head and yell, "Get it together girl!" But I'm sure that would be frowned upon.

"So what are you ladies up to?" Tanner puffs out of his chest, stretching the cotton of his shirt so you can see every ripped and defined edge of his abs.

I look at him like he's the dumbest person I've ever encountered. "Waiting to get something to eat." I leave the *obviously* off. I almost expect him to invite himself.

Instead, he says, "Oh, yeah. Well I guess I'll be seeing you ladies around."

"Mmhmm," I hum.

He nods and heads off on his way—and not a moment too soon because the buzzer finally buzzes.

"That's our table." Makenna jumps up and rushes over to the hostess who already stands waiting with four menus.

We get seated near the front, where it's the loudest so conversation is near impossible.

Regardless, it's nice, and I find that I really like Makenna and Celine.

I know I need to start making more time for friends in-between all the time I spend doing homework and with Bennett.

Everyone needs a life, after all.

CHAPTER FOURTEEN

BENNETT

IT'S REALLY A SHAME THAT MURDERING SOMEONE IS frowned upon, because right about now I want to put the blade of my skate against Tanner's throat. The freshman is asking for it.

He slams into me from the side, sending me into the glass. It vibrates from the force of my weight hitting it.

I groan, biting down on my mouth guard. I see red and go after the fucker.

He's light and fast on the ice, but I've been doing this longer and with players a lot tougher than him. I don't know why the kid has it out for me, but I'm really fucking sick and tired of it.

"James!" Coach yells at me. "Focus! Don't let Wallace distract you! Protect your fucking center!"

I groan again, knowing I have to follow Coach's orders.

I skate as hard and as fast as I can to Michael, who moves furiously down the ice with his stick and the puck. Tanner tries to swipe the puck, but Toby—the left wing—blocks him. I skate up to Michael and he glances at me for only the briefest of seconds. In his eyes, though, I see the same love I have for the sport. This is his life too.

He smacks the puck into the net and the goaltender is unable to stop it.

We all hoot and holler—like as if this is a real game where the score counts.

"Let's call it a day, gentlemen," Coach calls from the box. "We've got a lot of work to do to be ready for your first game in a month." He shakes his head and pinches the bridge of his nose. "A *lot* of work," he reiterates. "James, we need to talk." He gives me a solemn look. I don't like his tone of voice. Something tells me I'm really not going to like what he has to say. "Come see me after you shower. I'll be in my office."

I nod once, letting him know I understand.

The team skates off the ice and I fall in behind the last guy.

I've been doing good with these guys. Really fucking good. But suddenly, I fear it hasn't been good enough.

When I get to the locker room, I shuck off my gear and shower as fast as humanly possible. I get dressed in a pair of jeans, t-shirt, with a sweatshirt thrown over top. It has the school mascot on it—a tiger.

I grab my bag and head down the hall to Coach's office. I knock on the door once and his raspy voice calls, "Come in."

I allow myself one deep breath before I open the door and step inside.

"Hey, Coach. What's up?" I try to sound as chill as possible, but it's hard. Luckily, I'm a master at keeping myself in check.

"Coach Matthews called me," he says, referring to my coach for the Plymouth Hunters. "He said the last drug test you did for the team over the summer came back positive for steroids."

My world falls out from under me. My fists clench at my sides. "He's lying." And he is. The fucker—because he can't use me for his endeavors he's going to try to destroy me.

Coach shrugs. "I want to believe you, Bennett, but he faxed me over the papers, and I can't deny the truth in what

I see." He looks at me sadly, like a father that's been let down.

"Coach," I plead. "Give me another drug test—I promise you I'm not on anything. You *know* me." I pound my fist against my chest. "You know me," I repeat.

He looks tired ... Defeated, almost. I'd expect him to be angry in this situation, but it's like the fight has gone out of him. "I plan on giving you a drug test," he says, and opens a drawer. He holds out a white clear cup for me to pee in and I take it. "This way I can be sure you don't have time to sober up if you're on anything." He leans back in his chair. "There's something else, Bennett."

What else could there possibly be? "What?" I ask, scared to know.

"Your probation has been changed to a suspension for half of the season."

"You have got to be fucking kidding me!" I roar. I completely lose it then, shoving everything off of Coach's desk. I scream until the veins in my neck feel ready to burst. "He's ruining my life!" Melodramatic, maybe, but Coach Matthews has it out for me. He's a complete asshole—if he can't own me, make me one of his puppets, he'll break me. Completely fucking ruin me.

When I can finally regain my wits, I pick up the stupid fucking cup I need to pee in and point at Coach. "Don't trust anything that man tells you. He's a fucking slime ball."

Coach surprises me by saying, "I know."

I march out of his office and pee in the cup, dropping it

off in the sports clinic. They won't find anything. I'm squeaky clean. But I don't put it past Coach Matthews to have covered his tracks some way, somehow.

I need to go to Boston.

Tonight.

———

I KNOCK ON GRACE'S DOOR.

I'm a jittery mess, and I should be on my way to Boston, but I can't go alone. I'm scared if I go alone I just might strangle the man.

The door opens a second later and Grace stands there in the shortest pair of shorts I've ever seen and a skin-tight top.

"Do you always study dressed like that?" I gawk at her. I wouldn't be surprised if there's drool in the corner of my mouth.

She looks down. "I like to be comfy. Why are you here?" She looks around the hall like she's afraid we'll be spotted together.

"I don't know," I sigh, shoving my hands in my pockets. "Some shit happened and I need to go to Boston tonight. Can you come with me?" She looks back into her room and then at me. "Are you not alone?" My tone sounds way too jealous for my liking. Giggles sound in the room and I grin. "Slumber party? Are there going to be pillow fights? Why didn't you invite me, Princess? I'm hurt." I pout, clutching my heart.

She sighs. "Celine and Makenna are here *studying* which has somehow turned into fingernail painting. I'm still really studying, though—so no, I can't go to Boston tonight. It's already eight, Bennett, and that's like a three-hour drive."

"*Please*," I beg her. "I can't do this alone. Bring your books. You can study on the way. We can stay at my place in the city and come back in the morning. Tomorrow's Saturday so you can't argue about missing class," I remind her.

She bites her lip and I know I've worn her down. "Okay," she says softly. "Give me like fifteen minutes to pack and change and I'll meet you at your car."

"No, I'll wait outside," I tell her. "I don't want you walking across campus in the dark by yourself." I pause, my brows furrowing. "Wait, fifteen minutes? Princess, we're only going to be gone overnight. You don't need to pack your whole closet."

She rolls her eyes. "My books, laptop, and a change of clothes, Bennett. That's all. Promise." She promptly closes the door in my face.

I chuckle. "Well then."

I stuff my hands into the pocket of my sweatshirt and head outside to the steps to wait. If we're spending the night at my apartment I don't need to pack anything and I have my gym bag with me so I can at least wash that stuff tonight. I'm sure Grace will shit her pants at the sight of me doing my own laundry. She seems to think I'm incapable of doing most things. I like to think I just might surprise her.

The air is growing cold as we move into October and I love it. It's my favorite time of the year. I love the change of the leaves and the crispness in the air—something in the air just smells of *hockey*. I might play the whole year between training and scrimmages, but fall time means real games. It means the rush and high of a win and the crushing feeling of defeat when we lose.

My phone rings in my pocket and I pull it out, seeing my sister's name light up the screen.

"Hey, Bina," I say into the speaker.

"Bennett, what the hell?" I hear something slam in the background, like a kitchen counter or something.

I take a seat on the step and pinch the bridge of my nose. "What did I do now?"

Something else slams and she curses. "Our sports reporter cornered me today, with this gloating smirk on his face, and informed me that he had exclusive news that you've been suspended for doing steroids. I told him that was an outright lie, but is it, Bennett? Are you on steroids? Do I need to come there and haul your ass to rehab? Because I will. You might be a giant, but I can do it. Don't underestimate me, Bennett James."

"Shit, Bina." I sigh, defeated.

She squeaks and I'm scared she's about to cry. "No, Bennett. *No*."

"Bina, it's complicated," I say.

"So you're doing steroids?"

"No," I say firmly. "I'm not. But Coach Matthews has made it look like I am."

"Why would he do that? I don't believe you." Yep, she's about to cry.

"Dammit, Sabrina, I'm your *brother*. Who are you going to believe? Some shitty sports reporter or your family?"

"It doesn't make any sense, though." She bangs something else, it sounds like she's rattling in the silverware drawer. "Why would he fudge a drug test?"

I sigh. "I can't talk about this with you, Bina."

"Is it because I'm a reporter or your sister?"

"Both," I answer, feeling a headache coming on. "There's just a lot of shit going on right now." I rub the back of my head. "The last drug test I did for Matthews was when I was still playing for the team so that was *months* ago. Just let this go, please?" I beg her. "All I want is to make it through this season and get traded to another team."

"Traded? You want to *leave*?"

I look toward the lights dotting campus. "Yes. I have to."

I have to get away from Matthews before he ruins my life.

All because of what I saw.

"Why? What's going on?" She pesters. "Talk to me, Bennett. I'm your sister."

"That's exactly why I can't talk to you. You don't know what I'm up against. This guy ... I don't trust him."

"Your coach?"

"Yes."

She grows quiet. "I'll look into it."

"Bina, no," I beg.

But it's too late, she's already hung up.

"That sounded intense."

I look up to find Grace standing over me. It's the second time she's stumbled upon me in a heated conversation.

"Yeah." I sigh. My voice sounds tired, like all the fight's gone out of me, but the fight is really only beginning.

"Are you going to tell me why we're taking an unexpected trip to Boston in the middle of the night?"

"It's not the middle of the night," I counter. She raises a brow. "I'll explain in the car."

Explain what I can, at least.

"You better." She slings her duffle bag into my chest, and I cough from the unexpected impact with my gut. "You dragged me out of my dorm room, the least you can do is carry my bag." Her green eyes sparkle with laughter.

My lips quirk into a smile and we fall into step beside each other, walking across campus.

We get to her favorite coffee spot and I point. "I want some. You?"

She nods eagerly. "I'm going to need it if you expect me to study in the car—riding in cars make me sleepy," she admits with a sheepish smile.

I smile down at her. Her face is clear of makeup, showing a small smattering of freckles across her nose, and her hair is pulled back in a sloppy ponytail. She's beautiful. She's always beautiful. And I actually like being around her—which is something I didn't expect.

We head into the coffee shop and place our order. Grace tries to fight me on paying for hers—arguing that I bring her coffee every morning—but then I remind her that I dragged her out of her room for a three-hour long road trip and then she stopped arguing.

With our coffees in hand, we walk the last little bit to the garage where I park my car.

I drop my gym bag and Grace's into the trunk and start the car. We sit there for a few minutes while I put in the address.

I've calmed down some since finding out what Matthews did, but I know my temper will rise once more when I get to his place.

Confronting the fucker is probably the last thing I should ever do, but I can't sit idly by while he destroys everything I've worked for—so that my word counts for nothing against his. I've already done a good enough job destroying my image, but he's determined to make sure I never play in a professional game ever again. I promised to keep my mouth shut about what I saw, but my promise must count for nothing and he wants to silence me forever.

"What has you so worked up?" Grace asks as I fix my phone in its spot to navigate me.

"Hockey stuff."

She crosses her legs and pulls out a textbook from her

backpack, plopping it in her lap. "That's the most evasive answer you could've possibly given. Elaborate." She flips through her textbook, looking for the right page.

"I got suspended for drug use. Steroids."

She slams the textbook closed. "What?"

I pull out of the garage and into traffic. "I'm not on anything," I tell her.

"I know," she replies immediately. "That's why I'm confused."

My head whips to her. "How do you know?"

She looks at me with a puzzled expression. "Because I know you."

I glance at her briefly before my eyes dart back to the road.

Because *she* knows me? My own sister didn't believe me.

"Why?" I ask.

"Why what?" She begins flipping through her textbook again.

"Why do you think you know me?"

She snorts. "Bennett, I pretty much spend every waking moment with you that I'm not in class or studying. I *know* you pretty damn well at this point—and I'm not an idiot. I'd know if you were abusing anything." She reaches over then and jabs me in the chest.

"What the hell was that for?" I nearly run off the road trying to get away from her before she can poke me again.

"Checking to see if your boobs are sensitive. Isn't that

what happens if you're taking steroids. You become a woman?"

"First, off they're *not* boobs—they're pecs, get it right, woman. Secondly, I have no fucking clue."

She shrugs and sits back in the seat. "I was just making a point." A playful smile tugs on her lips. I knock her textbook off her lap and onto the floor. "What was that for?" she cries, quickly picking it up and looking it over like it's an injured bird.

"Forget studying. Distract me."

"Bennett," she groans. "I have to study."

"And I'm about to go and murder my coach for telling everyone I'm doing steroids when I'm *not*."

"Wait, your *coach* is the one that lied about the drug test? It's not some fuck up somewhere else?"

My jaw clenches. "It's him," I say in a rough tone. "He's fucking up my life. If I hadn't gotten injured, he would've found a way to get me off the team then. This is his latest ploy because I'm getting better—good enough to go back."

"I didn't know that," Grace says softly, and I swear there's sadness in her gaze when she looks at me.

"Aw, are you going to miss me, Princess?" I mock. I know I shouldn't have said it, but that's what I do—I always fuck up a good thing.

"Only in your dreams," she shoots back.

I grin. "You love me, admit it."

She snorts. "Now you're really stretching the truth." She picks a piece of lint off her book.

We grow quiet and I let her study, but about an hour into the drive, I break the silence. "Thank you," I say softly.

She looks up from her book with tired eyes. "For what?"

"For coming with me." I swallow thickly, my fingers tight around the wheel. "This ... This is hard for me. This whole situation. And I probably shouldn't even be doing this, but I have to speak to the fucker and I know ... I know if you're waiting for me I won't do anything stupid."

Grace's tongue slides out the barest bit to moisten her lips. "You're welcome. I could tell you needed me, so I'm here. I'm here for you, Bennett," she reiterates.

"Thanks." I reach over and take her hand in mine, entwining our fingers together

"Bennett ..."

"Yes?"

"You know no one can see us, right?" she asks.

"Yeah?" I say, a questioning tone to my voice.

"Then why are you holding my hand?"

I let go like my hand has caught on fire. "Oh, sorry," I mumble awkwardly.

"It's okay," she says, and I swear she's blushing but it's too dark to tell.

We don't speak much for the rest of the trip. I arrive at Coach Matthews McMansion in the suburbs a little before midnight.

"Sit here," I tell Grace.

My blood is boiling once more. Coach's shiny red Ferrari sits in his driveway—the man likes his cars—and I wish I had a fucking baseball bat so I could beat the car to a pulp. It'd be a shame to hurt a car that nice, but it's tainted with Matthews' filth so it's already ruined.

I march up to the door and ring the doorbell again and again and again.

I'm not worried about waking up his wife and daughter. He doesn't have a family anymore. Just an endless barrage of perky-boobed blondes since he divorced his wife two years ago.

I see a light flick on and then Coach Matthews appears through the glass in the door. It distorts his image, but I'd know the man anywhere.

He's a legend. He played professionally as long as he could and was one of the best players in history—still is, I guess. When he couldn't play any longer, he turned to coaching.

Before I became a part of his team, I revered him. I wanted nothing more than to be Joseph Matthews. The way he commanded the ice was unparalleled.

When I first joined the team, he was just your normal hardass coach.

But then things changed and I found out who he really is.

Scum and a liar—he uses his position to gain what he wants.

He swings the door open, his dark hair—graying at the temples—is ruffled and there's lipstick stains all over his neck and bare chest.

"James," he greets. "Mary, Sherrie, Terry, and I were just getting started. Would you like to join us?"

I punch him straight across his already crooked nose. I hope it hurts like a bitch.

He falls to the ground from the force, not having expected that.

I point a finger at him. "That's for fucking with me. Remember what I know about you? You better watch yourself," I warn.

He grins up at me like there isn't blood pouring from his nose. "And who will people believe? The man whore drug abuser or the living legend? Hmmm ...?"

I shake my head, my jaw clenched. "Don't fuck with me, Matthews. I'll fuck you right back."

He grins, and I walk away before I do something stupid—like hit him again.

I get back in the car and Grace stares at me wide-eyed. "You punched your coach," she states.

"I did," I pant, breathless. I think I'd been holding my breath and hadn't realized it yet.

"Is your hand hurt?" she asks, grabbing ahold of my hand and drawing it to her. She inspects my knuckles, touching her fingers lightly to the tender skin.

"Nah, I'm fine." I gingerly remove my hand from hers so I can put the car in drive. I want to get out of here before Matthews calls the cops or something. As we pull out of the neighborhood, I glance at her. "Are you okay to stay at my place? I can get you a hotel room if you're more comfortable there?"

She shakes her head and looks away from the window to me. "Your place is fine."

"Okay," I say, my throat catching for some odd reason.

We arrive at my place thirty minutes later and I park in the garage beneath the building.

"This place looks swanky," she comments. "At least from the outside. Garages all look the same, no offense."

I laugh and get out of the car, grabbing our bags. "None taken," I say when she gets out. "It is a pretty nice place I admit. I like it."

She follows me to the elevator and I press the button for my floor.

"Not the penthouse?" she asks, pointing at the P button and raising a single brow.

I laugh. "No, not the penthouse. Didn't want that. This is plenty big for me."

She nods. "Not the penthouse," she repeats.

"Making a mental note, Wentworth?"

She smiles. "Maybe. I'm deciding that maybe you're not as douchey as I originally thought."

I put a hand to my heart. "Aw, I'm touched."

She punches me lightly in the stomach, her lips twitching with laughter.

The doors open and I lead her down the hall to my place. I set our bags down and dig my keys out of my pockets. I unlock the door and it swings open with a slight squeak.

I pick our bags up again and motion for Grace to head on in.

"Home sweet home," I say, coming behind her.

I close the door and flick the lights on, dropping our bags on the floor again.

She looks around, and I wonder what this place looks like from her eyes. Probably pretty plain. The walls are white and gray and the kitchen has the same color scheme topped off with stainless steel appliances.

The floors are all some sort of dark hardwood—no rugs. My couch sits in front of a large flat-screen TV and every gaming console I could get my hands on. There's a wall of windows across from us that overlooks the city of Boston. It's the reason I bought an apartment in this building: the view is unparalleled.

Grace crosses her arms over her chest and looks out the windows.

"It's beautiful," she comments.

I step up beside her, our arms brushing against each other, and I swear she shivers.

"It is," I agree.

But I'm looking at her.

I'm always looking at her.

CHAPTER FIFTEEN

GRACE

"Wanna watch a movie?" Bennett asks, moving away from the window.

I know I should go to bed, but tomorrow *is* Saturday, so I don't have to be up early. "Sure." I shrug. "But let me go change into something comfier."

He grins. "Oh, right, your sexy PJs."

I smack the back of his head, and he laughs uproariously.

"Where can I change?" I ask, looking around.

"Oh, right." He grabs my bag and leads me down the hall to a bedroom. He turns on the light and steps back after putting my bag on the bed. "My room's the one at the end of hall. Your bathroom is just across." He taps the closed door.

"Thanks." I close the door behind him so I can change.

The bedroom is plain with white walls and oak furniture. The bedding is a basic gray that matches the color scheme of the rest of the house. But considering this is a bachelor pad, I guess it's better than it could be. I mean, there could be a pinball machine in here.

I close the blinds and change out of my clothes into a pair of sleep shorts and a loose shirt. I add a pair of knee-high socks because I'm *always* freezing.

I find Bennett sitting on the couch, changed into a pair of sweatpants—shirtless.

Kill me now.

The man's body is a work of art between all his muscles—seriously, hockey must be really good for the body—and the tattoos. There's a spear between his shoulder blades and I wonder if he got it to represent the Plymouth Hunters.

He looks up when he hears me. "What do you want to watch?"

"You pick. I'll probably fall asleep anyway." I yawn as if

to prove my point. I sit down beside him, careful to keep a distance between us.

He notices and shoots me a shit-eating grin. "What are you afraid of, Princess? That if you get too close you won't be able to get enough? Come on, you can look ... and lick if you want."

"You're so gross." I push his shoulder and he falls back cackling.

Then, just because I can, I grab his arm and lick his firm bicep over a tattoo of a leaf.

He laughs even louder. "That's not what I meant for you to lick," he chortles.

I blush and mumble, "I know."

He touches my cheek, and I reluctantly lift my eyes to his. He stares at me intensely, and for a moment, I think he's going to kiss me, but just as quickly, he pulls away and says, "I'm picking *Snow Dogs*."

"What?" I say, confused. "Wait, the moving with Cuba Gooding Jr.?"

"That's the one." He presses some buttons and the movie begins to play.

"I cannot believe you own *Snow Dogs* let alone want to watch it." I shake my head. "You keep on surprising me."

He smiles. "As do you, Princess."

He wiggles around and gets comfortable and the movie starts.

My eyes grow heavy and he sighs, lifting his arm in invitation. I look at him reluctantly. I know I shouldn't, but ...

I move and snuggle against his side, resting my head on his chest.

Since I can't see, I can't be sure, but I'd swear he kisses the top of my head.

This ... This feels good.

Normal even.

And I have to remind myself over and over again that it's not real.

We're not a couple, and I don't even know if we're friends.

Besides, he's using me to get what he wants, just as I'm using him to show me how to be bad.

It's not real.

It's not real.

It's not real.

Then why does it feel so damn right?

I BLINK MY EYES OPEN, TAKING IN MY UNFAMILIAR surroundings. I'm confused at first but then I remember coming to Bennett's apartment after he confronted his coach.

I'm in the guestroom, but the last thing I remember is falling asleep on the couch so Bennett must have carried me to bed.

I sit up fully, the sheets pooling at my waist. The beginning rays of sunlight break through the blinds, and I glance at the clock on the nightstand. It shows that it's a little after seven in the morning.

I don't know what time Bennett will want to head back, so I decide to get up and be ready. I head across the hall to shower and find that there aren't any towels or soap.

I sigh and tentatively tip-toe down the hall to his room. I push the door open and find that his bed is rumpled from sleep, but empty.

He probably went to the gym or something. I figure there's no harm in raiding his bathroom for what I need, but as soon as I reach the half open door, I realize that was a mistake.

He's just turned the shower on and he opens the glass door, stepping inside.

He doesn't know I'm there.

I should turn.

Run.

Get my ass out of there.

But I can't.

I'm frozen, held prisoner by my own body.

It's wrong, but I stare at him. At the smooth planes of his back and the firmness of his ass.

Standing here is so wrong. *So wrong*. I'd be embarrassed to know he was watching me like this, and yet still I cannot move.

He turns then and I stifle a gasp by biting my lip. My whole body clenches, and a shiver runs down my spine.

He's beautiful. He'd probably sneer at me if I ever said that out loud, but it's the truth.

I lick my lips and I stare at him for only a few seconds longer, before I force myself away. I run back to the safety of my room and dive under the covers. Now that I'm away from his potent presence, I feel ashamed of my actions. He had no idea I was there and I was staring like some kind of pervert. But even with my shame, I still feel so incredibly turned on. My body is tight all over with the need for a release I've never really had.

"Hey."

I squeak at the sound of his voice. *He saw me.*

I pop my head up from beneath the covers, pretending to just be waking up. He stands in the doorway in a pair of loose shorts, his chest glistening with water and his hair damp.

Fuck, he's way too good-looking for his own good.

"Good, you're up," he says. "Wanna go get breakfast?"

"Sure." My voice is high-pitched and not at all natural.

He raises a brow. "You okay?"

"Just peachy." *I mean, it's not like I stared at you naked or anything.* "Mind if I shower first?"

"Go ahead." He peeks in the bathroom and pops back in the room. "I'll grab you a towel and stuff. I forgot I never stocked that bathroom."

"Cool. Thanks," I squeak again.

He looks at me with concern and then shrugs and walks away.

I breathe a sigh of relief. He doesn't know—if he did, he would've said something. Bennett can't keep quiet about anything.

I shower as quickly as possible and then we're out the door with our bags in hand.

Bennett drives a few blocks over from his apartment to a small restaurant hidden between two larger buildings. The place is quaint and doesn't seem to belong in the bustling city, but I like it.

"They have the best waffles," Bennett tells me, sliding his menu to the end of the table.

I slide mine over too. "Waffles sounds good."

He grins. "So, what do you think of Boston?"

"I've been here before. I like it. No place beats home for me, though." I shrug.

He crosses his hands together. "Home is always special, isn't it?"

I nod as a waitress comes over to take our order. Bennett and I order the same special and both of us get waters to drink.

Bennett runs his fingers over his face, and I can see how tired he looks.

"I'm sorry about your coach," I say. I might not know what's really going on, but it's obviously pretty bad. I hate that Bennett is so torn up about it—he's a pretty carefree guy, so this is really eating at him for it to be so obvious on his face.

He shrugs like it's not as big of a deal as it is. "Thanks

again for coming with me." He slides the peppershaker back and forth from hand to hand. "I ... It meant a lot."

I give him a small smile. "I'm glad me being here made you feel better." *And I'm glad you know I wasn't staring at your dick this morning.* The thought alone brings color to my cheeks.

"Why are you blushing?" he asks wish a slight chuckle.

"No reason." I look away and up at the TV that plays a news morning show.

"Is it because you saw me naked?" My mouth pops open and he grins. "I thought I saw you." He chuckles. "I never would've expected *you* to be a peeping Tom."

My face turns as red as a tomato. "It was an accident."

"But you didn't run away," he comments. I have no comeback for that and he knows it. "I take it you like what you saw?" He raises one brow. The waitress leaves our drinks and I rip into my straw. "I'll take that as, 'Oh yes, Bennett, you have the finest ass I've ever seen.' I'm sure your thoughts on my cock were much dirtier."

I nearly pass out in the booth. "*Shut up.*"

"Don't be such a prude, Grace. It's just a word. *Cock.* Say it."

"No." I shake my head.

"Don't make me stand on the table and shout it," he threatens. "You know I will."

He pushes his hands against the table and begins to stand. "Cock," I whisper.

He tilts his head to the side. "That was pathetic,

Princess. You sound like you're scraping dirt off your pointy shoes and it's killing you inside. Say it like you mean it."

My eyes shift around uneasily. "Cock," I say it a little louder.

He grins. "You can do better than that."

"Bennett," I hiss. "We're in a restaurant."

"I don't care." He leans back in the booth, stretching his arm along the back. He's the picture of ease. Meanwhile, I'm squirming.

I look around again and everyone in the restaurant seems to be occupied.

"Cock," I say louder this time.

"That was good." He grins like the cat that ate the canary. "Now say, "Bennett, your cock is a glorious—"

I throw his ice-cold water on him. I expect him to be mad, but instead, he busts out laughing. The waitress comes running over with napkins.

"Oh, my God, what happened?" she asks, handing him the napkins. She stares at his chest a bit too long where the wet cotton sticks to him. She blushes and looks away quickly.

"Nothing. Just my girlfriend being silly." Bennett wipes at his shirt and the table and looks up at the waitress with the most innocent of smiles. "I guess going shirtless would be frowned upon?"

"Uh ... I mean, I wouldn't mind, but my manager would probably ask you to leave." She blushes and holds her tray up to her chest like a shield.

"It's okay." Bennett winks. "I have a shirt in the car."

"I'll be right back," he tells me, tapping his fingers against the table.

"I'll get you another water," the waitress says before walking away.

Bennett isn't gone long. He returns in a thin muscle shirt that's almost completely open at the sides. I think he's trying to kill me. How is it possible that he looks so hot all the time without even trying?

"It's a bit chilly for this," he pulls on his shirt as he sits down, "but it's all I had in my gym bag that was clean." He sniffs it then. "Yeah, it's definitely clean."

"I'd apologize for throwing water at you, but it would be a lie." I sip at my drink innocently.

Bennett brings his hand to his mouth to hide his smile. "You're something else." He shakes his head, stifling a laugh.

The waitress brings him a fresh water and he flashes her a smile. "Thanks." She nods and disappears again. Bennett yawns. "I should've ordered some coffee, but I guess it's good I didn't. I can handle water being thrown at me. Coffee, not so much." Bennett leans back in the booth, stretching his arm along the back. "Are you sure you have to get back to campus? Maybe we should do something."

"Like what?" I ask as the waitress sets our plates down.

He shrugs. "I dunno. Go to a park or something."

I snort. "You? In a park? Won't you get mobbed?" I pour syrup onto my waffles.

"Possibly, but it's a nice day. Probably one of the last we'll have until it gets bitterly cold."

"True," I agree. "Sure, I guess we can go for a walk. I'm sure someone will snap a photo and your manager will see it—good PR. I can see the headline now, 'Bennett James Goes for a Walk'," I joke.

He throws his straw wrapper at me. "Ha-ha, you're hysterical. I actually wasn't thinking about the media," he admits.

"Oh?" I take a bite of waffle—Bennett was right, it's one of the best waffles I've ever had.

"No." He takes a bite of his. "I just thought it would be nice."

My fork hovers near my mouth. "Really?"

"Well, yeah." He looks away awkwardly.

"Um, okay then. A short detour won't hurt anything."

He smiles. "Good. Now eat."

"Always so bossy." I shake my head.

When we're done, Bennett wads up his napkin on the table and gives me a *look*. You know, the look someone gives you when they know they're about to say something you're not going to like.

"So, you still want to try out life on the bad side?"

"Yes," I answer hesitantly.

"Then run."

"What?" I look at him dumbfounded.

"Run," he repeats. "Number Two on 'Bennett's Guide to Being Bad': Dine and Dash."

"You ... You want me to get up and leave without paying? No, Bennett."

"Grace." He gives me a stern look. "This was your idea. I'm only following through on what you asked for."

My eyes shift around the room and I bite my lip. "Okay." I take a deep breath. I can do this. "I can't do this."

He laughs. "*Yes*, you can."

I measure the distance between where we sit and the door. Another deep breath.

And then I'm up and running out the door. I keep running all the way to Bennett's car. I can hear him running behind me, his steps heavier as they thump the ground. He unlocks the car and I dive inside.

He gets in and starts the car, pulling away quickly like we've just robbed a bank and not ditched our bill.

I lean back in the seat, my chest rising and falling heavily with each labored breath. "That was ... invigorating. Can we do it again?"

He laughs outright and shakes his head. "I think we better stick to things that won't get us in too much trouble. But it's good to know you have a wild side, Grace." He winks.

My heart is still beating a mile a minute and I'm not sure it'll ever slow down. "Am I sweating?" I feel my forehead. "I feel like I'm sweating."

He laughs. "No, you're not sweating."

"I thought I'd feel worse about that," I admit, finally buckling my seatbelt. "But I feel so *alive*."

"That's how I feel on the ice," he says with a forlorn smile.

My high instantly vanishes and I touch his arm with hesitant fingers. "You'll get this mess straightened out."

Bennett looks away from me, and I know it's his silent way of saying he's not so sure.

I settle back into my seat, realizing he doesn't want to talk.

I look out the window at the passing scenery as he speeds down the road. We'll be back to campus in no time if he keeps this speed up, and while I should be happy to get back to studying, I kind of don't want this mini-trip to be over.

I'm beginning to realize that I like Bennett way more than I should and it's only going to hurt me in the end.

But it's too late now.

CHAPTER SIXTEEN

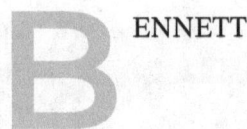ENNETT

IT'S THE FIRST HOCKEY GAME OF THE SEASON AND I'm not with my team like I should be. *Pissed* doesn't even cover what I feel. I glare at the TV screen mounted to the wall in the bar. Coach Matthews orders the guys around on the ice, and I might hate the fucker, but I'd give anything to be out there with my team. They probably don't want me there, though. I haven't heard from any of the guys while I've been gone, not while I was hurt and not now. There's no telling the lies Matthews has spewed.

Matthews ... the fucker is good.

But me? I'm better.

He thinks he has the upper-hand, but he's wrong. He's always underestimated me, and I'm going to use that to my advantage.

"You look like you could use another drink." The bartender slides another beer across the shiny wood top to me.

"Thanks."

"You're welcome." She winks and sways her hips suggestively before heading over to fill an order. She has glossy dark hair, a decent rack, and nice ass. A few months ago, I would've put on the charm and been fucking her before the night was over. But I'm a "new man" the "reformed bad boy" that "loves" his "girlfriend". I have to keep up pretenses as far as the media's concerned, and that means no cheating on my perfect girlfriend. Except, she's not my real girlfriend, which means no sex for me.

It really fucking sucks to be me right now.

I groan and scrub my hands down my face.

My life is one big clusterfuck, and I need to figure out how to fix it.

My drug test for Coach Harrison came back negative—like I knew it would—so he's continued to let me work with his team, but I'm restless. I want to be back with my team playing *games*. Practice isn't enough. I need the thrill and high of playing in an arena full of screaming fans. But Coach Matthews is dragging out this drug thing and he's probably using it to buy more time to find some other reason to keep me off the team.

I've been laying low and doing my best to be the NHL's new golden boy—unfortunately, I didn't anticipate the *bad boy* stigma being so hard to shake.

Grace and I need to up the ante. We've been too tame.

I just hope she's ready to play the game.

I drag Grace, Elle, Ryland, Makenna, and Celine to the next home game for the Plymouth Hunters. I'd only intended to bring Grace, but Elle overheard and fangirl shrieked while begging me to get tickets for her and Ryland. I don't even know how Makenna and Celine got into it—two girls that live across the hall from Grace and Elle—but somehow it's now the six of us. So much for my "date" with Grace.

Grace took some convincing to get here. She didn't want to go, and I had to remind her that she was my fake girlfriend and we needed to put on a show.

She just has no idea *what* kind of show I have in mind.

I take her hand as we descend the steps into the arena. It's slow going as fans of the team stop me to sign stuff. I don't mind, though. I smile and sign whatever the hell they want me too—except for a very large pair of boobs that's shoved in my face. Men that are happily in love with their girlfriend don't sign another girl's boobs.

We finally make it to our seats and Grace and I wind up in the middle.

"It's louder than I expected," she says, looking around, unsure.

She's adorable when she's nervous. "People love hockey. There's more to life than shopping, Princess."

She wrinkles her nose. "I know that." She pauses. "Speaking of shopping, you still need to let me get you some new clothes." She looks at my jeans and sweatshirt in distaste. I don't think there's anything wrong with my style—or lack of one—but I do know dressing nicer would go a long way in reforming my image.

I sit up and pull out my wallet, grabbing a credit card. I hold it out to her between two fingers. "Go nuts."

Her lips part and her eyes widen. "Seriously?"

I nod and she takes it. "Buy yourself a date night outfit too." I wink and I swear her breath catches.

"R-Right," she stutters, sliding the card into her wallet.

Beside her, Elle squeals. "This is the best day of my *life*!"

I laugh under my breath. I never would've pegged Grace's emo roommate to be into hockey, but I guess it shows you should never judge a book by its cover.

Makenna and Celine are on my side and I can hear them gossiping about how hot hockey players are. Considering we're sitting near my teammates in the box, I won't be surprised if a few them don't set their sights on Makenna and Celine and take them home. Hell, I'd roll Elle into that too, but I'm pretty sure she's hung up on Ryland, which I find hysterical seeing as they look like complete opposites.

But, again, don't judge a book by its cover.

I play the part of the attentive boyfriend by asking, "Do you need anything, baby?"

Grace jumps slightly and looks at me with startled eyes. "No, I'm good."

She's uncomfortable, and she's going to blow our cover if she keeps this up. Everyone thinks we've been dating since the start of the school year so her unease isn't going to look good.

I touch my fingers lightly to her flushed cheek and her lips part. "You have an eyelash," I say as an excuse to touch her. She buys it. I brush the invisible eyelash away and she ducks her head. I take her hand in mine and relax into the seat.

The game begins, and my stomach plummets as the guys skate out onto the ice. I should be there. My grasp on Grace's hand tightens as I hold myself back from jumping out on the ice and making a spectacle of myself.

"Bennett?" she asks nervously.

"Yes?"

She looks at me and then out to the ice. "Never mind."

"What is it?" I coax.

She shrugs. "I just wanted to say I'm sorry you can't

play. I know it must be really hard for you to sit here and watch your team play without you."

I release a pent-up breath. "Yeah, it really fucking sucks." I don't see the point in lying.

I'm tense for the first period. My team is behind by *a lot*. Luckily, they catch up in the second period and I can relax. When the second intermission comes, I know it's show time.

"Are you enjoying yourself?" I ask Grace, dropping my arm over the back of her seat.

She lifts her head and smiles. "Actually, yes."

I grin and lean close and her breath catches. "Smile," I whisper in her ear. "There are cameras on us."

"What are you up to?" she whispers back as I lean even closer.

I don't answer her.

Not with words anyway.

I take her face between my hands, allowing myself one second to marvel at how small her face is in my grasp, and then I lower my head and kiss her in front of all the thousands of people filling the stadium. I hear the shouts of, "Ooh!" and "Yeah, kiss her good," and I know that our image is being projected on the screens. I don't let that divert my attention, though. Instead, I kiss Grace like it's only the two of us. At first, she's tense in my hold, but she gradually relaxes and I can feel her throat vibrate with a moan. She kisses me back with a fervor I didn't expect and I feel her fingernails dig into my shoulders. I angle her head back, deepening the kiss and the cheers grow in volume.

I break the kiss before it reaches R-rated levels and press my forehead to hers. We both breathe heavily and I swallow thickly. It was supposed to be just a kiss, but suddenly it feels like so much more. Like *I* want more. Like maybe I wish it was *real*.

I am so fucked.

CHAPTER SEVENTEEN

GRACE

"Wake up! Wake up! Wake up!"

"What the hell? Go away." I try to shove Elle off my bed, but her skinny ass isn't going anywhere.

"Wake *up*," she demands. "You're famous."

That gets me to sit straight up in bed. Elle bounces by my feet, absolutely giddy.

"What do you mean?" I ask.

"Look." She shoves her phone in my face. "This is everywhere."

I snatch the cellphone from her hand and look at the screen. An image of the kiss Bennett and I shared at the hockey game is plastered across the screen along with an article about us. I scroll down. It talks about how we've been dating for a month now—nearly two months actually, but whatever—and that I am a freshman. They even list my hometown and talk about the fact that I'm a Wentworth and therefore worth billions.

A fact I've kept a secret about myself. Not even Bennett knows. I mean, it's not a huge secret but since we keep to ourselves and don't really infiltrate with the high society life outside of our home state, it's not common knowledge.

"You have to be kidding me," I mutter.

"I can't believe you didn't tell me you're rich. I mean, I kinda guessed it based on the way you dress, but *billions*? I had no idea."

I shrug. "It's not important. It's old family money. My dad owns a mechanic shop now. He didn't want any part in the business. My uncle Trent has more to do with the business than him, but still not much. It's just not a big deal."

Elle raises a brow like she begs to differ. "But you're like … royalty or something."

I snort. "Hardly. We live in a normal house, in a normal neighborhood. We're a normal family. I promise you."

She takes her phone from me and hops back to her side of the room. "This doesn't change anything," she says softly. "Just so you know, you're still Grace to me and I still think you're way too prissy."

I snort. "Thanks, Elle."

I shove the covers off and decide to get ready for the day. It's Saturday but I still have a helluva lot of homework to do.

I dress comfortably in a pair of jeans and a sweater and apply my makeup. I don't feel like messing with my hair, so I gather the long dark strands into a ponytail.

When I'm ready, I grab my backpack and a stack of books. "I'm going to study at the coffee shop," I tell Elle.

"Cool." She nods, looking at her phone. "I'm going to meet Ryland for breakfast."

"Have fun," I tell her with a small wave, but she's too busy looking at her phone to see.

Outside, the air is nippy, and I curse myself for not grabbing a coat. I still haven't adjusted to the cooler temperatures here. Back home, it would be ten degrees warmer than this.

The campus is beautiful, though, with its cobblestone paths and old gothic-style buildings. I had a hard time picking a college, especially with my parents begging me to stay close to home, but I know I picked the right one. This is where I'm supposed to be.

I step into the coffee shop and inhale the smell. To me, a coffee shop smells like home and comfort. I love it.

I step into line and place my order for a coffee and sandwich and then snag a seat in the back where it's quieter. I scatter my books around the table and place my order card where someone will see it.

Before I can sit down, my phone rings shrilly in purse.

I pull it out and see MOM flashing on the screen.

"Hey, Mom," I answer in a bright tone. I try to call her at least once a day in the evenings, but I forgot to yesterday after the hockey game. I came back to the dorm and crashed. Hockey games are exhausting even when you're not the one playing. "I'm sorry I forgot to call you."

"That's not why I'm calling, Grace."

I know instantly that I'm in trouble. Parents just have that *tone* they get and you know it's game over. "What did I do?" I cut to the chase.

"Apparently, you have a boyfriend and didn't tell us."

Shit. I completely forgot to tell them about Bennett. I mean, it's kind of hard to tell your parents you're fake dating someone you told them you weren't dating—sounds like total bullshit, right?

"I'm sorry," I say.

"I'm hurt that you wouldn't tell me. We talk every day. I understand not telling your dad, but *me?*"

The hurt in her voice kills me. "I forgot with all that I have going on."

"Hmm," she hums like she doesn't really believe me. "You have a bigger problem on your hands, though."

"What?" I grip the phone tighter and tip my head at the guy that brings my coffee and sandwich.

"Your dad saw the same photo I did—it's *everywhere*—and he's on his way to campus."

"No," I gasp.

"Yes."

"He's going to kill me." I close my eyes and drop my head into my hand.

She laughs. "No, he's going to kill Bennett. Your brothers are with him."

"Not both of them," I cry.

Granted, Dean is more of a lover than a fighter but *still*, I'd rather not deal with the two of them. Maybe I could distract Dean with some Pokémon cards. I wonder if anyone on campus sells them? Lincoln, on the other hand, will be more difficult to distract. He might be my little brother, but he's still insanely protective and as a football player he's huge.

"Why didn't you come with them?" I ask.

She sighs. "Your dad grabbed his keys, yelled that he was picking up Dean and was gone. I saw the photo on his computer which is how I found out, so I put two and two together and figured he's on his way there." She pauses. "Plus, I tracked his iPhone."

"Mom, you stalker." I laugh.

She laughs too. "Hey, you do what you have to do."

"I was going to study, but I better go warn Bennett."

"I hope he's treating you well," she says, worry in her tone. "I googled him—because I mean, he had to be someone important for your picture to show up on the internet—and he's been pictured with a lot of women, Grace. So be careful."

"I will, Mom. Promise."

"I love you."

"Love you too." I hang up and eat my sandwich as quickly as possible. She didn't say when they left, but I know it'll take them at least ten hours without stopping, so I have some time.

I throw away my trash and gather up my stuff again and head over to Bennett's dorm. I figure I can tell him and he can skip town if he wants. Granted, it's not like my dad and Dean are all that threatening: they're both tall and slender, whereas Bennett is tall and bulky like Lincoln—but Lincoln *is* young—besides, I really don't think it will come to a fight. At least, I really hope not. But if my dad googled Bennett like my mom did, he might be pissed enough to hit him.

I make it to Bennett's dorm and a guy that's going out lets me in.

I've only been to Bennett's dorm two other times—he usually comes to mine—but I remember where it is.

I bang on the door but there's no sound on the other side. "Bennett," I hiss. "Open this door right now. Bennett." I bang some more.

The door behind me opens up and a guy with messy

brown hair and sleepy eyes glares at me. "Can you keep it down? It's Saturday."

"Do you know where Bennett is?" I ask.

He shrugs. "Probably the rink."

"Thanks," I mumble and the guy disappears back into his room.

Fucking great. The hockey arena is all the way on the other side of campus and I've already hauled my heavy books around this far. Bennett will be lucky if I don't chuck one at his head when I find him. After all, this is *his* fault. If he hadn't kissed me in a stadium full of people we wouldn't have this problem.

But oh, my God, *that kiss*.

I spent all of last night thinking about it. I've never been kissed like that. But what sucks is that I know it wasn't real. It was all for show. Bennett knew it would be projected on the screen and that it would invariably end up online and in the tabloids. I *knew* what I was agreeing to, but it still hurts, and that's what really sucks. I have to keep reminding myself that it's not real. So far, that isn't working, though. When I agreed to Bennett's stupid idea to be his fake girlfriend, I thought there was no chance I'd fall for the egotistical hockey player. But I've gotten to know *him* and he's really not so bad.

I head back across campus to the arena. Since it's the weekend it's open to the public. It's big but I follow the signs and eventually find myself entering into the seated area. I walk down the steps and I can hear the slapping sound of a hockey stick against a puck. Bennett just looks a small speck from where I stand, but the further down I go, the closer I get. He hasn't heard me. He's too focused on slinging the pucks into the net. I drop my stuff into one of the seats and then stand in front of the glass so I can watch him better.

Once he's shot all the pucks into the net, he skates down the ice and climbs over a wall. He tears his helmet off and spits out his mouth-guard. His hair drips with sweat and he pushes the longer strands out of his eyes. He picks up a bottle of water and gulps it down.

I head over to him. "Hey," I say softly.

He startles and nearly drops his water. "Fuck, I didn't hear you." He wipes some water off his jersey.

"Sorry, I didn't mean to sneak in. You were just really into it."

He flashes me a lopsided smile. "I take it you missed me? Come back for another kiss?"

I push his shoulder but of course he goes nowhere. "Hardly. I came to warn you."

"Warn me?" He raises a brow and takes another sip of water.

"My dad saw the photo of us and he's on his way here."

I expect Bennett to look scared but instead his grin only grows. "Aw, overprotective daddy? I should've known Princess would have one."

I roll my eyes. "Sometimes I think about killing you just to shut you up."

He laughs. "You're funny."

"I was serious." I cross my arms over my chest. "My brothers are with him too."

He chuckles and says, "Okay. We'll take them out to dinner then."

"Bennett," I cry. "How can you be so blasé about this?"

He shrugs and takes another large gulp of water. "Because it's not a big deal. Your dad getting pissed over a photo is the least of my problems. You're not even my real girlfriend."

My jaw drops, and before I can stop myself, I slap him right across his too smug face.

He looks at me, stunned, and I stare back.

I can't believe I just did that. It's not like me at all but Bennett infuriates me more than anyone else can.

Only seconds pass before I turn and run.

I'M HALFWAY BACK TO MY DORM WHEN I REALIZE I left my backpack and books sitting on one of the seats in the stadium.

I halt in my tracks and groan. I feel so incredibly frustrated. I don't know why I even bothered warning Bennett, because he's right: this isn't real so it's no big deal to him anyway. It *is* a big deal to me, though, and that's where the problem lies. I don't like keeping secrets and I definitely don't like my dad being mad at me, but it's not Bennett's problem, it's mine, and that's something I have to come to terms with.

I know I should turn around and go back to get my stuff, but I don't want to face Bennett again. I *hit* him—and not a little smack, either. I've never been a violent person, but something about what he said struck a chord and it *hurt*. I know we're not a real couple but I did think we were friends and what he said isn't something you'd say to a friend.

I decide to go back to the dorm like I'd originally planned. Thankfully, Elle is still gone. I pull back the covers on my bed and burrow myself beneath them, wishing they'd swallow me whole.

I feel ashamed of myself and I hate that icky feeling. It sucks.

I don't know how much time has passed in my burrow of shame when someone bangs on the door. I know instinctively that it's Bennett even before he shouts, "Grace, let me in."

"Go away," I yell back, my voice muffled by the sheets.

"Don't make me break down this fucking door because I will. Try explaining that one."

"Ugh." I throw back the covers and march over to the door, throwing it open.

Bennett's changed into a pair of sweatpants and a long-sleeve shirt, my backpack and books in his arms. He comes inside and drops them on my bed.

I close the door and lean my back against it, putting as much distance between the two of us as I can.

"I pissed you off," he states. His cheek is tinged red where I slapped him, but the stubble on his cheeks helps camouflage it. Even still, it glares at me.

"Yes," I reply. "But I still shouldn't have hit you." I look down at the pale-pink polish on my toes.

Suddenly, his sneaker-covered feet appear in my line of vision and then his fingers touch my chin and he lifts my head up so I'm forced to look at him. I know he can see the shame in my eyes.

"I'm a dick," he says seriously, no traces of humor in his eyes. "I deserved it. I shouldn't have said that to you."

I try to step back, but of course, the door's still behind me so there's nowhere for me to go to get away from him. "You're right, though," I start, pushing his arm down so he's not touching me anymore—I can't think straight when he touches me, "I'm not your real girlfriend. I'm nothing to you." I move around him and to my bed.

He grabs my arm before I can get too far and keeps me from retreating. "That's not true, Grace. You're not nothing. You're ..."

"I'm what?" He licks his lips and his eyes dance over my face. "See, you don't even know." I shake my arm from his hold.

He shakes his head roughly. "I don't know how to describe it. I've never had a girl that's a friend, but I guess that's what you are. I like you."

I sit down on my bed and push my books to the bottom. "You can go now," I tell him, not even looking at him. "I'll deal with my dad on my own when he gets here."

Bennett stands there not saying a word.

I force my gaze to his and glare. "You can *go*," I say harshly. He looks at me strangely and stalks forward. "What are you doing?" I ask nervously.

Before I can blink he lifts me up and my legs wrap involuntarily around his waist. He crushes his lips to mine and I startle, not having expected that. I grab onto his shirt to push him away, but instead, I pull him closer. My body doesn't seem to realize what my mind wants to do.

This kiss is different from the first because it's *real* and not for show. I know it shouldn't be happening, but I'm powerless to stop it. In fact, I'm hungry for more.

I shouldn't want to kiss Bennett.

I shouldn't like it.

I shouldn't, I shouldn't, *I shouldn't*.

But I do.

His tongue tangles with mine and I *moan*, desire pooling in my belly. I've liked plenty of guys, but none of them have ever made me tingle all over the way Bennett does. The kiss in the arena was electric but this one makes that one seem like a peck on the lips. This is intense and all-consuming. It makes me feel things—*want* things—that I shouldn't want with Bennett, of all people.

He breaks the kiss and I find that my arms have wound around his neck. Our breaths mingle together in the space between us, and his hazel eyes stare into mine with as much confusion as I feel.

He sets me down easily and keeps a hold on my waist. His teeth dig into his lip and I know he's warring with himself the same way I am.

"Grace," he whispers my name and I hear the pain in his voice.

I lean my head against his chest and breathe out. "I know."

CHAPTER EIGHTEEN

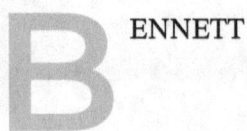ENNETT

Grace's mom ends up talking some sense into her dad and he and her brothers end up heading home before they make it even halfway to campus.

It's too late to change what's happened between us, though.

I kissed her again, and this time there was no one to witness it so I can't blame it on our arrangement. This was all me.

I was a dick to her in the arena because of the first kiss —because of what I felt—and then like the fucking idiot I am, I kissed her again and screwed it up even more.

I ruin everything. I have to figure out a way to move past this and I think I have.

It involves adding another item to "Bennett's Guide to Being Bad".

An item I don't like at all.

I hold the door open to the bar and let Grace go in front of me.

I chose a bar away from campus with a crowd that might not recognize us. I keep my baseball cap low over my face to reduce the chances of someone noticing me. Grace chooses a table in the back and I take the seat across from her. A waitress appears at our table for our drink order. I ask for a beer and Grace sticks with her standard water.

"Mind telling me why we're here?" she asks, looking around. Her nose wrinkles in distaste. I don't blame her. This place isn't exactly the nicest. Thankfully, there are a few college-aged guys around which plays perfectly into my plan.

"I thought we could add something to the guide." I shrug.

She narrows her eyes. "*Here?* What are you up to?" I

give her an innocent look, which she obviously doesn't buy. "I'd have rather taken you shopping."

"You can buy me whatever you want, Princess, but I'm not going with you. I don't shop."

"I can tell." She narrows her eyes on my thin long-sleeve shirt.

I shrug. "It's just not important to me."

"Again, I can tell." She laughs and takes her water when the waitress sets it down.

"Can I get you guys anything to eat?"

"Um, I'll have the cheeseburger," Grace says.

"Same here." I haven't even looked at the menu, but a cheeseburger sounds fantastic.

"That'll be ready soon." The waitress smiles and heads off.

"So—" Grace leans forward, the gesture giving me a small glimpse of cleavage when her shirt falls "—tell me why we're here, Bennett? Don't beat around the bush." I calmly lift my beer bottle to my lips and swig it down. "*Bennett*," she warns, raising one elegant brow.

"Third on 'Bennett's Guide to Being Bad'." I hold up three fingers. "Kiss a stranger."

Her mouth parts, and she glares at me like she wishes she could kill me with her gaze alone. Then, her eyes glitter with amusement and she shakes her head while laughing softly. She stares at me head on. "I can do that."

My fists clench beneath the table. It's what I want. To

see her kiss someone else so I'll be reminded she's not mine, but I'm not happy about it, and from her calculating gaze, I guess she's figured that out.

"You're a real piece of work, Bennett." She shakes her head, her hair swishing around her shoulders. "Did you think because you kissed me that I'd fallen head over heels in love with you? You're more conceited than I thought."

No, that's not what I thought, but I did think that *my* feelings were stronger than they should be. I had to find a way to squash them and I figured seeing her kiss someone else would be the best bet.

Grace stands and picks up her purse. "Game on, asshole."

I turn around just in time to see her tap a guy at the bar on the shoulder. He turns around and looks at her questioningly. Before he can say anything, she takes his face in her hands and kisses him—and I mean she *kisses* him. It's not a fucking peck on the lips like I expected and I'm pretty damn sure there's tongue involved. I shouldn't be pissed, I'm not allowed to be, but I am. I really fucking am.

And then Grace lets the guy go and goes down the line to the other three guys sitting at the bar, kissing them all. I hear the sound of glass shattering and realize I've knocked my beer off the table.

Grace kisses the last guy, turns to see me watching, and fucking *bows* with this look on her face like *I've got you*, and then leaves.

I sit for a few more seconds before I finally get moving. I pull my wallet out of my back pocket and throw some bills on the table before running out of the bar after her.

I stop when I see she's not waiting by the car.

I look to my right down the lit-up street, and she's not there, but when I look to the left I see her heading that way talking on her phone.

"Fucking hell," I mutter under my breath and run after her.

I catch up to her easily and tug on her arm, grabbing the phone from her hand and ending the call.

"Hey!" she screams, trying to snatch the phone from my hand. "I was calling a cab."

"And I have a car right over there that I can drive you back to campus in."

She glares at me, and I swear there's a fire in her eyes. "Did you ever think that maybe I don't want you to drive me back?" She laughs humorlessly. "Oh, wait, you think the sun rises and falls because you breathe. Right, I forgot," she mutters and starts walking again.

"Grace," I plead.

She whips around. *"What?"* she yells. "What do you want? Tell me, Bennett, because I'm incredibly confused." She holds her arms out at her sides. "You're the one that kissed *me*, remember? And don't play dumb, I know that's why you came up with that stupid kiss a stranger thing. That was a dick move." She crosses her arms over her chest.

"I'm your fake girlfriend, Bennett. I *get* it, so you don't have to keep reminding me. Can we move on now?"

My teeth smash together and I scrub my hands down my face. "Jesus Christ, Grace, this isn't about you, it's about me."

She rolls her eyes. "Of course it is. Everything's about you, Bennett."

"You don't understand," I tell her.

"Then make me understand!" she yells.

"I don't understand it myself, so how can I possibly explain it to you?" I counter.

She shakes her head. "You're ridiculous. Give me my phone back. I'm calling a cab."

"No," I say firmly.

"*Why?*" she snaps.

"Because I care about you, and I'm not letting you stand out here alone to get in a cab with some stranger."

She snorts. "Oh, so I can't get in a car with a stranger but I can kiss them? You sure make a lot sense."

"Fuck," I curse. "Just get in the car, Grace."

"*No.*"

"You leave me no choice then."

"Wh—"

She starts to speak but I pick her up and throw her over my shoulder.

"Bennett!" She beats my back. "Put me down."

"I'll put you down in a minute."

"Ugh, I hate you." She slaps my ass like that'll get me to drop her or something.

"Keep lodging your insults, Princess, they just bounce off of me."

I unlock my car and open the passenger door, dropping her inside. She immediately tries to push past me and out of the car. I grab her by the shoulder and give a gentle push back.

"Grace," I say, "I know you're pissed, but I also know you're a smart girl and the safest alternative is to let me take you back to the dorm."

She groans but stops fighting me and sits back in the seat.

I take her silence as her defeat.

"I'm glad you could see things my way." I start to close the door.

"Watch yourself," she warns. "I'm *this* close to slapping you again." She holds up her thumb and forefinger a tiny bit apart.

I chuckle and shake my head. "Try it, Princess. I'll be expecting it from now on."

She harrumphs and crosses her arms over her chest. I close the door and jog around to get in the driver's side.

She doesn't speak to me on the drive back to campus, but I didn't expect her to.

I park as close to her dorm as I can get and let her out. She doesn't look at me or say goodbye as she gets out.

I watch her walk away and just before she disappears, I whisper, "I'm sorry."

And I am. She doesn't know how much I wish things were different. That *I* was different. That I could be the guy she deserves.

CHAPTER NINETEEN

Grace

BENNETT AND I SINK BACK INTO AN EASY RHYTHM. We forget that our kisses happened and completely ignore what transpired at the bar. I continue to play the part of the perfect girlfriend and he's still ... *Bennett*. Thanksgiving came, and I headed home *alone* despite the fact that my parents requested Bennett join me. I didn't want to deal with that drama so I didn't tell Bennett they asked. I told my brothers the real deal between Bennett and me and they promised to help me out with my dad.

Classes are back in session now for a few weeks before Christmas break. In other words, it's time for finals. Shoot me.

I knock on his door and hear shuffling so I know he's there. The door opens a moment later and I push myself inside armed with loads of shopping bags.

I drop them on the bed and turn to him. "Try them on," I demand. "And here's your credit card."

He eyes the stack on the bed and then looks at the card. "Fuck, did you catch the thing on fire with how many times you swiped it?"

I sigh. "I know you can afford it. Besides, I got a lot of things on sale. Just because my family is rich doesn't mean I don't know how to bargain shop."

He shakes his head and picks up a bag, pulling out a pair of khaki pants. "I'm going to look like a prep."

I stick my hands on my hips. "No, you'll look like a *man*. You know, like someone that has their shit together."

He chuckles. "Touché." He pulls the rest of the items from the bag and holds up a maroon-colored sweater. "This looks like I'm going to play polo."

I snort. "I'm pretty sure they don't wear *sweaters* to play polo."

He shrugs. "Still ..." He lays more items out on the bed. "I like that." He points at a brown leather jacket.

"Stop looking at the stuff and try it on," I demand. I'm eager to see Bennett in something other than jeans and a t-shirt. He has a killer body and he's hot, but he usually dresses like a bum.

"You want me to drop my drawers right here, right now, Princess?"

"Yes," I say, my impatience growing.

"I'm not wearing underwear," he says with an impish smile.

I don't believe him so I call his bluff. "I've already seen everything," I remind him, my mind briefly flashing back to that morning in his apartment.

He chuckles. "True. I forgot you like to look at my cock."

I roll my eyes. "You're ridiculous."

His smile only grows. "Sit back and enjoy the show, Princess."

I shake my head and move around him and rummage through the bags. "Try this first." I thrust a pair of *nice* denim jeans at him and a button-down shirt.

"Yes, ma'am." He takes them from me and drapes both across the back of his desk chair. He smirks at me as he grabs the bottom of his shirt and crisscrosses his arms as he lifts the shirt up. He does it slow, purposely teasing me, and my breath catches at the sight of the reddish-blond hair trailing from beneath his belly button and disappearing into his jeans. He chuckles, having heard the small sound I made. I wish I could take it back so he didn't hear it and know that he affects me. We've been doing better since that night at the bar, and I don't want to ruin this easiness between us. I hate to admit it, but Bennett's become my friend, and I don't want to jeopardize that.

He removes his shirt completely and drops it on the floor, and I can't help it: I stare at his chiseled chest and muscular arms. Bennett is a big guy, but he's still on the leaner side, and I like that about him. He doesn't look like one of those gross body builders. He's just the right amount of muscled.

I slowly raise my eyes to his, and I expect to find amusement there but instead I'm shocked to see lust. I stumble a step back, breaking our eye contact.

"You should ... uh ... try that on," I stutter.

He doesn't say anything. Instead, he proceeds to undo his belt and drop his jeans. And surprise, surprise, he *is* wearing underwear. I knew it.

Bennett grabs the new jeans and puts them on. They fit him so much better than the ones he normally wears, and when he turns with his back to me to put the shirt on I nearly groan at how good his ass looks in them. People are going to be looking at him even more than they usually do.

Bennett buttons the shirt and tucks it into his jeans.

"What do you think?" he asks.

"You look hot," I tell him honestly.

"I don't look like I work at a bank?" he asks.

I laugh and shake my head. "Definitely not."

He walks into his small attached bathroom and looks in the mirror. "Hey, I actually like this," he calls out. "You're good at this," he comments, stepping back out and unbuttoning the shirt.

"Thanks." I sort through the bags and set aside the next outfit for him to try.

This time, he wears a pair of tan-colored pants and a gray sweater. "I look like a grandpa," he comments, suppressing a laugh.

"*I* like it."

He grins. "This is what turns you on, Wentworth? Men in sweaters?"

I shrug. "No, men with *style*."

"Ah—" he nods "—and I have none?"

"I don't think what you normally wear can be considered a style." I laugh and point to the next outfit I want him to try. It's a navy suit with a purple shirt and a gray tie. "You need suits for interviews, right?" I ask him.

He nods. "Yeah, that's a nice one."

"It cost a lot," I admit. "But I figured it was a good investment."

He sighs and a dark look flashes over his eyes. "If I ever get to play again."

"You *will* get to play again," I tell him.

He gives me a sad look. "We're days away from December. Matthews is getting exactly what he wants."

"Whatever happened with the steroids thing?" I ask. He never told me anything more, and I didn't want to ask because I hate how sad he looks when he talks about his team and asshole coach.

"Coach Harrison had me do a drug test, which of course came back negative. The league had me do one too, also negative—so, thank God Matthews wasn't able to tamper with it. But Matthews is still keeping me benched. So that's why I'm still here. Coach Matthews won't let me even practice with the team, and at least Harrison lets me train with the college team." Bennett lets out a long-winded sigh.

"Can't the guys on your team do anything to help you?"

He sighs again. "No one goes against Matthews, *ever*."

I frown as he changes into a different pair of pants. "Why is Matthews so great?"

Bennett buttons his pants and zips them, holding out his hand for me to hand him a shirt. I hand him a navy sweater. "He was a hell of a player back in the day. One of the greats. He's someone a lot of people admire, and when he started coaching, everyone was vying to be on his team." He shakes his head and he looks pissed. "He's not what he seems, though. He's a liar and a cheat."

"You admired him? Before? Didn't you?" I question.

Bennett winces. "Yeah, I did," he admits.

"What did he do?"

Bennett shakes his head. "The less you know the better."

"Did he kill someone?"

Bennett snorts. "Princess, I'm really beginning to worry about your obsession with killing, but no, it's not that."

"Then what?" I plead. "You can tell me. It's not like I'm going to spill the beans to someone."

Bennett sighs and begins taking off his clothes. "I don't want to talk about it."

"Did it have to do with steroids?" I ask.

He freezes in the process of taking the sweater off so I can't see his face. He lowers his arms again and the shirt falls. "What makes you say that?"

"I'm right, aren't I?" I grin. "That's why he made that drug test look like *you* were doing steroids."

Bennett's lips pinch and he pulls out his desk chair, taking a seat. He claps his hands together and looks at me seriously. "You can't tell anyone, Grace. I mean it."

"Yes!" I do a little dance. "I was right!"

"Stop it," Bennett scolds but his tone is light.

I cease my dance and mime zipping my lips. I sit on the edge of his bed and lean toward him. "So," I begin, "you saw your coach doing steroids? Big deal—he's the coach, not a player, so I don't see where that's an issue."

Bennett shakes his head and lays his hands on his knees, spreading out his long fingers. "No, Grace, I saw the coach *giving* a player steroids—not just any player, our Captain."

I gape at him. "That *is* a big deal."

"Exactly." He pinches the bridge of his nose and leans back in the chair so far that I'm afraid it's going to topple over. He moves forward and the legs come crashing back down against the linoleum floor. "I got injured shortly after that so I couldn't play and he wasn't worried about me. Then, I think he hoped I wouldn't get well enough to play again, now that I've proven him wrong, he's stuck grasping at any fucking straws he can get his hands on to keep me off the team."

"Can't you just switch teams?" I ask.

He glares at me like I've committed some sort of sin. "It doesn't work like that. I signed a contract. I'm legally bound to this team for the remainder of the season."

"Okay, so then can't you be traded to another team?" As soon as the words leave my lips, my stomach flops. If Bennett's traded that means he has to move and he won't be in Boston. Then, I realize, that regardless, he'll probably only need me a few more months at the most, and after that, we'll probably never see each other again. I should be glad to be rid of him, but I'm not. I can't imagine a day where I don't see Bennett now. I've grown used to his presence.

Bennett shakes his head roughly. "He'd be too scared for me to go to another team. He'd think I could still spill the beans and that would be bad."

"Why don't you?" I ask, my eyes narrowing.

He sighs and looks away. "I idolized the guy for a long time. A long fucking time. And it … I don't know. I guess I felt like I owed it to him to keep my mouth shut, but then he started fucking with me."

"So tell someone," I urge.

He shakes his head resolutely. "Who are people going to

believe? The legend player turned coach or the alcoholic womanizer asshole?"

I snort. "You're none of those things. Okay, maybe *one* of those things, but you're not as bad as you think."

"Aw, thanks, Princess." He presses a hand to his heart. "So which of those two things am I not?"

"Well, you're definitely not an alcoholic. A few drinks here and there isn't a bad thing. And you used to be, but you're not a womanizer anymore."

He chuckles and rubs his jaw. "So that makes me an asshole?" He fights a smile.

"Ding, ding we have a winner." He shakes his head at my antics. "So," I say, growing serious, "what are you going to do?"

He shrugs and stands, pulling off the sweater and dropping it on the bed. "I have no idea, but I'm sure I'll think of something."

He tries to sound positive, but the look on his face tells me he feels anything but sure of himself. I wish I knew how to help him, but he's on his own with this one.

CHAPTER TWENTY

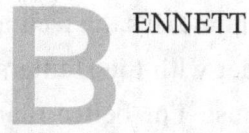ENNETT

MICHAEL AND I HAVE BEEN RUNNING DRILLS FOR hours. I've gotten to know the guy pretty well, and he's a nice dude with a future in hockey ahead of him. I'm sure of it. I don't tell him that—I don't want to give him false hope—but I already caught sight of some scouts at one of the home games, and I'm certain they were checking out Michael. He's one of those players that exudes magic on the ice.

We skate off the ice and head back to the locker room to shower and leave.

"Thanks for helping me out, man," I say, tying the laces on my shoes.

Michael shrugs into his jacket. "No problem. Glad I could help. Besides, I need all the extra ice time I can get." He grabs his bag and slings it onto his shoulder. "I'll see you in the gym tomorrow. Coach says he wants us there early."

I nod and shove my stuff into my bag. "See you later."

Michael leaves and I'm alone in the locker room. I can't help but take a moment to look around. It still looks the same as when I was here a few years ago. Ugly blue tiled walls and floors. Rows and rows of gray lockers and wooden benches. It's your standard locker room, but to me, it feels like home.

But it's not the room that feels like home. It's the feeling of *belonging*. I always felt like an outsider with the Hunters. Most of the guys don't like me because I'm better than them. I'm not being cocky, it's true, and no one wants someone better to come along because it jeopardizes spots on the team. In other words, older players begin to shake in their skates and fear being kicked off the team.

Playing for the Hunters was my dream since they're my home team, but the reality could never measure up to the dream. It wasn't that professional hockey is harder than college hockey, though it is, it's just ... it's not a good fit. We don't mesh well. And maybe, with a different coach, we'd come together as a team, but I don't see Matthews getting booted—though, I wish every day it would happen.

I don't know what my next step with Matthews is, but I know I have to get people on my side to back me up, which means I need to start by reaching out to the team. Not all of the guys hate my guts, so I think there are a few who'd be open to going to a bar and getting a few drinks and talking. I don't know exactly what I'll tell them, but I know it can't be the truth. At least not yet.

The *truth*.

Fuck.

I still can't believe I told Grace. I mean, she kind of guessed it so it doesn't really count, but ... Who the fuck am I kidding? I should've never involved her in this. When she guessed right, I should've lied or done something. Anything but let her in on the truth, because if Matthews finds out she knows I don't know what he might do and I swear to God if the fucker hurts her I'll make all of Grace's axe murderer worries come true and kill the asshole.

I slam my locker closed and grab my bag, lumbering out of the arena. I'm exhausted. I've been pushing myself too hard, but I've had to do something to distract my mind. Being around Grace helps, but she has classes and even more studying than normal with her finals coming up.

I should head back to my room and get some rest, but my feet have a mind of their own and lead me right to

Grace's door. It's getting late, after ten, and I debate for about thirty seconds on whether or not I should knock on the door before I finally do.

I knock lightly, just in case she or Elle has fallen asleep studying, but loud enough that someone awake should hear.

I hear footsteps treading lightly across the floor and then the door eases open a crack. "Bennett?" Grace pokes her head out. "It's late. Are you okay?" She's probably having flashbacks to the night I showed up flustered and begged her to go to Boston with me.

"I'm okay," I assure her. "I just wanted to see you." As soon as the words leave my mouth I want to take them back, but Grace just nods and doesn't seem to read into them. I shouldn't want to see her, though. This *thing* between us is supposed to be a business deal more or less an agreement between two parties who have no interest in each other. But that lie is getting harder and harder to tell myself. No interest in Grace? I'd have to be a blind fucking monk to not be interested in Grace. She's fucking gorgeous. And sweet. And her smile ... Oh, fuck, her smile is the best.

"I was just about to go to bed," she tells me, not opening the door up any wider.

"Can I stay here tonight?"

Where the ever-loving fuck did that come from? Stay *here*? For the night? Together? I have completely lost my mind. But it's too late to take it back now.

She looks back into her room and then at me, biting on

her plump bottom lip. It kills me when she does that. It's an innocent gesture, one she does when she's nervous or uncomfortable, but there's something infinitely sexy about it.

"I ..." She pauses and I'm about two seconds away from leaving when she finishes. "Okay."

My eyebrows shoot up my forehead. "Seriously?"

She shrugs. "We're just going to sleep, so I don't think it's a big deal." She opens the door wider to let me in.

"Where's Elle?" I ask, noting the empty bed.

Grace sighs. "Your guess is as good as mine. I'm betting with Ryland."

I nod. "I'm not surprised."

"Me either." She sits back down at her desk at her open laptop. "I have to work on this paper some more. It'll probably be an hour before I can even think about sleep." She sighs and glares at the screen. I kick off my shoes and drop my bag on the floor before flopping on her bed. She laughs. "I'd tell you to make yourself at home but you already have."

I cross my arms behind my head and smirk. "I thought you letting me stay was invitation enough." I wiggle around.

She shakes her head. "Don't distract me, this is important."

"You do realize that fuels me *to* distract you."

She narrows her green eyes on me. "Go get me a cupcake then, Bennett."

"Why?"

"Because that means you'll be gone long enough for me to almost finish this *and* I'll have a sweet when I'm done. It's a win-win."

"Yeah, a win-win where *I* don't win," I counter. I stand, though, and put my shoes back on. "I'll get you a cupcake, because I'm the best fake boyfriend ever." I bend down and kiss her temple. Her breath catches and she looks at me with surprised eyes. I quickly step away and open her door. "I'll be back in a little bit."

"Mmhmm," she hums, turning her gaze back to her computer but I don't miss the flush in her cheeks.

I ease the door closed behind me and head down the hall to the elevator.

"Hey, Bennett," a pretty blond says when I stop beside her to wait for the elevator doors to open.

"Hi," I say, giving her a quick-once over and then training my eyes back on the elevator doors.

Guys with girlfriends don't check out other girls—even when your fake dating. Pretty sure it's a law or something.

"I'm Beth," she says.

"Okay." I know I sound cold and I don't mean to, but if she's expecting me to flirt it's not going to happen.

The doors open and we step onto the elevator together.

"What are you doing in the girls' dorm?" she asks, flipping her blond hair over her shoulder so that I can get a better shot of her cleavage. I force myself not to look, but it's really fucking hard when there's a pair of tits right beside you. I mean, I'm a guy, we like to look. It's a fact of life.

"Visiting Grace," I bite out between my teeth.

She lets out a musical laugh. "And leaving so early?"

I know what she's implying but I don't bite. The doors open and I step out into the hallway. "See you later, Barb."

"It's Beth!" she calls after me.

I disappear outside, and Beth, thankfully, doesn't follow.

I head across campus to get Grace's cupcake. I choose the chocolate one with chocolate frosting and chocolate sprinkles. My girl likes chocolate.

Holy fucking shit. Did I just address Grace as *my girl*? What the fuck has gotten into me? She's not my girl. She never will be. I don't want her to be.

I stop in my tracks in the middle of campus. I don't know why I keep lying to myself. I do want Grace. For the first time in my life I actually *want* a girlfriend, but the timing ... The timing fucking sucks. With everything going on with my team and coach I can't afford any distractions and Grace would be a distraction.

I breathe out and watch my breath fog the air.

I've never felt so conflicted and at a loss as to what to do.

I know I can't tell Grace how I feel, though. She's as affected by me as I am by her and I don't want to give her false hope that something more will ever come of this. I can't promise her a real relationship. Not while my career is on the line.

I walk around campus for a while, just thinking, before I finally make my way back to her dorm. I don't bother knocking and let myself in.

Grace jumps and nearly falls out of her chair. "You scared me."

"Sorry," I say, closing the door and locking it. "Did you finish yet?"

"I think five more minutes will do it." she sighs, and I notice how tired her eyes are.

I hold up the clear plastic in my hands. "Well, I brought cupcakes."

"My hero." She claps her hands together and pretends to swoon.

"Are you mocking me, woman?" I set the cupcakes on the end of her desk and rid myself of my shoes again. I really hate wearing shoes.

She laughs. "No. Maybe a little."

I shake my head. "I buy you cupcakes and you mock me. I see how it goes."

She smiles and holds up her hand, wiggling her fingers. "Five more minutes." She turns back to her computer and I remove my shirt and start on my pants. Grace squeaks, "What are you doing?"

I pause with my belt undone. "Getting ready for bed."

"By taking your clothes off?" Her eyes nearly pop out of her head.

I suppress a grin. "Princess, I'm not sleeping in my pants and you've already seen me naked so there's nothing to be afraid of."

She looks like she's about to faint. "Yeah, but ... but ..."

"Hey, I have to be comfortable when I sleep, so boxers it is."

"Maybe you should go back to your dorm and sleep there," she pleads.

"Too late." I chuckle. "You already said I could sleep here."

She whimpers and looks at her computer and then back at me like she can't decide which she wants to look at. Her gaze steadies on me and she squares her shoulder. She lifts a finger and points it at me like a mother about to scold her child. "No cuddling."

I grin. "Wouldn't dream of it, Princess."

She breathes out a sigh and returns to her paper. "That better be the best cupcake I've ever had."

I step out of my jeans and dive under her covers. "Fuck these are the softest sheets I've ever felt," I comment, wiggling my toes around.

"Bennett," she hisses. "I'm working." She points at her computer screen.

"Oh, right." I mime zipping my lips.

It doesn't take her long to finish, and when she does she flips the lid closed on her computer and lets out a groan. "That paper was total bullshit, but let's hope the teacher buys it." She stands and stretches her arms above her head and rummages through her drawers. She holds a few items of clothing to her chest and says, "I'm going down the hall to change. Think you can manage to behave yourself for that long?"

I prop myself up on her pillows. "I'll be a perfect gentleman. I promise not to search through your drawers and smell your panties."

Her face twists into a scowl. "Okay, that's gross."

She quickly ducks out of the room and I make myself comfortable in her bed. It's the same kind of lumpy mattress that I have but her nicer sheets and blankets make up for it. Although, she has enough pillows on here that I could make a fort and live comfortably in it. I toss some of those suckers on the floor. With two of us on the small bed we need all the room we can get. Grace said no cuddling but it's kinda hard when there's no room.

She comes back a few minutes later and I groan. "You have got to be kidding me."

"What?" she asks innocently.

"You're wearing *that* to bed?" I indicate her super short shorts and tight long sleeve top. Oh, fuck me, I can see her nipples puckering beneath the gray fabric. "You're trying to kill me. You really are."

She laughs and grabs the cupcake box and slides into bed beside me. "Scoot over," she demands.

"Where?" I counter. "Into the wall?"

"Well, if you hadn't dumped all my pillows on the floor you wouldn't have to sleep against the wall." She sticks her tongue out and then giggles.

Grace's laugh has quickly become one of my favorite sounds in the world. It's soft and feminine just like her.

"Hold this." She hands me the cupcake box and then

leans over to grab her iPad off the table. "Wanna watch something on Netflix?" she asks, putting in her passcode.

"Is that your subtle way of asking me if I want to Netflix and chill?"

Her dark brows furrow together, and I know she's pondering over what I said. When she figures out the meaning, she gasps and smacks my bare chest. "Ew, you pig!"

I laugh. "I was kidding, but it was totally worth saying to get that reaction."

She wiggles her cute little butt around trying to get comfortable. "I can't believe I said you could stay the night here. Aliens must have taken over my brain. Yeah, that's it. Definitely aliens." I shake my head and open the cupcake box, grabbing mine. "What do you want to watch?" she asks.

"You pick," I tell her.

She laughs. "You really shouldn't have said that." She clicks on some show called *New Girl*.

"I'm sorry, I take it back. Let me pick." I try to take the iPad from her but she snatches it away. I somehow end up dropping my cupcake right on my chest, smearing icing all over myself.

Grace stares at the mess and then breaks out in hysterics. "I'm glad you find this amusing, Princess. Now I'm going to have to eat your cupcake."

She gasps. "You wouldn't dare."

"I really want a cupcake," I tell her, pretending to grab hers from the box.

Her hand shoots out and wraps around my wrist, keeping from going any further. I could break her hold easily, but I don't want to.

"You wouldn't have even gotten cupcakes if I hadn't asked for them," she says, her eyes flicking from me to the cupcake.

"Hey, I'll eat this one—" I point to the fresh one "—and you can lick this one off of me."

"Not happening, dude. Keep dreaming."

I snort. "When did I become *dude?*"

"When you threatened to eat my cupcake."

"Come on, just give me one little lick," I plead, but suddenly feel like I'm not talking about the cupcake anymore.

Her lips purse and she shakes her head. "No."

"Please?" I jut out my bottom lip and lean closer to her. She smells like heaven and hell all wrapped into one cute package.

She shakes her head almost imperceptibly and inches just slightly closer to me.

I swallow thickly, staring at her lips. "I want to kiss you again," I confess. "Really kiss you."

Her eyes widen in surprise. "Haven't we already *really* kissed?"

I shake my head. "No."

She lets go of my hand and says, "Then kiss me."

I expected her to kick me out again, or to flat out say no, but I definitely didn't think she'd actually say yes. I don't hesitate for a second—I don't want to give her a chance to change her mind.

I cup her cheek in my hand, rubbing my thumb over her smooth skin and then I lean in, pillowing my lips over hers. The light contact isn't enough, though, and I press more firmly as her fingers grasp at my hair and her leg hooks around my waist. My tongue swipes into her mouth and she lets out the softest sound I've ever heard. It's a cross between a moan and purr and I'm eager to make her do it again. My hands move to her waist and my fingers dig into the indent above her ass. She tastes minty from her toothpaste but sweet too, like she's just sucked on a piece of candy. She rolls her hips against mine and I stifle a groan. This girl is going to kill me, but I'm pretty sure I'd willingly welcome death at her hands.

Her hands move from my hair to wrap around my neck and she rocks her hips more. If this was any other girl I'd have her naked in no time but this is Grace and I can't do that to her. I can't add her to the list with a bunch of other faceless girls. She doesn't belong there. Grace is special. She's the kind of girl that when you have her, you find a way to keep her. She's the kind of girl you marry. But me? I'm not the kind of guy that gets the girl. I always fuck it up. *Always*.

I kiss my way down her neck, over her collarbone, and then rest my head against her chest.

I breathe heavily and her fingers brush through my hair.

"Bennett?" she says softly after a minute.

"What?"

"We forgot about the cupcake."

"Huh?" I sit up and she presses more firmly against my growing erection.

She stifles a giggle and points at my chest. "The cupcake."

"Ah, fuck." I look down at the chocolate cupcake smeared all over my chest and her shirt now. Little pieces of chocolate cake cover her bed too. "Sorry."

She kisses my cheek in the sweetest fucking gesture I've ever had thrown my way. "It's okay. I can change the sheets and I have plenty of tops. I'd tell you to go down the hall to wash up, but you might scare the girls. I'll go grab you a wet cloth."

I chuckle and run my fingers through my hair. "Thanks, Princess."

She grabs another shirt before she scurries out of the room, and I deflate at the fact that I'm not going to get to see her change. I'm pretty sure if there's a God, he's laughing at me right now.

I stand up and will my dick to go down—like literally say a little prayer and I'm pretty sure that must be sacrilegious or something, but fuck it—and remove the sheets from Grace's bed, piling them in her laundry basket.

She returns with a wet cloth and in a clean shirt. This one is looser but somehow sexier. I'm pretty sure I asked to sleep here just to torture myself, because *come on*.

"Here you go." Grace hands me the cloth and then grabs a second set of sheets from the bottom dresser drawer.

She fits the clean sheets on while I scrub the cake and icing from my chest. When I'm clean, I add the washcloth to her laundry basket.

She sighs and wrinkles her nose at the basket. "Looks like I'll have to do laundry tomorrow."

"I can come entertain you while you do it." I waggle my brows.

She laughs and puts the comforter back on the bed. "Or you could do it for me?" she suggests with a pleading smile.

I mock-wince. "Sorry, no can do, Princess. Laundry is not my thing."

"Please don't tell me you pay someone to do your laundry."

I shake my head. "Nah, I do it. I just don't like it."

She flattens her hands over the bedding. "Get in."

"Yes, ma'am." I dive onto her bed and it bounces under my weight. I lift up the covers and pat the space beside me. "Come on, Princess."

She gets in beside me and grabs her iPad once more, finally starting the show.

I hand her the cupcake box and she takes it eagerly, her eyes lighting up. "I'd be nice and share this with you, but I really want the cupcake." She lets out a little giggle and takes a bite. I can't even be mad when she's so damn cute.

She starts the show, and before I know it we've breezed

through half the season. "Those two are going to end up together," I declare. I hate to admit it, but I'm hooked.

She nods and puts her iPad on the end table. "Oh, definitely." She agrees, wiggling around. We turned the light off a while ago, so both of our eyes have adjusted to the darkness. A little bit of light seeps in through the blinds.

Grace snuggles down under the covers and rolls to her side. "Goodnight, Bennett." She wiggles and her ass brushes my thigh. I let out a sound like I'm in pain. "Are you okay?" I can't mistake the real note of worry in her tone.

"Fine," I hiss out. "Pretty sure my dick hates me, though."

She snorts. "Tough cookies."

"Did you just say *tough cookies* when my dick is about ten seconds away from exploding?"

"Can you not use the word dick and exploding in the same sentence?" She rolls to her other side to face me and her breasts brush my arm. This is worse than her ass. "And yes, I said *tough cookies*. It's an expression."

"I know it's an expression and I hate it. Especially right now."

She shakes her head, and I see a flash of her white teeth as she smiles in the darkness.

"Go to sleep, Bennett," she says softly.

"You're cold, woman," I joke. "Stone-cold."

"Not my fault your dick has no self-control."

"Aw, look at you. You said dick without flinching. I'm proud of you, Princess."

"Dick is easy," she says, cupping her hands under her head. "It's the other word that trips me up."

I suppress a grin. "And by other word you mean *cock*?"

Even in the darkened room I know her lips are pressed into a thin line and her eyes are narrowed. "Yes."

"And here I thought I got you over that fear in the diner." I reach out to tuck a piece of hair behind her ear. "I guess we'll have to start all over."

"No." She puts her hand over my mouth.

I grin beneath her fingers and mumble, "Cock."

She shakes her head and fights a smile. She's so beautiful like this, barely illuminated in the darkness, her face free of makeup, and her hair wild. She's always beautiful, but I love getting to see her like this with her guard down.

Her hand falls away and I clear my throat. "Thanks for letting me stay the night with you."

"*Why* did you want to stay here?"

"I don't know," I answer honestly. "I guess I didn't want to be alone."

She nods. "I'm surprised you didn't go find someone else."

"Someone else?" I ask, confused.

Even in the dark I know she's blushing. "Yeah, another girl. I mean, I know enough about your reputation to know that you get around. It's not a secret."

I know I should keep my mouth shut, but I find myself telling her the truth instead. "I haven't slept with anyone since before my injury," I admit. "My sole focus became getting better."

"But you are better now."

I chuckle and tuck a stray piece of hair behind her ear, skimming my knuckles over her cheek as I do it. "I know that, but I have a girlfriend now."

"*Fake* girlfriend," she reminds me. "It's not like you'd be cheating."

"Yeah, but if the media caught wind that I was cheating …" I fall upon my media excuse easily. The truth is I want Grace—no one else. The thought of fucking another girl makes me sick and it's stupid since Grace will never be mine. I'm not good enough for her.

"Oh, I see." She looks saddened by that for some reason. She stifles a yawn.

"Go to sleep," I tell her. "You're tired."

"I am," she agrees. "School is kicking my ass."

She rolls over away from me, and even though there's only inches between us it feels like an ocean.

Within minutes the sound of her breathing changes and I know she's asleep.

I wish I could say the same for myself.

CHAPTER TWENTY-ONE

RACE

I WAKE UP TANGLED IN BENNETT'S ARMS. MY LEG IS tossed over his and my head rests on his chest with his arms wrapped around me. As I blink into awareness, I realize I should pull away but I also know I don't want to. The warmth of his body against mine feels like the most dangerous temptation out there.

I know he's all kinds of wrong for me, but that doesn't stop me from being attracted to him. In fact, I think it makes me like him more because he *is* different than the kind of guy I normally go for. My usual go-to is a guy from a good family that has lofty career aspirations like a doctor or lawyer or something and his idea of a fun time is going to the country club. But that ... That's boring. Bennett's anything but boring. In the last few months, he's made me feel more alive than I ever have.

I sit up a bit and admire the slope of his nose and the slight poutiness of his lips in sleep. He breathes evenly and I can see his eyes moving behind his closed lids as if he's dreaming. His chest is bare and covered in a light dusting of reddish-blond hair and freckles. His shoulders are wide and muscular, the perfect width for snuggling into.

I don't know what makes me do it, but I trail a single finger down his stomach and to the top of his boxer-briefs. Something compels me to slip my finger beneath, but before I can go much further, he snaps awake and his hand wraps around my wrist.

"What are you doing?" His voice is thick with sleep and he blinks tiredly at me.

"I don't know," I admit honestly, embarrassment leaking into me. "I ... I shouldn't have done that."

I try to pull my hand away but he won't let go, so I stay

trapped there with my hand beneath his underwear. I feel like the kid who got caught with their hand in the cookie jar and now there's no way in hell I'm getting any cookies.

"Why, Grace?" he asks, and I can tell he's becoming more aware and I swear there's lust in his eyes.

"Because I wanted to." The words slip out before I can stop them.

He lets go of my hand and crosses both of his behind his head. "Go ahead," he urges. "Do whatever you want. I won't stop you and I won't touch you."

I know what he's really saying. He's giving me the freedom to explore *him* without having to worry about thinking he'll want me to return the favor.

"Are you sure?" I find myself asking.

"As long as Elle isn't going to bust in here and see you looking at my *cock* like it's a damn Oscar, then I don't care. Granted, I've been caught in a lot worse situations but let's not traumatize your roommate, okay?"

I laugh and glance at the clock. It's early, and I doubt I'll see Elle until after lunchtime.

"We have time," I say, biting my lip nervously.

I know there are some virgins out there that have explored oral sex and other things, but not me. I was more interested in my schoolwork and I just didn't like any guy enough to want to. I've always been curious, but there's never been any guy I was comfortable enough to do this with. Bennett, though, I trust him not to take this farther than I want to. Maybe that's weird since I *know* he's slept around and basically been a big ole man-slut but he's never tried to pressure me into anything. Yes, he makes sexual innuendos on an almost daily basis, but that's just his personality. I know he doesn't mean anything by it.

"Proceed," he says with a lazy look.

My heart accelerates behind my rib cage. This is a big deal for me. I think Bennett must realize this because he keeps his mouth shut at my hesitation instead of cajoling me.

I take a deep breath and then silently scold myself for being silly.

It's a dick, not a shark. It isn't going to bite my hand off.

I move my hand lower and I can feel the hard length of him. I swallow thickly, skimming my hand down and back up. He's already hard, and for some reason, this fact makes desire pool in my belly.

"Can I?" I ask hesitantly, nodding at his boxer-briefs.

"Whatever you want, sweetheart," he rasps. "I'm not helping, though. This is all you."

I hate it when he calls me Princess, but when he says *sweetheart* it does something funny to me. It makes me feel like he cares.

My heart races even faster as I tug his underwear down. He springs free and I moan. I don't know why I have that reaction since it's not like he's touching me or I'm touching myself, but seeing him like this turns me on.

I stare at his long, thick length and swallow thickly

before my eyes dance to his. I expect to see him silently laughing at me, but instead, his muscles are taut and his eyes are serious—like he's trying to hold himself back. I want to tell him it's okay—that he can touch me too, that I want him to—but a voice in the back of my head whispers *baby steps*.

I wrap my hand around him and drag it slowly up and down. He hisses between his teeth and I stop. My gaze darts to his and I fear that I hurt him.

"Did I do something wrong? I didn't hurt you, did I?" I ramble.

He shakes his head once, his jaw clenched. Between his teeth he hisses, "Keep going."

I stare at him a second longer, afraid he's lying, but he nods encouraging me to continue.

"If I do something wrong tell me," I beg him. "I want do this right."

"Trust me, there's nothing you could do wrong," he rasps.

I move my hand up and down again, circling my thumb over the head of his *cock*.

I breathe out heavily. I don't know why I feel so out of breath. It's not like I'm doing any physical exertion but I'm breathing like I just went out and sprinted a mile.

My eyes roam from his cock to his stomach and finally land on his face. His eyes are hooded, lips parted, and he stares at me like I'm the most gorgeous woman he's ever seen.

I move the sheet out of my way and lower my head.

"What are you doing?" he growls.

I look up at him, my mouth hovering inches away from his cock. "What do you think I'm about to do?"

He looks torn. "Are you sure? You don't have to do anything you don't want to."

"I want to," I rasp out. I've never been turned on so much in my life, but bringing Bennett pleasure seems to do the same for me.

He nods once and I wrap my lips around him.

He hisses out, "Holy fuck."

I'd be lying if I said his reaction didn't please me. I move my mouth up and down. He's big so I can't take much of him, but I work with what I can do and he seems to like it so that's what matters to me. I use my hand too and when it joins the mix his hips buck off the mattress.

"Grace," he whimpers my name and my core clenches.

I want to ask him to say my name again but I also don't want to stop what I'm doing, so I keep going. His fingers tangle in my hair, sweeping the long locks away from my face so he can see me. I lift my eyes to his and find that his hazel eyes are dilated.

I swirl my tongue around the tip and moan as I move down again.

His fingers tighten in my hair. "Fuck, Grace, I'm gonna come if you don't stop." I keep going. "Seriously, Grace, unless you want me to come in your mouth you need to stop."

I give him one last lick and then my mouth pops off, my hand doing the rest of the work. The muscles in his stomach tighten the moment before he comes. It spurts out on his stomach and he breathes heavily, his hand resting on my waist. His eyes stay on mine even though they're heavy-lidded like he's drunk.

I feel shy all of a sudden and I can't look at him any longer so I avert my gaze to the magazine clippings and posters on my wall.

"Hey." His voice is thick when he touches my thigh. "That is single-handedly the hottest thing that's ever happened to me."

I look to him nervously. "Really?"

He nods and his Adam's apple bobs as he swallows. "Oh, yeah. So fucking hot. You ... You're amazing." He reaches up and tucks my hair behind my ear. I lean into his touch and he holds his hand there against my cheek. "What made you want to do that?" he asks.

I shrug. "I was curious and I trust you."

He presses his lips to mine and kisses me softly. "You don't know how fucking good it is to hear that you trust me, sweetheart."

I pull away slightly and grab some tissues so he can clean up. He wipes away the stickiness and puts his underwear back on.

"Come here." He opens his arms for me.

I hesitate for only a second before taking him up on the

offer. I cuddle against his chest and he brushes his fingers through my hair.

I want to ask him what this means. How this changes what we are and what we've been doing, but I'm scared he'll say he wants things to continue as they are so I don't say anything. I just enjoy the moment.

CHAPTER TWENTY-TWO

BENNETT

I CAN'T GET WHAT HAPPENED BETWEEN GRACE AND me out of my head, and it's been three days. Three fucking days of me playing a *blowjob* on loop in my mind, but I wasn't lying when I told her it was the hottest thing to ever happen to me. Grace thinks that because she's a virgin she has no sex appeal, but she's so wrong. I'm more attracted to her than I ever have been to another girl. Most of the time I've slept with women I only just met. I never have the chance to get to know them. We fuck and I leave or she leaves. That's it. But I do know Grace and I ... I don't love her, but I like her. I like her a lot. I care about her more than I should and that made what we did so much more powerful. She hasn't said anything about it since it happened, and I don't know whether that's because she's embarrassed or doesn't want me to get my hopes up that it'll happen again. Thankfully, she acts normal, not like it scared her or anything. So that's good, I guess.

"James! What the fuck are you doing? Move!" Coach yells at me so loud that his voice echoes through the entire arena.

I'm supposed to be practicing with the team but my mind's not in it.

For the first time in my life, hockey isn't my sole focus. A girl is.

I skate down the ice and Tanner rams into me. I am *this* close to punching the fucker in the face. It's been months, and I'm pretty sure he's still pissed Grace is my girlfriend. He'd never be good enough for her, though. No guy is.

I shove Tanner into the glass and it vibrates with the force of his weight.

Tanner comes after me more than he does anyone else during practice. I usually go easy on him because he's a fucking freshman and has a lot of maturing to do, but fuck it, it's time to give the kid a taste of his own medicine.

He comes after me again and I ram him with my shoulder hard enough that he falls to the ice and slides away.

I chuckle around my mouth-guard and leave him to pick himself up.

Michael passes the puck to me and I sling it to another player named Roscoe who shoots it toward the goal. The goalie blocks it and we all groan.

"Stop playing like a bunch of girls!" Coach yells. "Arnett," he says, referring to Roscoe, "you can do better than that!" We play for another hour before Coach calls it a day. "Come see me after you shower, James. Don't come to my office smelling like a damn sweaty pig," he says gruffly before leaving us to go down the tunnel.

I feel like every time he asks me to come see him it's never good news. We're into December now and I'm still not back with my team. I'm losing precious time.

I shower as quickly as I can and change into a pair of jeans and a sweater that Grace got me. It's a little too preppy for my taste but I can't argue about the fact that I definitely feel a hell of a lot more professional in the clothes she picked. I just have to get used to them.

I head down to Coach's office and knock once.

"Come in and shut the door behind you," he orders.

I take a deep breath before I open the door. If shit's about to hit the fan, I want to at least brace myself before it happens.

I step into Coach's shoebox-size office and wonder again why the man likes this tiny hole for an office.

"Bennett," he says my name on a sigh and leans back in his chair. It squeaks from his weight and for a second I think he might fall, but apparently, the chair is in a lot better shape than it looks. "What are you still doing here?"

"I keep asking myself that too, Coach."

"You're a professional player, Bennett," he says, like I don't already know. "You don't belong out there with a bunch of college kids. Go back to your team."

I look away. "Coach Matthews won't let me back. They're investigating me."

"Investigating you?" Coach's brows knit into a line. "What the hell for?"

I shrug. "I told you, Matthews hates me."

Coach snorts. "So you keep telling me, but you won't tell me *why* he hates you. You must have done something."

"I didn't do anything," I snap, offended that he'd suggest that it's my fault. I've done a lot of shitty things, but I'm not a bad person.

Coach slams his hand down on the table. "Then tell me what it is. You must know." A vein in his forehead pulses—a telltale sign that he's pissed. "A coach doesn't keep one of his best players benched for no reason."

"You think I'm one of his best players?" I don't know why I latch onto those words. I guess maybe after all this time I needed affirmation that I am a good player. After a while you begin to doubt yourself.

"You don't need me to tell you that you're a damn good player." Coach picks up a pen and taps it against his desk. "Now, stop pussyfooting around and tell me what the hell is going on," he demands. He narrows his eyes on me and gives me the look that he used to give me when I went to school here—the one that says he'll keep me in this room until I spill the beans.

I told Grace—well, she figured it out—so I don't see the point in not telling Coach Harrison. Keeping it a secret isn't doing me any fucking good. Matthews is still coming after me.

"I caught Matthews giving Greg Paulson steroids. The fucking team captain."

Coach says one word. "No." He doesn't say it like he doesn't believe me but like he doesn't want to believe it's true.

I nod once. "He threatened to ruin my career if I told anyone and I know he could. I got injured just after it happened which I'm sure thrilled him. Even though I haven't told a soul, except you now." I leave Grace out of it, because even though I trust Coach, I don't want there to be any chance of her getting dragged into this. "He's doing everything he can to keep me off the team until my contract runs out at the end of the season and here's the thing: if I don't get to play soon, no other team will want to draft me."

Coach nods, rubbing his hand over his jaw. "We'll just go public with this then."

"No," I say quickly. Coach looks at me quizzically

waiting for me to elaborate. "Do you really think anyone will believe me?" I ask. "You know what kind of reputation I have, and God knows what kind of lies Matthews is feeding the higher ups. I need proof. Right now, it's my word against his."

"Then we have to get you back with your team." Coach nods at his words. "That's the only way we can get proof. Unless you think the player you saw will talk?" He raises a brow and waits for me to answer.

"Why would he? If he admits to doing steroids, then he's in a fuck ton of trouble."

Coach makes a noise of agreement. "You're right." He rubs his fingers over his lips, a sign that he's deep in thought. "Let me think on this. I'll ... I'll come up with a plan."

I nod and leave him. I didn't want to get Coach Harrison involved in this but he's one of the smartest men I know. If he can't help me then no one can.

"My parents want you to come visit for Christmas and New Year's."

I choke on the pasta I was swallowing. "What?" I ask when I can breathe again.

Grace sighs. "My parents want to meet you over Christmas break. They asked me to invite you to Thanksgiving but I got you out of that. They won't let it go, though."

I wipe my mouth with a napkin and look around the restaurant. Someone snaps a photo of us on their phone and whispers to the people they're with.

My gaze slides back to Grace and I can tell how nervous she is. She hates asking me to do this.

"All right, I'll go."

"Really?" She swirls spaghetti around her fork. "I mean, if you can come up with a good enough excuse for them I'm sure they'll let it go."

"Nah." I shrug. "It won't be so bad."

Grace chuckles like she thinks it's cute that I believe that. "Just remember that they think we're really a couple so prepare for an intense inquisition."

"I'll live," I tell her.

She takes a bite of her spaghetti, chews, and swallows before speaking again. "There's also this huge party my family throws every year on New Year's Eve in the mansion my dad grew up in. You'll need to bring a tux."

"I can do that."

She breathes out a sigh of relief. "I really thought you were going to run screaming from the restaurant when I told you."

"It's your parents, Grace, not Kim Jong-un."

She giggles. "I'm semi-impressed that you know who the president of North Korea is."

"Oh, is that who that is?" I joke.

"Funny." She shakes her head. "I'm going to head home after my finals next Thursday and you can come whenever."

"Why don't I go then?" I ask her. "I can drive you home."

"You want to drive me home?" she asks. "It's like ten hours without stopping—and you have to stop for gas, food, potty breaks," she rambles.

"I don't mind." I take a bite of my food. "It'll be fun."

The idea of a ten-plus-hour road trip with anyone else would have me wanting to poke my eyes out with a spoon, but not with Grace. I think it would be fun.

"If you're sure, I'd love that. It saves me from having to ride the train. I *hate* the train."

I chuckle. "I'm surprised your parents wouldn't pay for you to fly home."

"They would," she admits. "But it's so much cheaper to go by train. I don't like them to spend money on unnecessary things."

I bend my head to peer under the table. "Says the girl wearing a thousand-dollar pair of shoes."

"I have my priorities." She laughs.

There's a speck of spaghetti sauce in the corner of her lip and I reach across the table to swipe it away. I lick the sauce off my finger and her eyes widen with desire.

We're playing a very dangerous game, one where someone gets hurt, but both of us seem helpless to stop it.

CHAPTER TWENTY-THREE

GRACE

"You're bringing all of this?" Bennett looks at all my bags sitting by the door of my dorm.

"Yes. I'm going to be home for three weeks. I need this stuff."

He shakes his head like he can't believe it. "You're going

home. How could you possibly need this much? I'm only bringing one bag and it's not like I have stuff waiting at your house for me."

I shrug. "I'm a girl, we need a lot of stuff."

"I'd like to point out that I'm a girl and I don't need that much stuff." Elle points to the two duffle bags she has packed.

"Yeah, well you're also flying home," I reason. "It's always better to pack light for a flight."

"We need to get out of here," Bennett says, grabbing three of my bags. "We're already late."

"I'll meet you outside," I tell him. "I want to say goodbye to Elle."

He nods once and leaves us alone.

After our disastrous first encounter, I would've never thought Elle would end up becoming one of the best friends I've ever had, but she has. We're only off for three weeks, but I'm going to miss her.

"Stop looking at me like that," she warns.

"Like what?" I try not to laugh.

"Like you're going to cry. I know I'm awesome but I'm not that awesome."

"Come here, you loser," I say and pull her into a hug.

We sway back and forth and she whispers, "I'm going to miss you."

"I knew it." I laugh, letting her go.

There's a knock on our door and we turn to the open doorway to find Ryland. His dark hair is damp from a shower and he wears a pair of jeans and an Addams University sweatshirt. "Are you ready?" he asks Elle.

She nods. "I'll see you in three weeks," she tells me and hugs me again.

"Bye, Grace." Ryland waves.

"Bye." I wave back.

Elle still insists they're not dating, but I don't know whether she's trying to fool me or herself. Ryland offered to drop her off at the airport since it's on his way home, but I think there's more to it. She'll tell me when she's ready, though. I don't feel right to press her when I'm keeping so many secrets of my own.

They leave and I grab my last two bags, locking the door behind me.

Bennett is waiting outside on the steps like he promised and we walk over to his car in the garage. My arms are screaming by the time we get there. I probably shouldn't have packed so much but I would never admit that to Bennett. I'd never hear the end of it.

Bennett loads my stuff in, squishing it in beside his one lone bag. It won't all fit in the trunk so he ends up having to put two of my bags in the back seat.

When we finally get on our way, it's after ten.

Bennett had wanted to get on the road by seven.

He turns on the radio and puts his sunglasses on. "Ready, Princess?"

I nod. "You bet."

I'm excited to go home for longer this time. Thanksgiving break wasn't long enough. I'm sure it'll be hard to come back to school, but I need this. Family time is important.

A song comes on the radio and I smile when I recognize it. "That's a Willow Creek song," I tell Bennett—like he doesn't already know, which *of course* he does since they're only one of the biggest bands in the world.

"I know," he says with a chuckle.

"My brother is dating the drummer's daughter," I tell him.

He glances at me with a surprised expression. "No shit?"

"Yeah, she's a friend of mine. She's Dean's best friend, though. It was kind of inevitable that those two ended up together even though they were oblivious to it for the longest time."

"Hmm," Bennett hums.

"They went on a road trip this past summer and the rest is history." I don't know why I'm telling Bennett this. It's not like he cares, but the words keep coming. "I envy them," I admit.

His head snaps toward me and then back to the road. "Why?" he asks.

I shrug. "They found love in their best friend. That's special."

"All love is special," he counters.

"I know, but ... I guess I feel like I'll never have any kind of love."

He chokes on a laugh. "Are you kidding me? You're

beautiful Grace. Sweet. Funny. Amazing," he says the last on a sigh. "Any guy would be lucky to have you."

"Really? Because I don't see any lining up." I hold up a hand. "And *don't* say it's because they think I have a boyfriend. I know that rarely stops most guys, and when I was in high school it was the same thing."

"Maybe they're intimidated by you," he suggests.

I snort. "Intimidated by me? Are you crazy?"

"Well," he starts, "in your hometown, they probably knew you came from a rich family, right?"

I nod. "Yeah, it's common knowledge around there."

"Okay," he says. "Take that and your whole take charge attitude and it scares a guy away."

"Take charge?"

"I don't mean that in a bad way," he says quickly. "I just mean, you're kind of bossy."

"Is there any *good* way to take bossy?"

"Fuck," he curses, and pinches the bridge of his nose. "I'm saying this all wrong. What I mean is, you're a leader and a lot of guys are intimidated by that."

"Are *you* intimidated by that?" I don't know why I ask that, but I'm insanely curious of his answer.

He grins. "Hell no. I fucking love it. You don't take anyone's bullshit, and I find that insanely attractive."

I press my lips together. I want to ask him if that means he finds *me* attractive, but I'm scared to push my luck. If he hasn't realized I've developed real feelings for him I'd like to keep it that way. Something tells me that anyone that falls in love with Bennett gets their heartbroken, and I don't want to be added to that list.

———

WE STOP FOR THE NIGHT AROUND SEVEN O' CLOCK. We got stuck in traffic thanks to a nasty wreck so we still have a good six hours to drive tomorrow.

"You can shower first," Bennett tells me, opening the door to our room and dropping our bags on the floor. "I'm going to go grab us something to eat from that restaurant next door. I'll be right back."

I nod as he immediately ducks back out the door.

I don't hesitate to get in the shower. I didn't have time this morning since I was already behind and I don't know why, but sitting in a car all day makes me feel gross. I turn the shower on and let the room steam up. Bennett insisted on us staying in a nice hotel, and I'm thankful for that. I drop my clothes on the floor and step under the spray. I feel my coiled muscles instantly relax and I sigh. I'm glad Bennett asked if I was okay to stop and didn't insist on continuing down the road. I don't think I could've lasted another six hours in the car. Luckily, when we were growing up we usually flew everywhere when we went on vacation, but on those rare occasions when we drove, I was always the one complaining. Being cooped up in a car never bothered my brothers, though.

I step out of the shower and grab one of the fluffy white

towels embroidered with the hotel logo and dry off before wrapping it around my body.

I stupidly didn't bring a change of clothes into the bathroom with me but I was too eager to get in the shower. I open the door and find that our bags are no longer right there, which means Bennett is back.

"I got you a cheeseburger. I hope that's okay," he calls from the bedroom area.

"Yeah, that's fine." I pad in there and find him standing over the bed pulling Styrofoam boxes out of a paper bag.

He looks up when he hears me and makes a strangled sound.

I don't move. I don't think I even breathe.

"Grace," he whispers my name like it's the only word he knows.

I feel like everything between us has been leading to this moment. Like we're at a crossroads and one choice will define how everything ends. I always make the safe choice. *Always*. But fuck it, the safe choice is boring, and I'm so sick of it.

I drop the towel.

Bennett makes a strangled sound and he swallows thickly. He doesn't look away, and his eyes ... They're burning with a fire. He doesn't move toward me, though, and I realize he's giving me the choice. The choice to pick up my towel and pretend this never happened or the choice to grab the reins and take what I want.

I take a step forward and he doesn't move away. I take that as a good sign.

Another step and then another until I'm right in front of him. My hands slide up around his neck, tangling into the hair that's grown slightly shaggy since I first saw him.

"What are you doing?" he asks, breathing heavily.

"I want this," I tell him, sliding my hands down his chest. "I want you."

"Why?" he asks. "Why me? I'm not good for you."

"I trust you," I tell him. "I *like* you." More than I should. "I want this to be you."

He shakes his head, his jaw clenched tight. "There are plenty of other guys that would be so much better for you, Grace. I don't want you to regret this."

"I want *you*." I plead with my eyes for him to understand. "How can I regret something I want so bad?"

He still looks unsure. "I don't want you to hate me."

"I won't," I promise.

"You might," he counters. "Sex complicates things."

"Everything is complicated, not just sex."

He swallows thickly. "I feel like such an asshole."

"Why?" I ask, my brows furrowing together.

"Because I want this," he whispers, taking my face between his hands and crashing his lips to mine.

He backs me up against the bed, and I fall onto it with his large body over mine. I feel vulnerable naked while he's fully dressed, but I feel confident he won't stay that way for long.

My legs wind around his waist and I rub against his jeans. My hands skim under his shirt over his toned stomach, pushing the shirt up as I go. I want it off and he obliges, breaking the kiss long enough to tear it off and throw it into the corner of the room. My heart beats so fast that I think it might fall out of my chest.

He kisses my neck and down my chest, over my breasts, before swirling his tongue around each nipple. I'm pretty sure I whimper. He moves further down, kissing my stomach and then stops, looking at me for affirmation.

I nod. I don't want him to stop. Ever.

He hooks my legs over his shoulders and swipes his tongue over my pussy.

I really do whimper that time. My fingers grasp at the sheets, his hair, anything to keep me from flying away.

He lifts his head enough to ask, "Does that feel good?"

"Don't stop," I plead.

He chuckles but does as I said. I've never experienced anything that can compare to the pleasure he makes me feel. This is unlike anything else, and it's amazing.

My body tingles and I fall over the edge of a cliff. At least, that's what it feels like. My vision goes fuzzy and I forget to breathe.

Bennett moves back up my body and kisses me. He bites my bottom lip and tugs on it just slightly. I reach for his belt buckle, my hands shaking from the aftershocks of my orgasm.

Bennett grasps my hands, stopping me.

"Are you sure?" he asks again. "We can stop right now. This doesn't have to go any farther than this."

I shake my head and push his hands off. "Shut up."

He chuckles and rolls to the bed, taking me with him so that I'm on top. I undo the buckle and move onto the button and zipper. I move fast—scared that he'll change his mind. I'm not worried about myself. I'm sure. I want this more than anything.

When I have his jeans completely undone, he rolls me back over and then stands, getting rid of his jeans and underwear in one movement.

"Eager, are we?" I ask, propping up on my elbows. I groan when he wraps his hand around his cock and gives it one sure stroke.

"There's a hot naked girl lying on the bed. *Of course* I'm eager." He reaches for his jeans and pulls out his wallet. He fumbles through it and pulls out a condom, holding it between his fingers.

"I don't know whether I should be mad or glad that you have that in there." I narrow my eyes on him.

He chuckles and rips the foil. "Better to be prepared than not."

He rolls the condom on and then stalks toward me. I lie back on the bed and his large body falls on top of me. He holds his weight above me enough that I can feel him, but I'm not crushed.

He takes my chin between his fingers and tips my head down, staring into my eyes. "I probably shouldn't admit this, but you have no fucking clue how badly I've wanted this—wanted *you*."

My throat catches and I reach up, rubbing my fingers over the stubble on his cheek. We don't say anything. We don't need to. A thousand words can be conveyed in one look.

He kisses me and pulls back, nuzzling his lips against my ear. "This is going to hurt you," he warns, "and I'm so fucking sorry for that."

I brush my fingers through his hair, noting the worry in his eyes. "I'll be okay," I tell him. "I'm ready." I mean that in more ways than one.

He guides himself inside me and I close my eyes, bracing myself for the pinch.

He starts in slowly and I hiss. He immediately stops. "What? What did I do?" he asks, touching my face tenderly. "Grace?"

"Do it fast," I tell him. "Like ripping off a Band-Aid."

He chuckles. "Sex isn't like a Band-Aid, Princess."

I narrow my eyes on him. "Last time I checked, you didn't have a vagina to know what this feels like. Just do it, Bennett."

He rolls his hips slightly. "Definitely no vagina." He winks.

He bends and kisses me, but doesn't move any farther inside me. His tongue tangles in mine and I grasp his shoulders, ready to push him away so I can yell at him to get a move on with it, when he *does* push all the way into me. I cry into his mouth and I'm pretty sure I bite his tongue or lip. He doesn't scold me, though.

He holds steady there and looks down at me as I fight tears. I *knew* it would hurt, but I guess I didn't think it would be *this* bad.

"I'm sorry, so sorry, sweetheart," he murmurs, and he looks truly distraught at causing me any sort of pain.

I want to tell him it's okay, but there's not any air in my lungs to speak with. He seems to know to give me a minute, and eventually, the pain turns to a dull throbbing and my fingernails are no longer digging into his shoulders.

"I'm okay," I assure him. "Promise."

He looks at me doubtfully. "Tell me when you're ready for me to move."

"Not yet." I nearly scream the words, clamping my legs around his waist.

He chuckles softly and lowers his head, sweeping his lips over mine in a tender caress. He's being infinitely sweet with me—sweeter than I ever imagined. He deepens the kiss and I completely forget about the pain. He moves to my neck, kissing the sensitive skin there and my hips rock slightly against his. The pain is minimal now, merely a dullness remaining. But I still find myself scared to tell him to continue in case it starts up again. He seems fine to wait, though.

I grasp his cheeks in my hands and bring his lips back to mine. I kiss him deeply, my tongue tangling with his. He tastes like cinnamon and something sweet that I can't quite pinpoint.

With a shaky breath I say, "You can move now."

He pauses, giving me the chance to take back the words if I don't really mean them, but he must see the truth there because he slides out the smallest amount and back in. It hurts, but not like before. It's duller now.

I can tell he's holding back, however.

"I can take it," I tell him. "Don't hold back."

He looks uncertain and breathes out, "I don't want to hurt you."

"You won't," I promise. At least, not now, like this. He does have the power to hurt me—to break my heart.

He grabs my waist and angles my hips up. He moves faster, but not too fast, and for that, I'm thankful. He's slightly rough, though, in the way his fingers dig into my skin, and I love that—I love that he's so close to losing control that he has to hold onto me.

He stares down at me like I'm the most beautiful woman he's ever seen and I'd be lying if I didn't say I don't feel that way when he looks at me. More than beautiful: he makes me feel alive in a way I never have before.

He lowers, his chest pressing mine, and angles his hips so he's pressing deeper into me. My eyes nearly roll back into my head.

"Do that again," I beg.

He does, chuckling when he sees what it does to me.

I force my eyes open and look down to where we're

joined. The sight turns me on and I clench around him. Bennett's eyes darken with desire.

"That turns you on," he rasps out. "Watching me fuck you."

It does, but I have no words to tell him. My thoughts have turned into a kaleidoscope of colors and I can't think straight. The only thing I feel and know is pleasure.

He rubs his fingers against me, and I jolt in surprise at the feeling.

"Did I hurt you?" he asks, worried.

I shake my head.

He rubs his fingers harder and I nearly black out from the pleasure. I come around him, my fingers digging into his arms, and when I come back down to Earth I see that I've bitten his shoulder.

Oops.

Bennett doesn't look upset, though. Instead, he looks even more turned on than he was before.

He moves a little faster and bends to kiss me. He growls into my neck when he comes and then rolls off of me before his weight can crush me. He surprises me by reaching for me and holding my body against his side. I hook my leg over his and we both try to gather our breaths.

As my senses come back I can't believe that really just happened, but I don't regret it.

Not at all.

"Are you okay?" he asks me a few minutes later when he's caught his breath.

I nod, burrowing my head into the space where his neck meets his shoulder. His hand rests on my thigh and he circles his thumb there. He kisses my forehead tenderly before sitting up and leaving me in the bed.

I can't move. My limbs have turned to Jell-O.

He moves around the room but I'm too tired to turn my head and see what he's doing. He comes back a minute later with one of his t-shirts and coaxes me into a sitting position. He puts the shirt on me and climbs into bed beside me, pulling the covers over us.

"Are you hungry?" he asks. I shake my head and he chuckles. "Are you still speechless?" I nod and he cups my cheek, turning me to look at him. "It's not because you're upset, is it?" He sounds worried now.

I shake my head. "Just tired."

He chuckles and kisses the end of my nose. "Get some sleep, sweetheart."

I do, and it's the best sleep I've ever had.

CHAPTER TWENTY-FOUR

BENNETT

I HOLD GRACE'S HAND THE ENTIRE SIX-HOUR DRIVE from the hotel to her house. I don't know how last night changes things, I don't really want to think about it and complicate everything, but for now, I'm content to just let things be.

Grace looks out the window, her dark hair curling around her shoulders and dressed in a skirt and blouse. She's beautiful. The most beautiful girl I've ever met—inside and out.

"We're almost there," she says, and it's unnecessary since I know that too thanks to my navigation system. She sounds worried, though. She's been unusually quiet, and I hope to God it's not because she regrets having sex with me. I'd never forgive myself.

"Are you okay?" I ask her and immediately cringe. She's probably ready to duct tape my mouth shut for asking that question so many times.

"Fine." She gives me a small smile, but it does nothing to alleviate my worries.

"Grace," I probe, but she quickly shuts me down.

"I'm fine, Bennett."

My teeth grind together. She's most definitely *not* fine. I might be a guy, but I'm not an idiot, and I know when someone's upset. We're five minutes away from her house, definitely not enough time for a decent conversation, and they know we're due there in a few minutes since she sent them a text. In other words, I can't pull over and demand she talk to me. I'll have to try to corner her later.

We pull into the driveway of a large two-story home. It's decorated for the holidays with lights and greenery and what looks like Santa's legs sticking out of the chimney.

Grace looks at me sheepishly. "My dad goes all out for Christmas."

"Not your mom?" I ask.

"She likes the holidays, but my dad's a bit ... eccentric. It's all or nothing with him."

"Gotcha." I nod, undoing my belt.

The front door opens, and a short, thin woman with dark hair the same color as Grace's comes running out with open arms.

Grace gets out of the car and the woman—who I'm assuming is her mom—basically tackle hugs her. I get out of the car, trying not to laugh at the two of them.

"I missed you so much," her mom says, swaying back and forth as she hugs Grace.

"Missed you too." Grace's voice is muffled against her mom's shirt. They pull apart and Grace waves her hand toward me standing by the car. "This is Bennett." I expect her mom to shake my hand, or stand and glare at me, but instead she comes barreling toward me and hugs me just as tight. Grace laughs. "And this is my mom, Olivia."

Olivia releases me and looks me over. "You did good," she tells Grace with a wink.

Grace's cheeks flame and she hisses, "*Mom*."

Something tells me the next three weeks are going to be fun.

Lots of fun.

———

Grace's dad and older brother Dean are working, and her little brother is still in school, so for the next few hours, it'll only be us. I'm okay with that. I'm not *worried* about her dad and brothers but I do want them to like me, but my gut says that's doubtful. After all, Grace is the only girl, so of course they're going to be protective. I doubt I can charm them, either—plus, I'm sure after the magazine debacles they've googled me and that *definitely* wouldn't gain me any points with them. I'm just going to have to bide my time and see how things go.

Olivia shows me to one of the guestrooms—all the way down the hall from Grace's room, might I add—and then I go back out to the car to carry our bags in while Grace and her mom catch up.

I still don't understand why Grace packed so much stuff, but I guess girls need a lot of shit.

I bring her bags into her room. It's just as girly as I expected and the color scheme matches what she has in her dorm with lots of white, gold, and blue. The floors are a shining hardwood and she has a fuzzy white monstrosity covering them. Grace and her damn rugs ... and pillows. So many fucking pillows. Not only are they all over the bed but there's even a pile of them on the floor to create a makeshift seating area. A chandelier hangs from the center of the ceiling and illuminates the room. It's prissy, that's for sure. And big. Grace might've classified this house as *normal* but it's still huge. I grew up in a small house that could fit inside this one three times.

I head back out to my car and grab my own bag. Before I can escape into the guestroom, Grace's mom calls out, "Bennett, come join us in the kitchen."

I sigh. I figured I'd get a chance to chill on my own for a while.

I drop my bag on the bed and turn around to go downstairs. All along the upstairs hallway are pictures of the entire family in various stages of life. My mom has a similar wall at home.

I meander through the house and into the kitchen. Grace and her mom sit at the kitchen table with a plate of cookies. It's a magazine worthy picture. Especially the way Grace glows with happiness when speaking to her mom. When she hears me, however, she grows flushed and her hands shake nervously. My gut nosedives with fear that she regrets last night. I was scared of this—terrified that she'd regret losing her virginity to me. Now that we're here, I don't know when I'll get the chance to ask her about it and I'm not very good at reading people.

"Have a seat, Bennett," her mom says, pointing to the chair beside Grace. "The cookies are fresh out of the oven. Double chocolate chip, they're Grace's favorite," she explains.

I pull out the chair and take a seat. I don't really want a cookie but I take one anyway since it would be rude not to. I take a bite and it's actually pretty damn good. Olivia smiles at me, pleased.

"So," she starts, "you play hockey?"

I nod. "I've been benched so far this season, but yeah."

She smiles and glances at Grace. "Grace said you're training with the coach at the university."

I nod again and finish the cookie, wiping the crumbs on my jeans. "Yeah, that's right."

"How'd you guys meet then?" she asks. "*Grace*," she says in a jokingly disgusted tone, "won't tell me and I'm curious."

I shrug. "Bumped into each other on campus. Things kinda just happened from there."

You know, the usual, I sweet-talked your daughter into pretending to be my girlfriend and then took her virginity.

Olivia frowns. "Oh, okay."

Grace laughs. "Were you expecting something more climactic?"

Her mom purses her lips. "Well, yeah."

Grace shakes her head, fighting a smile. "Sorry to disappoint you."

Olivia turns to me. "So, are you from the Boston area?"

I nod. "Born and raised in the town over from the university."

She nods. "Do you have any brothers or sisters?"

"A sister," I answer. "Sabrina. Speaking of," I stand, "I better call her back. She's been blowing up my phone all day."

"Oh, of course." Olivia waves me off. "Family comes first."

"Thanks." I smile at her and excuse myself from the

room. I head upstairs and close the door to the guestroom. I sit on the end of the bed and call back Sabrina, praying to God that it's nothing bad.

She answers with a clipped, "Hello?"

"Hey, you called?" *Like fifty times.*

"Mom said you won't be home for Christmas and New Year's."

"That's right."

"*Why?*" she whines. "We always have Christmas as a family."

I'm sure my mom told her that I'm with Grace for the holidays, but I play into her. "I'm with my girlfriend and her family." I pinch the bridge of my nose.

"Your girlfriend," she repeats. "You're spending the holidays with *her* family and we've never even met her. It's not like we live far away, Bennett. We could've had a family dinner and we could've met her then."

I sigh. "I don't know what you want me to say."

"That you're a stupid fuck and you'll introduce her to us when you get back."

"I'll introduce you to her when we get back," I repeat.

She tsks. "You forgot the first part *little brother*."

She says *little brother* like it's meant to be an insult. I'd tell her to be more creative but I don't want to argue with her. "Uh-huh, I'm a stupid fuck, Bina. We know this."

She laughs. "Thanks. I'm going to miss you," she says in a sad tone. "I think we've spent almost every Christmas together."

"Yeah, I know. I'm sorry I won't be there to help you burn those monstrosity of a pair of pajamas mom gets us every year."

Sabrina laughs and I can tell it's genuine. At least she's feeling better about all of this. "She picks the ugliest ones on purpose, I swear."

"What were they last year?"

"Leprechauns," she giggles. "Not *elves* but leprechauns. Those might've been the best yet."

"I don't know," I hedge. "The year with narwhals was pretty epic."

"Ooh," she cries, and I can hear her smack her hand against something. "What about the year with the unicorn that was shitting rainbows—but the rainbow was green and red for Christmas?"

I snort. "Those were good too."

Sabrina grows quiet on the line. "I'm worried about you, Bennett."

"Why, Bina? I'm good."

"You're such a shitty liar. Seriously, the worst."

I chuckle. "Nah, it's just because you're a reporter. You see through everyone's bullshit."

"Damn straight." She laughs but it sounds forced this time. "I know I tell you all the time, but seriously, Bennett, if you ever need to talk about things I'm here."

"Off the record?"

She snorts. "Yes, fucktard, *off the fucking record*. You're my brother. I would never leak anything you tell me to the media. Don't you have more faith in me than that?"

"Sorry, Bina," I sigh. "I've been screwed over by a lot of people in this business. It's hard not to question everyone after a while."

"But I'm not people," she counters. "I'm family."

"True," I sigh. "We'll talk later but I better get back to Grace and her mom."

"Oh, of course," Sabrina says. "You better call me, douche-canoe. I mean it."

"I will."

"Love you, Bennie."

I chuckle. "Love you too, Bina."

I hang up and collapse back on the bed. I hate not telling my sister and parents what's going on with Coach Matthews but the less they know the better. I hope Coach Harrison is figuring something out because I have no fucking clue what to do.

How do you knock down someone who rules the world?

CHAPTER TWENTY-FIVE

GRACE

AFTER LINCOLN COMES HOME FROM SCHOOL AND gives Bennett the cold shoulder, Mom decides it would be best to meet my dad and Dean at a restaurant for dinner. I guess she figures they have to act somewhat respectfully in public.

My mom insists that Bennett and I ride in the car with her and Linc, which I'm thankful for. I can tell Bennett's looking to get me alone so we can talk about last night, but I can't wrap my head around my thoughts to even talk about it with him. I don't regret it, that's for sure, but I'm scared. My feelings for Bennett were already complicated and now it's worse. I've never wanted anyone the way I want him, but I know I can't have him. He doesn't do girlfriends—at least, not real ones—and I'm sure last night meant nothing to him. How could it have? He's been with a lot of women and I'm nothing special. I'm just ... me.

"You're quiet," Mom comments during the drive to the restaurant.

"Lost in my thoughts," I explain. I glance behind me at Bennett and Lincoln in the back of the Land Rover. Linc glares at Bennett like he's the most disgusting person he's ever met. "Linc," I hiss. "Stop it."

Linc's lips curl into a snarl. "But he's a *hockey* player."

Bennett's snorts. "Dude, I'm sitting right here. Besides, what's so wrong with hockey players?"

"Football is better," Lincoln quips. He plays for the high school team, and his whole life revolves around the sport. His love and passion for it is funny since no one in my family is that much into sports. My dad and Dean are pretty much nerds.

Bennett turns in his seat. "Football, huh?" He then launches into a bunch of stats and team names that mean nothing to me. Apparently, Bennett not only knows hockey, he knows football as well. I can see Lincoln warming up to him now, and that makes me happy. This thing between us might not be real but he did get suckered into spending three weeks in Virginia, so I'd hoped the experience wouldn't be entirely miserable for him.

My mom turns into the lot and I scan the parked cars for my dad's and Dean's, but they're nowhere to be seen. I let out a breath I didn't know I was holding, relieved that we beat them. This way we can avoid a confrontation in the parking lot.

My mom parks the car and we hop out, heading inside to get a table.

There's five-minute wait and I sway nervously beside Bennett, scared that my dad's going to walk in any second and deck him across the face. It's not a likely scenario. We *are* in public and my dad isn't that mean, but I can't seem to shake the fear. Luckily, the buzzer goes off and we're taken to a table before they arrive.

My mom points for Bennett and me to take two seats beside each other and then she takes the end seat beside Bennett, while ordering Linc to take the one across from Bennett. I don't call her on it but I see exactly what she's doing—and I'm silently grateful for it.

The waiter comes by for our drink order, and since I'm too busy freaking out to pay attention, Bennett orders a water for me.

"Calm down," he whispers in my ear. "It'll be fine."

A few minutes later, I see my dad's tall form enter the

restaurant. He looks tired from a hard day of work and my brother comes in behind him. They're both tall with angular cheekbones and a sharp gaze. My dad's brown hair has slight speck of gray in it now and my brother's brown locks hang unkempt in his green eyes—green the same color as mine, courtesy of our dad.

I hold my breath, waiting for the shit to hit the fan. I startle when I feel Bennett's hand on mine. He gives it a reassuring squeeze and the look in his eyes alleviates my worry slightly.

"Hey, Princess," my dad says, coming to kiss my forehead.

I expect Bennett to make a comment on the princess thing but he wisely keeps his mouth shut.

"Hi, Dad. I missed you." I reach up to hug him. He moves to take his seat and Dean hugs me then. They both smell like oil and grease from the car shop, but I don't mind it. It's normal and smells like home. "This is Bennett. Bennett, this is my dad, Trace, and my brother, Dean."

Dean eyes Bennett over my shoulder. "Hey," he says, giving Bennett a head nod. It's polite and more than I expected.

"Hey." Bennett holds out his hand for Dean to shake. "I'm Bennett."

"I know," Dean says coldly. His tone of voice suggests that he's done some research on Bennett and he's none too pleased. So much for that politeness.

"Right," Bennett says awkwardly, letting his hand fall when Dean doesn't accept it.

Dean takes his seat across from me and picks up the menu. My dad has yet to acknowledge Bennett. It's like he's not even here. I can handle the silent treatment over yelling or flat out hostility, though.

I clear my throat. "Dad," I say firm enough to get his attention. He lowers the menu and his eyes portray the sadness he's trying to hide. "This is Bennett." I know he already knows that but it felt rude not to make some sort of official introduction.

He grunts in response and narrows his eyes on Bennett. "So, you're the dirt bag that dragged my daughter into your media firestorm?"

"*Dad*," I hiss. "Stop it."

Bennett touches his fingers to my knee under the table, silently telling me that he can handle it. I know he can, but the problem is he shouldn't have to. Yes, this isn't real between us, but my dad doesn't know that. He should, at least, treat Bennett with some respect.

"I admit the media isn't in my favor, but I wouldn't say I *dragged* Grace into it." I don't miss the twitch of his lips as he tries to hold back laughter because that's exactly what he did.

"Mmhmm," my dad hums in disbelief.

This is going nowhere and we don't even have our food yet. Which tells me this is going to be one long-ass dinner.

Bennett clears his throat and takes a sip of his water. I

hadn't even noticed the waiter bring them and I grab my glass as well, taking a huge sip to quench my suddenly dry throat. I don't do well with awkward situations.

"Bennett plays hockey," I say stupidly. Of course, they already know this and we talked about him some when I was here for Thanksgiving but I hate the quiet awkwardness that has settled in the air. My family is *never* quiet: with three kids and a dad that's a bit outlandish, there's never a dull moment with the Wentworth's so when things *do* get quiet it doesn't feel right. I shake my head. This is stupid. "Dad," I say calmly. "You don't have to like Bennett, but you do have to accept him. I'm a big girl now. I'm grown up and on my own and I've chosen to have Bennett in my life. He's not going anywhere anytime soon and this would be a lot easier on me if you'd be nice to him. When you're rude to him, it's a slap in the face to me, and that hurts." I take a deep breath. I'm not normally so forward, but I'm learning that I have a voice and it's okay to use it.

The table is silent. My brothers, mom, dad, and Bennett all stare at me like I've grown three heads.

I've always been more like my mom. Quiet, go with the flow, and easily embarrassed, but there are brief moments when I'm not afraid to speak my mind—also something I get from her. When she has something to say, you better listen up.

My dad speaks first. "Okay."

That's it. A simple *okay* but it speaks volumes.

I breathe out a sigh of relief. "Thank you."

The silence breaks, and suddenly, the table is full of chatter. My mom and dad are talking about his day at work, Lincoln and Dean talk about cars, and Bennett turns to me with a small crooked smile.

"You're amazing," he says with a bit of awe in his voice.

I blush. "I didn't say much."

He shakes his head. "Don't underestimate yourself. You defended me even though you didn't like speaking against your dad and that ... That means a lot. I know how much you love your parents and that you don't like to go against their wishes, so the fact that you'd defend me? Well, thanks, sweetheart." He leans over and kisses the side of my head quickly. No one at the table misses the gesture, but none of them say anything. In fact, I see what looks like approval in my dad's eyes.

The waiter comes for our order and I suddenly feel ravenous.

Idle chat is made through the rest of the dinner and then we head home. It's getting late, and after spending the day on the road, I excuse myself to shower and go to bed early.

Before college, I never realized what a luxury it was to have my own bathroom. The communal bathroom at school has been one of the hardest things to get used to. I like my privacy, and there's not much when you're sharing a bathroom with an entire floor of girls.

I take a longer shower than normal and change into a pair of pajamas. I blow dry my hair—sleeping on wet hair is *not* fun—and apply my moisturizer. I wonder idly if Bennett's come up to go to bed but I don't want to be caught seeking him out. After my rant at dinner, I think it's best not to rock the boat.

I move some of the pillows off my bed and turn back the covers. It's funny how in a short time my dorm room has become home to me and this room feels like a stranger's.

I burrow under the covers, stifling a yawn. There's a TV in my room but I don't really feel like watching it.

Instead, I think of last night—how it made me feel. Being with Bennett like that was more than I could've dreamed of. Yeah, it hurt, but it was … I don't know … *right*. Like suddenly something in the world aligned and everything was as it should be. I know that sounds as stupid as it gets, but it's the truth, and it scares me. I know Bennett doesn't see me as anything special—doesn't want this to be real, but I want it. I know I can't tell him that. It's not part of our agreement and he doesn't do commitment. I don't want to scare him away to the point that I don't have him in my life at all. I'd rather have him as a friend than nothing at all.

CHAPTER TWENTY-SIX

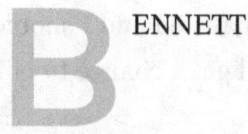

BENNETT

I WAIT UNTIL I KNOW FOR SURE THAT EVERYONE'S fallen asleep. It's after one in the morning when I finally creep into Grace's bedroom. It's pitch black, her blinds and curtains closed, and I can barely see to step across the floor. I bump into her dresser and curse when something rattles.

She stirs beneath her covers and I still. I was going to wake her up but I don't want to scare her.

She rubs her eyes and sits up. "Bennett? Is that you?" she whispers.

I nod, which is stupid since she can't see me. "Yeah," I croak.

She reaches up and flicks her light on. She blinks from the sudden flood of light and rubs her eyes. "What are you doing in here?" she asks.

"I wanted to talk to you." I walk over to her bed and sit down beside her. The bed dips with my added weight and she rolls a bit toward me. I itch to reach out and touch her. Kiss her. Hold her. But I don't. I'm so confused about what I want and I don't want to lead her on. It's better to act indifferent than to make her think …

Think what, Bennett? That this is real? Because it is.

I push my thoughts away. I don't want to hear them.

"About what?" she asks, trying not to yawn. There are circles under her eyes; I know she's exhausted and I should let her sleep, but I don't know when I'll get a chance to talk to her.

"I wanted to make sure that you were okay after last night." I swallow thickly as I think back on those moments. Fuck, I want to do it again, but I doubt Grace wants me the same way. "You were quiet today and I was worried you regretted it. I … I wouldn't be able to live with myself if I had done something you weren't one-hundred percent okay with." I rub my hands over my face. "I haven't always been the nice guy, Grace, but that's how I want you to see me. I want to be good because of you."

She laughs lightly. "So the bad boy wants the good girl to make him good, and the good girl wants the bad boy to make her bad." She lifts her fingers and strokes them against my cheek. "We're quite the pair, aren't we?"

I lean into her touch. I shouldn't, but the moment of brief contact feels like a lifeline. "Being bad is overrated," I tell her.

Her lips quirk up. "So is being good."

I wet my lips, my eyes flicking over her face. Her hair is a wild mess and her lips are slightly chapped, her cheeks rosy, and her eyes sparkling with amusement. I've never felt possessive over a woman before, but this one makes me crazy in ways I never imagined I would feel.

"Maybe there's a happy medium," I tell her. "And maybe —" I wrap a piece of her hair around my finger "—we can find it together?"

She's quiet, and the silence nearly kills me. Finally, after what feels like an eternity, she nods. "Together," she echoes and I smile.

"You never answered me, though—if you're okay?"

"I'm fine," she assures me. "Last night was ... amazing. I don't regret it. I couldn't."

I breathe out an embarrassingly loud sigh of relief. I had worried all day.

"Good," I say.

Her lips twitch the smallest bit and she says, "I wouldn't

be opposed to it happening again, either. I mean, if you wanted to."

I chuckle. "Trust me, I wouldn't mind." I wink.

She blushes slightly and lays her head down on the pillows. "Are we good now?"

I nod. "We're good. I'll stop worrying so much."

She smiles. "You better get out of here before we get caught."

I wince. Her dad finding me in here would definitely not score me any points.

I lean over and kiss her. It's a simple kiss goodnight, but it makes me realize something.

I'm a fucking liar if I think this is still simply an agreement between us—a deal struck to save my reputation.

This ... This is so much more.

"WHERE ARE WE GOING?" GRACE'S GIGGLES TRAIL behind us as I drag her down the street.

We've spent the past three days doing good things—baking cookies with her mom, helping at her brother's school for some holiday recital, and helping her mom plan some shmancy New Year's Eve party—now it's time to do something bad.

"I'm not telling."

Telling her would ruin the fun, and she'd probably

chicken out. If I completely blindside her with this, I have a better chance of getting her to agree.

I spot the sign for the shop and begin to slow down.

I had to search the internet before I found a place that I trusted to do this.

"Oh, hell no." Grace spots the sign and connects the dots. "I'm not getting a tattoo, Bennett."

I hold on tight to her hand, not letting her get away. "Come on Grace, a tattoo is like the true mark of a rebel. You have to do it."

"I don't even know what I'd get."

"I already have something picked out for you."

Her mouth drops. "You have to be kidding me. What?"

"I'm not telling. It's a surprise."

"*Bennett*," she practically shrieks my name, "you can't expect me to get a tattoo—something *permanent*—and not know what it is."

"You trust me, right?"

"Yes," she answers without a second of thought.

"Then you have nothing to worry about."

She sizes me up. "Do I get to pick one for you, then?"

I nod. "Absolutely."

She grins. "Then I'll do it."

Something tells me I might be in trouble. I don't argue with her, though. I open the door and let her go in first.

The shop is dark with purple walls and black curtains. Pictures of tattoos and other drawings line the walls. A man sits behind the counter, both arms covered in ink. I've gotten a few tattoos over the years but it's been a while since I got anything new. I'm mildly afraid of what Grace will pick for me, but I know she's feeling the same way.

"Hey, man, I'm Bennett," I say to the guy. "I think we spoke on the phone?"

"Oh, yeah, I'm Drew." He tips his head at me in acknowledgement. "You guys can come back here."

He leads us into a room in the back of the studio. I requested a private room since I thought it would make Grace feel more comfortable.

"Who's going first?" Drew asks.

Grace surprises me by saying, "Me, I guess. I need more time to figure out what you're going to get," she tells me, biting her lip and giving away how nervous she is.

"Take a seat then." Drew slaps his hand against the leather chair.

Grace takes a deep breath and sits down. "Please don't give me something stupid," she begs.

"Trust me, sweetheart, I've got this. You have nothing to worry about."

She surprises me by nodding and not arguing with me.

"What are you getting today?" Drew asks.

"This." I hand him a piece of paper where I sketched my idea. "I'm not the best artist so you can take that and make it better, but that's it."

Drew unfolds the paper and chuckles.

Grace looks at him in horror. "Is it bad? You have to tell me—this is permanent," she adds like he doesn't know.

Drew shakes his head. "It's not bad. You'll be fine."

Grace sighs and nibbles on her bottom lip. I take the seat beside her while Drew makes my drawing better. It's a simple design but it needed some improvement. Drew finishes and hands the paper back to me.

I grin. "It's perfect."

"Excellent."

He goes to work putting it on the transfer paper. "Where do you want it?" he asks Grace.

She looks to me. "You pick."

I'm surprised she's giving me so much control, but I'm not about to argue with her.

"There." I point to her wrist. Drew begins transferring the design to her skin and I warn, "No peeking."

She lifts her eyes to mine. "Then come sit over here and hold my other hand."

I chuckle and pull the other chair in the room over to her side. She turns away from Drew and holds her hand out to me. "Is this going to hurt?" She looks worried.

"It's not that bad." She looks doubtful. "Scout's honor." I lift my fingers.

"I think you'd have to have been a Boy Scout for that to mean anything." She jumps when Drew moves away to grab the ink and tattoo needle.

I gasp. "I can't believe you don't think I could've been a Boy Scout."

"Well, were you?" she asks with a raised brow.

"For like three years," I admit. "Then I discovered hockey and girls."

She snorts. "Of course."

"You're going to have to hold still," Drew warns.

Grace holds on tight to my hand. "It won't take long," I tell her, trying to comfort her. "It's small." She nods. "Have you figured out what I'm going to get?"

"No. I'm too nervous to think."

"Well you better hurry up and decide, sweetheart," I say just as the needle pierces her skin.

She winces. "I thought you said this wouldn't hurt?" she accuses.

I chuckle. "It doesn't hurt that bad."

"I'd beg to differ."

"Wimp," I joke.

She sticks her tongue out at me.

It doesn't take Drew long to finish her tattoo.

"You're not allowed to look at it until I get mine," I tell her. "Then we'll see them together."

She nods. "That seems fair."

"Does that mean you've decided what I'm getting?"

She grins like the cat that ate the damn canary and now *I'm* worried. "Yep."

We switch places and she whispers to Drew what he's supposed to give me. "Where do you want me to put it?" he asks her.

"I'd say his ass just because but that's too mean for even

me." She winks at me. "How about the same spot you did mine?"

"I can do that," Drew says, messing around at his station.

"Are you going to come hold my hand?" I pout and hold out my hand to her.

She laughs. "Aw, is the baby worried it'll hurt?"

I look at my other tattoos. "Nah, I just want my girl to sit here with me."

Her eyes flare at the *my girl* comment and she perches her cute ass on the chair I was sitting in a few minutes ago. She slides her hand into mine and her eyes linger on my face like she's searching for answers there.

Drew sketches out my tattoo and gets her approval.

She grins at the drawing. "It's perfect."

"Now I'm scared." I chuckle, rubbing my face nervously with my free hand before Drew starts.

"Don't be," she tells me. "You trust me, right?" she throws my words back at me.

"Yes," I answer, and I do. I surprisingly do. I don't trust many people—I've been screwed over a lot—but Grace is someone I know would never do me harm.

I can feel Drew outlining the tattoo but I still can't figure out what it is. He shades it in and Grace smiles as she watches. I look away, even though I want to peek. Grace didn't look at hers so I owe it to her to do the same until the big reveal.

Drew finishes and says, "Are you ready to see?"

"Fuck yes," I blurt.

Grace laughs. "You and your dirty mouth."

"Ready, Princess?" I ask her.

"You bet."

"We'll close our eyes while Drew uncovers yours," I tell her, "and then when he says ready, we'll look, okay?"

"Okay," she agrees.

We close our eyes and Drew removes the bandage from Grace's.

"One, two, three," Drew counts. "You can look now."

Grace and I both hold out our arms and look at the tattoos on our wrists.

I bust out laughing. "Good one, Princess." A red Sour Patch Kid is tattooed on my wrist. It's silly, but it's me, and every time I look at it I'll be reminded of Grace and that trip to Target. "This is perfect," I tell her. Grace is quiet, though, and I worry that she's mad about my choice. I bend, trying to see her face. She looks like she's close to tears. "Grace?" I prompt. She says nothing. "Fuck," I curse. "You hate it." She shakes her head. "You don't hate it, then?" A nod. "Fuck, sweetheart, talk to me," I beg. Her silence worries me.

"I hate that stupid nickname but this is … it's perfect." She smiles wistfully at the small crown-shaped tattoo.

I bend and kiss the top of her head. She looks so small and vulnerable and I can't help but show her some sort of affection. I mean—I'd like to do a whole lot more, but we *are* in public.

"Just so you know, I don't mean to call you Princess in a

bad way." She snorts. "Seriously," I add. "It just ... suits you."

She looks up at me, her hair falling behind her shoulders. "Why don't I believe you?"

I chuckle and hold up my fingers with a little space in between. "Okay, so maybe I *did* mean it sarcastically just a little bit."

"Only a little bit, huh?" She laughs, and her eyes sparkle with amusement.

God, I love this girl.

My thoughts stop me cold.

Love? I love this girl?

Fuck, I think I do. No, I *know* I do.

I've never loved another girl before—have nothing to compare this feeling to—but I know that's what it is.

Somewhere along the way, I fell in love with Grace.

I fell in love with her smile.

Her laugh.

The way she mocks me every chance she gets.

I fell in love with her love of chocolate and coffee.

I fell in love with every little thing that makes her *her*.

Six months ago, the thought of falling in love would've made me laugh, but something I've learned in my life is that things never seem to happen the way you expect them to.

I stare at her with a newfound wonder in my eyes, and she doesn't miss it.

"Why are you looking at me like that?" she asks. "Is there something on my face?"

Now that I know I love her—that I'm *in* love with her—I want to blurt the words out, but I don't want to scare her. I haven't even talked to her about making our arrangement official—becoming a *real* couple—but it's something that's been weighing heavily on my mind the past few days. Being near her twenty-four-seven has made me fall harder for her instead of scaring me away.

"Nah. You're perfect," I whisper.

"Then why are you looking at me like that?" She wrinkles her nose.

I shrug. "I was just thinking, I guess."

"About what?"

You. Us. A future. "About our awesome tattoos," I lie.

She laughs and looks down at the black outline of a crown. "Yeah, I think we both did good."

We finish up and pay and walk to a coffee shop we passed on our way here.

It's cold outside and the sky is a swirling gray, promising snow. Snow had already fallen on campus when we left, but the grass has been bare here.

I open the door to the coffee shop and let Grace go in first. The smell of coffee hits me as do the sounds of orders being placed and called out. There are a few people in line so Grace and I step up behind the last person. A few people in the shop watch us with curiosity. I'm learning that Grace and her family are practically local celebrities due to their wealth and ties to the band Willow Creek. I'm used to people staring at us because of *me,* and

I have to admit it's nice to have the tables turned for a change.

We place our order and I pay—no way in hell am I letting her pay—and then we stand off to the side to wait for our order.

I feel nervous—jumpy, even—because I know what I have to do and I'm scared she won't like it. Rejection isn't something I have to deal with often. At least, not with women, but Grace is always putting me in my place.

Our order is called out and Grace scurries forward to grab our mugs—yeah, they put it in mugs—before I can move. She has the biggest smile on her face as she turns back to me, and I'd like to think she's smiling at *me* like that, but she really fucking loves her coffee. I follow her through the coffee shop and to a back area with tables. She picks a table in the corner and sets our mugs down.

"Tattoo and coffees, I like this mix," she says, sliding into a chair.

I chuckle. "Funny, because you were opposed to the tattoo thing at first."

She lifts her mug and takes a tentative sip so she doesn't scald her tongue. She sets the mug back down and her lips quirk. "Hey, I changed my mind. I'm allowed to do that."

I want to ask her if that means I'm allowed to change my mind, but I bite my tongue. For now.

Grace holds out her wrist, admiring the crown tattoo.

"Are you sure it's okay?" When I thought of it, I knew it was perfect for her, but that doesn't mean she likes it.

She smiles and nods, wrapping her long fingers around her mug of coffee. Several rings adorn her fingers and her favorite watch sits on her wrist. "I really do love it," she promises. "What about yours?" She eyes my tattoo.

"It's fucking perfect."

Someone at a nearby table glares at me for cussing and I wave sheepishly.

Grace laughs. "You're going to get us in trouble."

"While we're being bad we might as well go full out," I tell her, waggling my brows. I pick up a sugar packet from the table and rub it between my fingers, waiting for her to speak.

"What do you have in mind?"

"Is there a bathroom here?" I ask.

"Why?" She looks scared now.

My voice lowers to a whisper. "I think you know why."

She shivers—and it's not because she's scared, but because she's turned on by this. Underneath her prissy attitude and dresses lies a wild heart. Anyone who says you can't be good and a rebel doesn't know how to live.

I stand and offer her my hand. We leave our mugs on the table and head down a narrow hall to the bathrooms. It's unisex—this couldn't get any better—and empty. I push open the door and she stumbles inside, breathing heavily. I know if I felt her chest I'd feel her heart beating madly behind her rib cage.

I close the door behind us, but I don't lock it. Her eyes

flick to the lock and she raises her brow in question. "Aren't you going to lock that?"

"No." I shake my head. "That's part of the thrill."

"Getting caught?" she asks, backing against the porcelain sink.

I shake my head. "*Thinking* you're going to get caught."

She swallows thickly as I stalk closer to her. I plant my hands on either side of the sink, caging her in.

"What are you going to do?"

I bite her bottom lip, pulling it between my teeth before letting it go. "Whatever you want to do."

"I'm in charge?" Her voice shakes and she reaches up a tentative hand to touch my chest.

I nod. "You're always in charge."

She smiles at that and leans in to kiss me. She doesn't have to lean far since she wears a pair of ridiculously long heels. My hands move to her waist and I can't get a good grip on her hips thanks to the heavy coat she wears. I find the tie around her waist and undo it, pushing the coat off her shoulders. It falls to the floor and she breaks the kiss with a laugh.

"I thought *I* was in charge?"

"You are." I go in to kiss her again.

"And yet you're already trying to get me naked."

I shake my head. "Just the coat. It was in my way."

"In the way of what?" She challenges.

"This." I grab her ass and she laughs, wrapping her arms around my neck.

"You're ridiculous."

I kiss her to shut her up. She kisses me back with fervor and the heat between us grows. I haven't gotten to hold her like this since that night at the hotel. It seems like there's always someone around us and we never get a moment alone.

Grace moans into my mouth, and it's the softest fucking sound I've ever heard, almost like a cat's purr. Her nails rake through my hair and she wraps her fingers around the strands, pulling my mouth down to hers. Her tongue tangles with mine and I groan as I hold myself back. I want to rip her clothes off and fuck her hard and fast, but I'm putting this in her hands. I won't push her to do anything she's not comfortable doing.

Her hands tentatively move down my chest to my stomach. She curls them under the fabric of my sweater and pushes it up and over my head. I'm wearing a shirt beneath it and she makes quick work of getting rid of that one as well. She glides her hands over my bare skin and my abs contract from the touch. She bites her lip and I know she's thinking deeply about what she wants to do next. It takes all my willpower not to touch her, or kiss her, or do *something*, but this is for her. Not me. This is her chance to be the bad girl. To take what she wants.

"We have to hurry," she whispers.

I startle at her words. "Do you really want to do this?" I ask her, gliding my fingers over her cheek. "We don't have to."

I don't normally give her an out when I'm making her do something 'bad' but this is something I would never force her to do.

She nods. "I want this. Please don't make me beg."

She doesn't have to ask me twice. I crash my lips to hers and she undoes my belt. I pick her up and back her against the wall. She wraps her legs around my waist and slides down my pants. I set her down long enough to grab a condom and put it on. She's in a skirt so that makes is easier. I pick her up again and move her underwear to the side before sliding inside her. I want to push in hard but this is only her second time so I move as gentle as I can.

She breathes into my mouth. "You're not going to break me. Fuck me."

If she's trying to kill me, it's working.

I move hard and fast. I don't make love to her the way I did the other night. A public bathroom isn't exactly made for slow sweet fucking. You either fuck as fast as you can or you don't fuck at all.

She holds onto my shoulders, her fingernails digging in so hard I wouldn't be surprised if she doesn't draw blood. She pants loudly and small cries leave her parted lips.

"Keep going," she encourages. "I'm almost there."

I bite her lip and the heat in her eyes nearly sets me on fire. "You love this, don't you?" I kiss her deeply. "You fucking love the thought of someone opening that door and seeing my cock inside you."

"Yes," she gasps, her eyes hooded with desire.

My fingers dig into her thighs and she clenches around my dick. I know she's close and I fight my own release so she can have hers.

Finally, she comes, and I groan into the skin of her neck as I come too.

Her whole body quakes in my arms and I hold on tight so that she doesn't fall. She lowers her legs from around my waist and little beads of sweat dot her forehead.

"That was…"

I silence her with a kiss. There are no adequate words for what that was.

She rights her clothes while I get rid of the condom and pull my pants up. My shirt and sweater lay scattered on the floor along with her coat. I pick them all up and hold out her coat to her. I slip my t-shirt on and tuck it into my pants before putting on the sweater.

Grace looks me up and down. "We look like we just fucked in the bathroom."

"That's because we did, sweetheart." I laugh and reach out to try to tame her hair a bit. It's a wild mess and I selfishly love seeing it that way—knowing it's from us fucking—but everyone else would know too.

She eyes her reflection in the mirror and wipes her smeared lip gloss off her lips and fixes her hair better than I did.

We can't put off the inevitable, so I open the door and we step out into the hall. It's—thankfully—empty.

Our coffee still sits on the table we had occupied and we sit back down, acting like nothing happened.

Grace raises her mug to her lips and takes a sip, her eyes shifting around the room. It's probably catching up with her, what we did, and I don't want her to freak out.

I take her hand and bring it to my lips, kissing the tops of her fingers.

She bites her lip and looks from our hands to my face. "Everyone knows," she hisses.

"Nah, sweetheart. We'd be in a police car if they did." She pales. "I was kidding," I hasten to add.

"Oh." Her shoulders sag in relief.

"Grace?" I say her name hesitantly. Now is the most wrong fucking time to bring this up, but I can't keep quiet anymore.

"What?" She looks scared, and I can't blame her: my voice shakes and I sound so unlike myself.

"What do you think about making this official? Us, I mean?"

Her eyes convey her surprise and her pouty pink lips part. "Like, you want us to be a real couple?"

I nod. I want it more than any-fucking-thing. So much so that for the last few days all I've thought of is Grace and hockey hasn't crossed my mind. That never happens. Hockey has always been my sole focus, but not anymore.

She doesn't say anything and that worries me. I start to take it back, to tell her to forget about it, when she gasps the softest, most perfect, "*Yes.*"

I breathe out an embarrassingly loud sigh of relief and take her face between my hands, kissing her. She smiles against my lips and lets out a quiet laugh.

"Are you sure about this?" she asks. "I know you don't date."

"I didn't, but you ... changed things. It's been killing me being this close to you and having to realize it was all fake."

"That was your idea," she reminds me. "For me to be your fake girlfriend," she adds like I didn't already know what she meant.

"I know, sweetheart, I fucking know." I press my forehead to hers, my hand winding around the back of her neck.

"By the way," she says with a smile, "it's worked."

"What has?" I ask, confused.

"You using me as your fake girlfriend," she whispers. "Look what Elle just sent me."

She holds out her phone to me with a picture Elle snapped of the inside of a magazine. The headline reads: **Meet Hockey's New 'It' Couple.** There are photos of Grace and I on campus, the one of our kiss at the game, and even one of me standing outside her dorm with coffee and cupcakes. The photo is out too far for me to read what it says, but from the headline, I'd say it's pretty positive.

I smile. "Thanks for saving my reputation." I draw her close and kiss her forehead.

She smiles. "And now it's real?"

"It's real."

CHAPTER TWENTY-SEVEN

GRACE

"I LIKE BENNETT," MY MOM SAYS, SHUFFLING clothes around on a rack.

When she asked me to go shopping, I *knew* she had an ulterior motive for getting me out of the house.

"I do too, obviously," I say, picking up a dress from the rack and holding it up to my body.

"That would be cute on you." My mom nods to the cobalt blue dress I hold.

"I need to get a dress for the New Year's Eve party," I tell her. "I don't think this is fancy enough."

Everyone goes all out for the annual Wentworth New Year's Eve bash and the dress I hold looks more appropriate for a winter formal.

"You're probably right," my mom says. "I need to get a dress too." She makes a face of disgust. I definitely didn't get my love of fashion from her. She's a jeans and t-shirt kind of girl while I usually wear a dress or skirt. Although, on campus I've been wearing jeans more often thanks to the frigid temperatures.

I move to another rack and flick through the dresses. The standard red and green colors make me want to pull out my eyeballs.

"Bennett seems really into you," she comments, getting back to what she *really* wants to talk to me about.

"He better be. I mean, we've only been dating for six months." *Or, you know, a week.*

"He hasn't always been a one-woman man," she tells me like I don't already know.

"I know, Mom," I say. "Things are different with me."

She looks unsure. "I just don't want to see you get hurt, Grace. This is your first real relationship and he's known to get around. Just ... be careful, okay?" she pleads.

"I am," I promise her.

She nods but I doubt this is the last I'll hear about this. She's a mom, so she worries twenty-four-seven.

"How about this dress?" She holds up a purple sequined number.

"For me?" I ask, and she nods. "I don't look good in purple."

She laughs and puts the dress back on the rack. "What about this one for me?" She holds up a strapless navy dress with silver detailing.

"I think that would be gorgeous on you," I tell her honestly. My mom is still young and can pull off anything she wants.

She drapes the dress over her arm. "I'm going to try it on."

"I'm going to keep looking for a dress for myself," I tell her. "Just holler for me when you're changed."

She nods and heads over to the dressing room a few feet away.

I pick up a gold and teal dress and look it over. It's nice, but still not the one. I put it back on the rack and keep looking. Thankfully, the store is full of dresses, so if I keep looking, I'm bound to find something eventually.

A few minutes later, my mom calls me over to check out the dress she chose.

She steps out of the dressing room with a wondering smile. "What do you think?"

I smile widely. "You look hot, Mom."

She rolls her eyes. "Oh, Grace."

"I'm serious." I laugh. "It looks great. You'll need a pair of heels, though."

At the word *heels* she looks I've just handed her a death sentence. "So you think I should get this one?" She turns, appraising herself in the mirror.

I nod. "As long as you like the way it looks and feels, go for it. It's a great dress."

She nods at her reflection and smiles. "Yeah, I think I'm going to get it."

She heads back into the dressing room to change back into her clothes, so I return to searching for my dress.

By the time she comes out, I think I've found it. "I'm going to try this one on," I tell her. "Wait for me."

I change into the dress quickly and step out of the room for my mom to see.

"Oh, Grace," she gasps. "You look beautiful."

I turn to look at my reflection in the full-length mirror. The skirt on the dress is long and fitted down my hips and thighs. It's done in gold and pink tone sequins while the top is white with short sleeves. It's simple but elegant, and totally me.

"I want this one," I say, fighting a smile. I love the way I look in the dress, but I really can't wait to see what Bennett thinks of me in it.

"Okay," she chimes. "Change and we'll checkout. Then how about we get some lunch? I'm starving."

"Sounds good. Do you mind if I invite Willow?" I ask,

referring to my friend and brother's girlfriend. "I haven't had a chance to see her since I've been back."

"Yeah, of course. That'll be fun."

I lock myself in the dressing room and change back into my navy skirt and white top and coat. My mom's waiting for me outside the changing room and she takes the dress from me so she can go checkout. While she does that, I send a text to Willow and browse the shoes and jewelry.

My phone vibrates in my hand with a text from Willow saying she'll meet us there.

My mom finds me, bag in her hand, and we head out to the car and to the restaurant.

We beat Willow there so we sit in the car to wait for her. She pulls up ten minutes later in her SUV and runs over to the car. I get out and she shrieks in excitement before squeezing me tight. Willow and I went through a rough patch a few months ago, nothing serious but our friendship needed some TLC, and now we're back on track.

"I've missed you." She smiles widely at me. Willow has the kind of smile that takes over her whole face, and it's infectious so I find myself smiling in response. Her blond hair is a wild mess of curls, like she forgot to brush it this morning, and her cheeks are flushed with happiness. Willow's one of those people who's almost always happy. The minute she's not smiling or bouncing off the wall, you know something is seriously wrong.

"I've missed you too." I let her go and we just stare at each other for a moment, taking in the small changes that have happened while we were apart. I notice her hair's gotten a little darker and she's cut it shorter so it now brushes her shoulders.

"How's college treating you?" she asks as we walk up the steps into the restaurant.

"Good," I answer. "I took way too many classes." I laugh. "But I like it."

She makes a face. "That makes one of us."

Willow should've been in her second year at NYU but over the summer she decided college wasn't for her. At, least not right now. Maybe one day she'll go back, or maybe not, and that's okay. I know Willow enough to know she's not going to sit on her ass and do nothing with her life.

"What have you been up to?" I ask her.

"Working on my blog," she answers. "I've been talking to Liam a lot and he's teaching me the basics of photography," she says, referring to her cousin who lives all the way on the coast of California. I haven't seen him in a few years but he's a professional surfer now.

"That's cool." I bump my shoulder with hers playfully as we follow my mom inside the restaurant. Someone immediately appears to take us to our seats.

"I haven't been here since your graduation dinner," Willow tells me, looking around with a wistful smile.

"Me either. Is Liam coming home for Christmas this year?" I ask her as we take our seats. I pick up the menu from the table and look it over.

"I think so," she says. "Mathias and Remy said they'd skin him alive if he didn't." She laughs.

"He has a girlfriend now, right?" I ask, trying to remember things she's told me over the last few months.

"Yeah. She's nice, but ..."

"But what?" I ask.

"I don't know." She shrugs. "She dragged him into a whole heap of trouble. It wasn't pretty."

"What do you mean?" I ask, confused.

"What rock do you live under?" she asks. "It was all over the news."

"I've been busy," I reason.

"True," she agrees. "Well, that's his story to tell, not mine." She waves her hand dismissively. "Now, let's eat."

"I MISSED YOU." BENNETT CLIMBS INTO BED BEHIND me and wraps his arms around me. I know I should kick him out, like I should've done every other night since we made this official, but I can never bring myself to do it. I like these stolen moments with him too much to give it up.

I roll over and kiss him, tangling my legs in his. "What'd you do today?"

"Played hockey."

"Really?" I ask surprised.

He nods. "Drove down to D.C. and hung out with the team there. I have a few friends there."

I rub the facial hair on his cheeks. "Do you think they might take you after your contract ends?"

He shrugs. "I talked to the coach some but I won't get my hopes up."

I frown. "I hate that you're not allowed to play with your team. I know you miss it."

He sighs. "I really fucking do, but I'm fighting an uphill battle with Matthews."

"Have you talked to that player? The one you saw him give steroids to?"

He shakes his head. "No."

"I think you should." I trace my fingers over his lip. "Look at the way Matthews is basically blackmailing you. You don't know what's really going on there. There might be more to the story than that guy being your coach's puppet."

He nods. "You might be right."

"We have a rink here in town—no fancy arena, that's for sure—but I want you to teach me how to skate."

His lips tip up. "Princess doesn't know how to ice skate?"

I shake my head. "I was more into dancing on dry land."

He chuckles and kisses the end of my nose. "Let's go tomorrow."

I nod and snuggle closer to him. "Just don't let me fall on my ass."

His chuckle rumbles against my ear. "No promises, sweetheart."

CHAPTER TWENTY-EIGHT

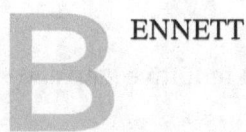ENNETT

G‍RACE FALLS ON HER ASS AFTER APPROXIMATELY five seconds on the ice. I bust out laughing instead of helping her up.

"You're such an asshole!" she curses me, trying to get up on her own, which results in her legs kicking wildly. Thankfully, we're the only ones on the ice. "Help me up, dickwad!"

I hold my hand out to her. "You're so nice to me."

"Yeah, well, you promised not to let me fall."

"Actually, sweetheart," I say sickeningly sweet, "I said *no* promises."

"Ugh, I hate you." She glares at me—and if looks could kill, I'd be dead. She holds onto my arm so tight that I'm afraid she's going to cut off the blood circulation.

"You know, for this to be classified as ice *skating,* we actually have to move."

"I'm not ready!" she cries, terrified I'm about to send her flying across the ice.

"Calm down, Princess. We'll take baby steps."

"Don't let me fall," she whimpers.

"Babe, you already did that, and chances are, you're going to do it again. It happens."

She gives me a mean look like she wishes a hole would open beneath me and eat me alive.

She takes a deep breath as we take a tentative step across the ice.

She lets out a small scream as we glide and tightens her hold on my arm.

"Grace, you're going to have to let go of me."

"No," she cries.

"Hold onto my hand," I plead. "I can't move when you're holding onto me like a goddamn spider monkey."

She slowly releases her vice-like grip on my arm and

entwines our fingers together. She shrieks as her legs wobble.

"I thought this would be easy," she mumbles.

I laugh. "Most people think that, but it takes some getting used to. You can do it."

"Not if I die first," she mutters, looking down at her feet.

"You're not going to die." I shake my head at her. I find her reaction amusing. She normally always has this take charge attitude like she can do anything. It's funny to see her losing her shit. "Come here, give me your other hand," I plead.

"You want me to swing around in front of you?" She gasps.

"Yes." I chuckle.

She whimpers, actually *whimpers*. I think it's cute but she'd be pissed if I said that.

She works herself up and pushes off with her feet to glide around in front of me, but of course, she fucking stumbles and starts to fall onto the ice again. I pull her up before she can fall and she smacks into my chest. I hold on tightly to her, balancing my weight so we don't fall.

"You're good at this," she gasps, and she actually sounds fucking surprised.

I laugh. "I *have* been doing this for years, sweetheart. Practically since I could walk. It's like a way of life in Boston. You learn to walk and then you learn to skate."

She shakes her head and holds onto my shoulders as I move us across the ice.

"Hey, this actually isn't so bad." She smiles up at me.

I laugh. "Well, it doesn't really count as *you* skating since *I'm* doing all the work."

She wrinkles her nose. "Thanks for bursting my bubble."

"Anytime." I kiss the end of her nose, and since I'm not paying any attention, we ram into the wall.

I lose my balance and fall to the ground with her on top of me.

Grace presses her lips together but can't contain her laughter. I laugh too and it feels so fucking good to be this carefree with someone. With Grace, I don't give a fuck about what I say or do, because I know she accepts me for *me* and vice versa. She's just so fucking perfect for me.

I tuck her hair behind her ear, my fingers lingering on her cheek. "I love you," I whisper.

I don't know why the fuck words leave my mouth, but I can't take it back, because it's true.

She makes the tiniest gasp and she looks at me with wonder and happiness and a million other things I can't even begin to understand.

The silence stretches between us and I worry that maybe I've scared her but then she smiles and kisses me. "I love you too," she murmurs between our pressed lips.

I and love and you have officially become my favorite words in the English language. I know that makes me sound like a lovesick sappy fool, but when you've never been in love and you *finally* find someone that makes you feel like a better version of yourself, the rest doesn't matter to you.

I take her face in my hands and kiss her deeply. My tongue slides into her mouth and she makes a soft sighing sound as her fingers tighten around my shirt. The ice is cold beneath me but I don't give a fuck. Nothing could make me move from this spot short of the zombie apocalypse, because zombies equal get the hell out of here.

Grace pulls back and looks down at me like she's truly seeing me for the first time. "I never thought things would end up like this," she admits, touching my cheek. "But I'm glad they did."

"Me too, sweetheart."

When I first asked Grace to be my fake girlfriend, that's all I wanted from her—to *use* her, and that fact makes me feel slightly sick, but I can't regret it, not when that led me to getting to know her and having her in my life.

We finally disentangle our bodies and I stand up, holding my hands out to her to help her up.

"I seriously didn't realize how much skill you have to possess to ice skate," she comments as we glide down the ice—well, I skate and she holds onto me.

I laugh. "And play a game on the ice," I remind her.

"Right," she groans. "Well, all I'm trying to say is you're pretty amazing."

"Aw," I laugh. "Was that a compliment?"

She glares at me. "You wish."

My laughter grows. "Really, because it sounded a whole lot like a compliment."

"I can't say anything nice to you, can I?" She sighs.

"Nope, sorry, sweetheart."

"Whoa," she cries when her feet skid a bit. "I think I've had enough of ice skating for the day."

I chuckle. "Are you sure?"

"Yes!" she screams when she starts to fall.

I hold her around the waist and skate over to the exit. I lift her onto the ground and then smack her ass. She stumbles onto the bench and turns to glare at me with fiery green eyes.

"Did you just *spank* me?" She looks shocked that I would do such a thing.

I grin and step off the ice. "I believe that's exactly what I did."

She shakes her head. "I want to say I can't believe you'd do that, but this *is* you we're talking about, so of course you would."

I hand her the skate guard for her blades and put mine on before taking off my skates. We walk back to return our skates and change into our regular shoes.

"Where do you want to go from here?" I ask her. "Back home?"

She shakes her head and bites her lip nervously, which tells me I'm more than likely not going to like what she has to say. "I was wondering if we could go by my dad's shop. I'd like you to see it."

I suppress my urge to groan. We've been staying with her parents for over a week, and even though things have moved past the awkward stage, they're still not great. I get along fine with her mom, but I still catch her dad giving me dirty looks. And I mean, I *get* it. What he knows of me isn't exactly the best. There are too many photos of me drinking and with various women. It doesn't take a rocket scientist to figure out what my lifestyle was, so I honestly can't blame him for being wary of me, but I also know I've been nothing but respectful of him while I've been here and kept my mouth shut in regard to the stupid stuff—usually perverted—that I usually say.

"Please?" Grace begs when I'm quiet for too long. "It's not that far from here."

What am I going to say? *No.* Not happening. It's not like I'm afraid of her dad, but I want him to like me.

"Sure." I nod, shoving my hand into the pocket of my pants to pull out my keys. "Just tell me how to get there."

GRACE GIVES ME DIRECTIONS TO HER DAD'S CAR shop and then sits on her phone. After a few minutes, she makes a choking sound.

My head whips in her direction and I nearly drive off the damn road. "What is it? What's wrong?"

"There's a picture of us online from the coffee shop," she says, her face going beet red.

"What's so bad about that?"

"*Bennett*," she says my name like I'm the stupidest fucking person she's ever encountered. "The. Coffee. Shop."

"Oh, fuck," I hiss between my teeth. "What does it say? It's not us in the bathroom, right?"

"No, of course not, it's just us sitting at the table laughing about something. Let me read the article. Give me a minute."

I clench my teeth and continue to drive, when what I really want to do is pull over and snatch the phone from her hand so I can read it myself. I'll be beyond pissed if somehow word got out about us having sex in the bathroom. I mean, I've done plenty of crazy shit before but I've never been concerned about it coming back on someone I care about—me, I can handle it, but Grace shouldn't have to.

After the longest minute of my life, she breathes out a sigh of relief. "The article is just talking about you coming home for the holidays and they speculate about when you're going to return to the team. It sounds like they think you and Coach Matthews have been planning some big return, like a publicity stunt or something."

I snort. "Yeah," I begin, "because everyone thinks he's a fucking god and not a complete dickwad."

Grace reaches over and rubs my arm, trying to offer me a small amount of comfort. I hate to tell her, but when it comes to Matthews *nothing* makes me feel better.

Grace puts her phone in her purse and says, "I'm just glad to know that no one knows about the bathroom."

"No one but us," I remind her with a wink.

She blushes and looks out the window. I love that a part of Grace is so shy, but she still has a wild side.

"Is this it?" I ask, pointing ahead of us.

"Yeah, that's the shop." She smiles.

As we draw closer, I can see *Wentworth Wheels* spelled out across the front.

"This is the shop," she says. "Dean lives in the apartment upstairs."

Dean doesn't say much to me. Whenever he's around, he looks at me with a shrewd eye like he's waiting for me to mess up. I guess I can't blame the guy. I mean, I'm protective of Sabrina, but it still sucks. Lincoln, on the other hand, has warmed to me. Even though he's younger than me, I like the kid. He's a good athlete and has a wicked sense of humor.

I park the car and follow Grace to the entrance.

"Dad's probably in his office," she says.

"Do you think we should've brought him lunch or something?" I ask.

Grace shakes her head. "Trust me, he's probably already eating."

There are several mechanics working beneath the hoods of various cars, and when they hear us they look up.

"Hey, Grace," one says with a lop-sided smile.

"Hey, Levi." She waves at him.

"Who's that?" I hiss. *I'm not jealous. Nope. I'm not.*

She laughs and swats my stomach. "Are you seriously jealous because I *waved* at a guy? Mr. Stick-My-Dick-In-Anything-That-Walks."

I snort. "Clever, and no, I'm not jealous." She eyes me. "Okay, maybe a little bit, but ... I'm new at this whole *love* thing. It's going to take me some time." I touch my fingers to her cheek.

I can tell my words please her, even though she tries to act like they don't. "Anyway," she says, stepping away from my touch, "that's Levi. He's the son of my mom and dad's best friends."

"Wait." I grin. "Your mom and dad got married and so did their best friends?"

She nods. "Yep. Luca and Avery. They don't really go together if you ask me—Luca doesn't say much and Avery is always talking. But hey." She shrugs in a whatcha-gonna-do way. "Dad's office is this way."

She leads me farther into the back of the shop and stops in front of a wooden door. She knocks two times and a gruff, "What?" greets us.

"It's me, Dad. I came to see you. *We* came to see you," she amends, looking up at me.

The door opens and her dad looks at her with a huge smile. "Well, isn't this a nice surprise. Come in." Then he looks at me and spits out, "Oh, and you."

I expect him to slam the door in my face but he surprisingly lets me in without a problem. The office is small and cluttered with papers, tools, and car parts. Her dad's arms are covered in tattoos and grease. The plaid shirt he wears hangs open over a t-shirt and he sits down in his office chair. I suppress a laugh when he picks up a cup full of fries and slathers them in ketchup. A burger also sits on the table. Grace was right, we didn't need to bring him something to eat.

"So what are y'all doing at the shop?" he asks, shoving some fries in his mouth.

"I wanted Bennett to see the shop." Grace shrugs and picks up a long, slender, metal tool and spins it between her fingers. "We just came from ice-skating."

Trace snorts and looks to me with a genuine smile. "I bet she fell on her butt as soon as she stepped on the ice."

"Dad," Grace whines.

"I'm right, aren't I?" Trace chortles.

"Yes." I chuckle. "But I picked her right up."

"Good man." He tips his head at me.

Even though the conversation is good, I don't even let myself think for a second that he might actually like me. I think he's just moving into the zone where he knows he has to tolerate me and it's better to be semi-pleasant. But I still wouldn't be surprised if he slammed the door behind me on the way out.

"Do you mind if I show Bennett around?" she asks.

"Not at all." He eats some more fries. "There's not much to see, though." He shrugs.

Grace laughs. "That's probably true. But this was practically my second home growing up so I wanted Bennett to see it."

Trace waves his fingers to the door. "Just say goodbye before you leave."

"Will do." She bends and kisses his cheek before grabbing my hand and pulling me out the door. I don't miss the flash of sadness in Trace's eyes when he sees my hand joined with Grace's. I'm sure it's hard seeing your kid growing up.

Grace leads me through the shop. It's a nice size, but not large, but I'm sure in a small town it's not necessary to have a big car shop. The tour consists of seeing the cars the guys are working on and tools, lots of tools.

At the end of her tour, Grace hops up on a work table. I place my hands on either side of her hips and lean in.

"What do you think?" she asks.

"I think it's pretty adorable how excited you get showing me pieces of your life."

She smiles and kisses me quickly, afraid someone's going to see us. "You know, I'm glad you came here with me." She wraps her arms around my neck.

I chuckle. "Me too, Princess."

At first, the thought of spending the holidays with Grace's family sounded like torture—I mean, we weren't even really dating at the time—but they're not so bad, and to have things work out with Grace the way they have … Well, that's pretty damn awesome.

I've never been one to believe in fate—in fact, I think it's pretty fucking stupid—but maybe everything really does happen for a reason.

"We better go," Grace says, pushing me away so she can climb off the table. "I promised my mom I'd go Christmas shopping with her."

I snort. "You mean you haven't done that already? I would've expected you to have your shopping done three months ago, Little Miss Perfect."

Grace sticks her tongue out at me. "I have a few more things I need to get, and knowing my mom, she needs to get everything. She's a notorious last-minute shopper. Thankfully, my dad is not when it comes to Christmas. He used to go all out when we were kids. He'd leave glitter on the floor and say that it was magic dust left behind by Santa." She smiles wistfully at the memories. "You can wait in the car. I'm going to say bye to my dad."

"Okay." I nod. "Where's Dean?" I ask, realizing we haven't seen him.

"Probably upstairs with Willow. They've been pretty much living together, so I'm *not* going up there to see them. I'm scared I'll walk in on something."

I laugh as she walks away. I know I shouldn't but I can't help but look at her ass as she leaves. It's small and firm and perfect like everything else about her.

When she disappears into the office, I finally tear my gaze away and go start the car.

Time seems to be passing at light speed. Before we know it, the holidays will be over and we'll be back at the school. I can't believe it's almost January and I'm still not back with my team. After we get back I'm going to have to make a trip to Boston and confront Matthews again. Demand my spot back on the team.

Yeah, that's exactly what I'm going to do. I'll soon be back on the ice in front of an arena full of people and all will be right in my world again.

CHAPTER TWENTY-NINE

Grace

"Is it really necessary to still make cookies?" Lincoln whines. "We know Santa's not real."

My dad swats him on the back of the head. "Of course it's necessary. It's Christmas Eve and it's Wentworth family tradition to make cookies."

Lincoln groans. "Heath is having a party," he refers to his best friend. "I wanted to go."

"You know we make cookies every year," my dad tells him, slipping on an apron. "So that's your problem to deal with, not mine." Linc mutters something under his breath and my dad narrows his eyes. "Don't push my buttons."

"Sorry." Lincoln picks up a spatula and looks at it like it's personally offended him.

My dad points at me. "You and Bennett are in charge of sugar cookies. Dean and Willow, you two will make peanut butter cookies. Lincoln, Mom, and I will make chocolate chip."

Lincoln whines, "Why do I have to work with you guys?"

"For starters, because you keep complaining. Secondly, because you're the youngest. Third, because there's no one else here to work with you so you're stuck with your lovely mom and dad."

Lincoln rests his arms on the island counter top. "Am I being punished for not having a girlfriend?"

"If you choose to look at it that way, then yes." My dad nods.

My mom stands off to the side, fighting laughter.

Bennett hisses under his breath to me, "Your dad takes his cookies very seriously, doesn't he?"

Before I can respond, my dad pivots around to face us. "I heard that, and yes, I do take my cookies very seriously. Cookies are important. Cookies are *happiness*."

Bennett presses his lips together, trying to contain his laughter. I can't blame him. When my dad goes on one of his tangents, it's pretty funny.

Dad claps his hands together. "Let's get to work."

The kitchen is large enough that each of our three groups has a separate work station. Mom, Dad, and Lincoln have the island, Dean and Willow have the area by the sink, and Bennett and I have the kitchen table.

"I hope you're good at making cookies," Bennett says, "because I haven't got a fucking clue what I'm doing." He looks around at the table. "Fuck, and there aren't even any directions."

I tap my head. "Right here, bud."

He makes a face. "Of course they are."

"Here," I begin, grabbing a glass bowl. "You cream together the butter and sugar and I'll handle the dry ingredients."

"How do I mix them?" he asks.

I give him an incredulous look. "With the beaters." I point. "It's already plugged in, all you have to do is turn it on, but *do not* put it on the high setting," I warn him.

"I think I can handle that."

"You better be able to," I mutter under my breath.

He chuckles and dumps the butter into the bowl and sugar. My dad and I had already gone around to each 'station' before we started and measured out the ingredients so there couldn't be any errors there.

I dump the dry ingredients in a bowl and stir them

together with a rubber spatula. I set it aside and grab Bennett's wrist.

"Careful," I warn. "You'll over mix it."

"Over mix it? Is that seriously a thing?"

I nod. "Yep. Now we add in the egg and vanilla." I do that since I'm terrified that it'll wind up with hunks of eggshell in the dough if he does it. "And then the dry ingredients." I stir those in with the rubber spatula.

When it's all mixed together, Bennett grins widely. "Hey, it looks like actual cookie dough."

I resist the temptation to roll my eyes. "Of course it does."

He shrugs sheepishly. "Sorry, I'm used to the stuff straight from the grocery store."

My dad hears this and gasps from across the room. "You've never made homemade cookies?" He sounds scandalized.

Bennett shrugs. "It was just easier for my mom, I guess."

My dad frowns at this but doesn't comment.

I bump Bennett's arm with mine. "It's time to start rolling out the dough to go in the oven. Like this." I grab a small amount and roll it into a ball between my hands before placing it on the waiting tray.

"Easy enough," he says, grabbing a gob of dough.

"Whoa." I grab his wrist to stop him. "You have way too much. You need like half that amount." I take some of the dough from him and make my own.

"I'm not very good at this," he says sheepishly.

I laugh and flick a piece of hair from my eyes that has fallen loose from my ponytail. "You'll get the hang of it."

He looks unsure, but by the time we've emptied the bowl of dough, he's making nicer looking cookies than I am. I set the tray on the island so my dad can put it in the oven. He always takes over for that part, saying there's some super-secret way to cook them so they stay gooey.

"All right, kids." My dad claps his hands together. "Go to bed so Santa can come."

"*Dad*," Lincoln groans. "We know Santa isn't real."

My dad narrows his eyes on Lincoln. "Of course he's real."

Even though all of us are old enough to not believe in Santa, my dad has never, not once, broken character when it comes to believing in him. In fact, we still get presents from 'Santa'. It's silly, but it makes my dad happy so who am I to ruin his fun? Plus, more presents, so yay me.

Bennett and I wash our hands before heading upstairs. I can still hear Lincoln groaning in his room. Even though I'm only in my first year of college, those years of teenage angst seem so long ago.

No one is in the hall so I pull Bennett into my room and close the door behind us.

I wrap my arms around his neck and he picks me up, my legs automatically winding around his waist.

He grins cockily. "Am I about to get my Christmas present?"

I kiss him teasingly and pull back all too soon. "No, I'm going to get mine."

His smile widens. "I like the sound of that even better."

These moments with Bennett are few and far between while we're here. We've only had sex the two times and the bathroom was hardly sufficient, not getting to feel him skin to skin. I feel ready to burst with the need to be with him.

"We have to be quiet," I warn him.

He chuckles and crosses my room to lay me flat on my bed, caging me in with his arms. "Of course," he murmurs, his eyes flashing with desire. The fact that *I* create that look in his eyes makes my body ache with yearning. I need to touch him. To feel him. To love him.

He kisses my neck, his lips warm and smooth. I rock against him, all too eager to get to the good part, but he grabs my hips to still me. I whimper and he chuckles.

"Patience," he murmurs. "Good things come to those who wait." He nips my chin and then moves to my lips, kissing me deeply and so passionately that for a moment I can't even feel the bed beneath me, it's like I'm floating on a cloud.

I want to beg, but I keep my mouth shut because I know Bennett would only find it amusing and it wouldn't work in my favor. Instead, I murmur, "I love you." Neither of us have said it since that day at the rink. I've wanted to, but when it's something so new to you there's a part of you that's still scared of the other person denying it.

Bennett makes a sound in his throat that echoes his

approval and then he braces his body weight on his arms above me and gazes down at me in a way that can only be described as worshipful. "I love you too. More than you know—more than I ever thought I was capable of."

I close my eyes as his fingers skim under my shirt and over my stomach. Being quiet will be hard, but I *need* this. I lift my arms so he can pull my shirt off and he rises up, gazing at me in my simple jog bra and pajama bottoms. It is arguably the most unsexy outfit ever, but he looks at me like I'm lying below him in the finest lingerie.

When he continues to stare, I whisper, "You next," and push at his chest.

He smiles crookedly and reaches for the hem of his long-sleeve t-shirt and pulls it off. He holds it against his chest, hiding his body from me so that he can drive me nuts a few seconds longer. I rip the shirt from his hands and toss it over my head. Where it lands, I don't know or care. I place my hands on his chest, palms flat, and move them over the smooth expanse of muscle. His skin is warm beneath my hands and I smile at the freckles dotting his shoulders. He breathes out slowly and I know he's holding back, giving me this moment. It's all too hard to get caught up in the frenzy of desire and rush things—like I wanted to do—but slow ... slow is better. Taking your time gives you a chance to appreciate the other person in a way you normally can't.

He takes my hands in his then and holds them above my head. I squeak in surprise at the sudden movement and he silences me with his lips. His hips rock against mine, and it's impossible to miss the hard press of his erection.

I hold onto his sides, wrapping my legs around him, and kiss him back. I kiss him with everything I have in me. Each and every press of our lips conveying the love we feel—the love that is still so new and scary.

His hand finds my right breast, and he rubs his finger over the fabric covering my nipple. I want to take off the bra, so I can feel the heat of his hand against my skin, but I remind myself *slow*.

He moves and grabs me by the waist, turning me and placing my head on the pillow. His body covers mine once more and I feel like I'm shrouded in the warmest blanket.

He skims his hands down the sides of my body and I shiver from the sensation of his light touch.

"You like that?" He grins, his hazel eyes darker than normal, closer to brown.

I nod as he brings his hands back up and I shiver again. He chuckles and drags his hands down, this time grabbing the tops of my pajama bottoms and slowly pulling them down my hips and legs. He drops them on the floor and covers my body with his. He kisses my mouth, my neck, over the small swell of my breasts straining against the bra, down my stomach and lower. He loops his fingers into the sides of my underwear and brings them down, letting them fall off my feet. I feel ready to burst as he stares at me and I'm scared I'll go off the moment he touches me.

Faster than I expect, he bends and pulls me forward

lifting my bottom off the bed and positioning my legs over his strong shoulders.

He gives me a wicked grin before his lips touch my pussy. It's even better than the first time since I know what to expect.

He moves his tongue in a circle around my clit and I claw at the sheets.

He pulls away and says, "If you're not quiet I'll have to stop."

I press a fist to my mouth in answer and he chuckles. His laughter rumbles against my thigh and then he licks me again.

I want to cry out, but I don't.

Quiet.

Quiet.

Quiet.

I chant in my head over and over again. The last thing I need is one of my parents—or brothers—coming to investigate the strange noises coming from my room.

I'm suddenly thankful that our house is fairly large and the rooms are spaced out with thick walls.

I bite my fist when I come, holding back my cry of pleasure, and for some reason, being forced to be silent makes me orgasm a thousand times stronger.

Bennett lets my legs fall gently to the bed and stands so he can get rid of his jeans. I sit up and tug off my bra, dropping it onto the bed beside me.

Bennett grabs a condom from his sweatpants and puts it on.

I raise a brow. "Did you know this was going to happen?" I whisper as he climbs back on the bed.

He chuckles. "Nah, I don't see the future, Princess, but I did hope."

"Missed me, huh?" I ask, taking his face between my hands. The stubble on his cheeks scratches the palms of my hands but I don't mind.

He grins and grabs my thighs, opening my legs and settling in-between them. "You have no fucking idea." He pushes into me, and in anticipation of my cry, he kisses me. His tongue flicks against mine and my fingers tangle into his hair. He rocks against me and my hips lift to meet his. We fall into a rhythm that our bodies seem to instinctively know.

He rubs my breast with his left hand and my body arches up to meet his palm. His lips move to my neck and he presses a soft bite to the area where my neck meets my shoulder.

"I'm scared I'll ruin this," he whispers into my skin.

I tug on his hair, forcing him to look at me. "You won't," I pant, my body straining.

He looks ... scared. "I really fucking hope not."

His lips crash to mine and he rolls so I'm on top. I roll my hips against his and close my eyes, forgetting his words, and getting lost in the moment.

CHAPTER THIRTY

BENNETT

I blink awake and Grace's darkened bedroom forms around me. I yawn and sit up, looking at the clock on her nightstand. It's early, a little after six in the morning. She rolls toward my body and reaches with her arms for me, making the cutest fucking sound when she finds my arm. I lie back down and she scoots even closer, looping her leg over mine. She burrows her head against my chest and I rest my chin on top.

"Merry Christmas, Grace," I murmur.

She stirs and lifts her head, blinking sleepy eyes at me. "Why are you up?" She asks, rubbing her hand over my chest.

I smile crookedly. "It's Christmas, sweetheart."

"Mmm," she hums. "Right. Merry Christmas."

She lays her head back down and promptly falls back asleep. I run my fingers through her hair, rubbing her scalp, and chuckle when she purrs in her sleep. I need to slip out from under her, go back to my room, but I don't want to. I want to take in every single second I have with her.

I give myself another ten minutes before I slip out of bed and her room. Thankfully, no one is in the hall, but I can hear someone in the kitchen. I walk quietly down the hall to the bathroom across from the guestroom I'm using. I shower and change into a different pair of sweatpants and a t-shirt. Grace said her dad insists on them staying in their pajamas until at least noon—not unlike my own family.

I grab my phone from my room and head downstairs, quietly so that I don't wake everyone up.

I find Trace in the kitchen and he pours a cup of coffee. "A package must've arrived yesterday for you." He nods at a small cardboard box sitting on the island. "I didn't see it until last night."

"Thanks." I look at the address on the box and smile.

"It's from my mom." I pick up the knife Trace already had sitting on the counter and use it to cut into the box. A card sits on top and I set it aside to see what sits inside. I move aside the tissue paper and then proceed to laugh my ass off. I reach in and pull out the pajamas. They're footy pajamas with that damn creepy Elf on the Shelf dude on them.

"That's horrifying," Trace comments.

"You're telling me." I chuckle and stuff the pajamas back in the box.

I pick up the card and open the envelope. My mom's slanted cursive greets my eyes.

Sabrina said you were worried about missing out on your pajamas. We could never forget you Bennett! We wish you were here! Don't forget to call.

—Mom

I smile and put the card away. Trace stands across from me, slowly lifting his coffee mug to his lips.

"Do you make it a habit of sleeping in my daughter's bed?"

I choke on my own saliva. "Um ..."

His shrewd eyes narrow. "Don't even think about lying to me."

"How'd you know?" I ask.

He shrugs innocently. "I looked in your room and you weren't there and the bathroom door was open. It was pretty obvious where you were." He lifts one brow. "Don't worry, I didn't open *that* door."

"I'm sorry," I say, because I don't know what else to tell him.

He sets his mug down and it clanks against the stone top. He crosses his arms over his chest and clears his throat. "I'm going to let you in on a little secret."

"What?" I ask, when it becomes obvious he's waiting for me to speak.

"I've been like you. Maybe not quite as bad, but I've been there. The meaningless sex and living the 'good life.'" He says *good life* with very obvious air quotes. "But let me tell you something, it's not that good, and when you find someone who changes everything—shakes the very foundation that you've built everything you believe on, then you hold onto them and never let go."

"Did Grace's mom do that for you?" I ask. "Shake your foundation?"

"She demolished it," he says stone-faced. He lowers his arms and places his hands flat on the counter, leaning toward me. "Grace is a good, sweet girl, and I'm not going to warn you away from her, I'm realizing there's no point, but what I can say is if you hurt her I'll make your life a living hell. I mean that whole-heartedly." He clenches his jaw. "One day, when you have a daughter, it'll change your foundation again and you'll understand where I'm coming from."

"I won't hurt her," I promise.

Grace means more to me than I ever thought possible

and the thought of anything hurting her, especially me, kills me.

Trace grows solemn. "I'm sure you mean that, but you will."

I physically rear back at his words. "Excuse me?"

He shrugs and picks up his coffee mug once more. "It's inevitable."

He stalks from the room, leaving me with those two words; words that bounce back and forth in my brain before settling my gut.

EVERYONE'S AWAKE BY EIGHT AND GATHERED around the large tree in the family room. Trace's mom joins us, as does Olivia's mom and step-dad—who's a hell of a lot younger than her mom, and looks hardly older than Olivia—and Olivia's little sister, Abby, who isn't much older than Dean.

Presents are passed around and laughter is had. It's nice, pleasant even, but I can't shake my conversation with Trace this morning.

Is it inevitable that I hurt Grace?

My gaze falls to her face. She's not wearing any makeup and her hair is pulled away from her face in a sloppy bun and she's wearing the same pajamas from last night. The ones I ever-so-carefully removed from her body. She smiles and shakes the present she holds. She's so happy, and it kills me to think of that smile disappearing because of me.

She tears off the wrapping paper and reveals a brand new, shiny gold watch. "Thanks Mom and Dad." She smiles at each of them and admires the gold band. She sets it aside and reaches for another present. I expect her to open it, but instead, she hands it to me.

"For me?" I ask.

She laughs. "Of course, silly. Did you think I would forget you?"

I grin. "Of course not. I'm unforgettable." I shove my hand into my pocket and hand her the small Tiffany blue box. She gasps and I can't stop my grin. That was the reaction I was hoping for.

"Bennett," she breathes my name and takes the box from my hand. She undoes the ribbon and it falls into her lap. Taking her time, she lifts the lid of the box off and reveals the necklace inside. "Bennett," she says again. She bites her lip and it looks like she's holding back tears. "It's beautiful," she finally whispers. She lifts the dainty rose-gold—that's what the salesperson called it, anyway—necklace out of the box and runs her finger over the small heart charm.

"I know it's pretty simple, but it reminded me of you, and I thought it would match that one watch you wear all the time."

She laughs and—yep those are definitely tears in her eyes—says, "You noticed my watch?"

I grab a stray piece of hair that's fallen loose from her

bun and rub it between my fingers before tucking it behind her ear. "Of course. I notice everything about you."

"It's funny you should say that." She nods at the box in my lap. I'd forgotten it was even there. "Here, help me put this on first." She hands me the necklace and turns with her back to me so I can slip it around her neck.

I fumble a few times before I can finally get the tiny clasp to attach. When I do, she grabs the necklace between her fingers and holds onto it.

"I love this, seriously." She smiles at me and leans over to kiss me.

I smile against her lips and murmur softly, "I love you."

She beams at my words and I hope, I really fucking hope that I continue to make her look that way.

She claps her hands together and says, "You next."

I rip into the paper and it reveals a plain white box in my hands. I take off the top of the box and I'm greeted by an explosion of green and red tissue paper. I move it out of my way and begin to reveal the items inside. A pack of Sour Patch Kids, a notepad—like the ones I piled in the cart that day in Target—and other little mementos from our time together. Each and every item brings forth a memory and the time and energy she put into thinking of each thing is what means the most.

"Creative," I tell her with a grin. "You did good."

This time, I'm the one leaning over to kiss her.

The rest of the presents are opened and then Olivia

dismisses us all to shower and change before we have a late lunch.

The day passes quickly, and I'm surprised by how much fun I have. I wasn't expecting today to actually be enjoyable—I know that's not very nice of me, but after how things have been with Trace, it was a legitimate assumption.

I can't help but think that I might actually miss these people. I'm sure I'll see them again, though, because despite what Trace said, I won't ruin this with Grace.

I won't.

I swear it.

CHAPTER THIRTY-ONE

GRACE

Break is going to be over before I know it. It's already New Year's Eve—the day of our annual party—and I only have a week of freedom left after that.

Bennett and I drove over to the Wentworth Mansion earlier in the afternoon so I could start getting ready and he was blown away by it. I'm used to it, so I forget how big it actually is. Bennett couldn't believe my dad and his brother grew up in the mansion. Sometimes, I can't believe it, either, for the fact that they're both so normal.

I have a room in the mansion—all of us kids do, and there are plenty more to spare—and that's where I've been since I arrived while a team of hair and makeup artists tends to me. I guess to some people that would be weird, but it's something we've always done for this night. It's the one night out of the whole year where I don't feel normal and I instead feel like royalty. I'm sure the parties were even more glamorous when my grandma had more control over it. My dad and uncle have definitely toned down the event some—but not much. It's still black tie: women wear ball gowns and men wear tuxes, but instead of the classical band my grandma prefers, there's always a more current band that you hear their music on the radio, and the food is more normal instead of fancy French dishes or something like that.

The hair stylist curls and twists my hair around. She pokes bobby pins into it and uses enough hair spray to kill the ozone layer above my head.

I asked the makeup artist for a soft pink and gold look to match my dress and hopefully she knows how to do *soft*. I'm going to be pissed if I come out looking like a clown. Now that I know what I'm doing, having someone else do my makeup is akin to torture.

"What time is it?" I ask and wait for one of them to reply.

The makeup artist looks at the clock on the TV. "After seven."

The party's already begun, so hopefully I'll be fashionably late and not obnoxiously late.

They finish and the hair stylist hands me a mirror. My eyes sparkle with a shimmery golden color and the winged eyeliner makes it pop even more. My lips shine with a shimmery pink gloss and my face glows. I turn my head, admiring my hair. She's curled it and pinned it all on one side so it cascades down my shoulder. Shorter pieces in the front are pinned back, making my hair look thicker than it is. It's an elegant look and I know it'll compliment my dress.

"Thank you, ladies," I say and stand. My dress is hanging in the bathroom.

They nod and begin to pack up their things.

I shut myself in the bathroom and remove my robe. I lift the dress off the hanger and slip into it, wiggling it up my hips. It's a fairly simple dress, compared to what I've worn in previous years, but I feel like it suits the woman I've become.

I slip my arms through the top of the dress just as there's a knock on the door.

"Grace, are you ready?"

My heart accelerates at the sound of Bennett's voice. As stupid as it sounds, I've missed him, and it's only been a few hours since I last saw him.

"Hang on," I say and flick the button on the door to unlock it. "You can come in."

He eases the door open and hisses between his teeth. "Damn, Grace, you look ... you look ... Fuck."

"I look fuck?" I suppress a laugh and turn around with my back to him. "Zip me up, please?"

He chuckles. "You definitely look fuck*able,* but that wasn't what I was trying to say."

"It wasn't? Should I be hurt?" I smile at him over my shoulder.

He steps forward and grazes his fingers along my bare back. I shiver and my body tightens all over. I want to grab him by the collar of his shirt and kiss him and then maybe fuck him right here in this bathroom, but I have to be good tonight. At least, until I'm seen at the party.

He sees the look in my eyes and his own grow a stormy brown color speckled with green and gold. "You're treading in dangerous waters looking at me like that," he warns, zipping up my dress.

"Maybe I want a little danger tonight," I say breathlessly.

I squeak in surprise as he grabs me by the waist and twists me around, shoving my back into the wall and caging me in with his body. I struggle to get enough air and my breasts brush his chest with each shaky inhale.

He ducks his head into the crook of my neck and bites the skin there. My eyes flutter close and my heart beats rapidly. God, I want him. The affect he has on me is unreal.

He pulls away and smiles at me cockily. "We have to go,

Princess. Thanks for actually wearing your ball gown this time." He winks.

I still struggle to get enough air, but I manage to hiss, "You're such an asshole."

"So you like to tell me. But we can't get carried away when I have a present waiting for you in your room."

"A present?" I raise a brow.

He stands to the side and raises his arm to sweep toward the open door.

"Go see for yourself."

I want to, only I can't move. I've only just realized that Bennett is wearing a tux and holy hell the tux is tailor-made for his body. It's cut to perfectly fit his muscular body and his blondish-red hair is slicked back and brushed to the side. He looks ... sophisticated, like some Duke from a foreign land.

Annnnd I'm turned on again. *Great*.

"Your present?" He raises a brow and chuckles.

"Oh, right." I shake my head and step out of the bathroom.

"Took you long enough. I was afraid you guys were doing the nasty and the thought alone made me want to throw up in my mouth."

I stop in my tracks and my jaw drops. "*Elle?* What are you doing here?" I shriek in excitement and run toward her, throwing my arms around her shoulders. I step back and appraise her dress. "Damn, you look good, girl," I compliment.

She's dressed in a floor-length black-sequined dress that flares out at the bottom on a mermaid cut with black tulle. Her dark hair is straightened and hangs in long thin sheets and her makeup is done in dramatic dark colors with a smoky eye and a purple-red lip color. She looks like a sexy vampire and the style suits her well.

"I can't believe you're here!" I exclaim and hug her again. "How did you do this?" I look to Bennett.

He shrugs. "Paid for a plane ticket." *Obviously,* he leaves unsaid.

"I know that." I laugh. "But I guess I should've asked *why?*" I turn to Elle. "Not that I'm not happy you're here, of course."

"Ryland is here too." She smiles at this and gets a wistful look in her eyes.

"Is this the part where you finally admit you're dating the guy?"

She shrugs and mumbles, "We're dating."

I grin triumphantly. "I knew it.

"Yeah, yeah." She waves a hand dismissively as Bennett steps up behind me and wraps his hands around my waist.

He rests his chin on my shoulder and says, "To answer your *why* question, it was because I felt like it. I know tonight is a big deal in your family, and I thought it would be cool for Elle and Ryland to come."

I tilt my head to the side and kiss the side of his cheek. "You're too sweet."

Elle gags. "You two are gross."

"Oh, stop it," I scold her with a smile. "You're just as bad with Ryland and that was *before* you admitted you were together."

Bennett chuckles and his laughter rumbles against my body. "Ladies, I think it's time for us to join the party."

Elle runs her fingers through her hair. "Will there be paparazzi here?"

I snort. "No, but there will probably be a photographer from our local newspaper."

Elle frowns. "I was hoping for paparazzi."

"Keep dreaming," I tell her.

I slip out of Bennett's hold and pad across the room to the dresser. I put on my earrings and other jewelry before slipping my feet into my heels.

"Ready," I chime.

Bennett crooks his elbow and extends it toward me like some dashing prince.

The three of us leave my room behind and head down the main grand staircase. As every pair of eyes in the foyer flicks up to us; I truly feel like a princess. Bennett smiles down at me and my heart does a happy dance behind my rib cage.

Ryland meets us in the foyer and he crooks his elbow, miming Bennett, and Elle takes it.

"The ballroom is that way." I point.

Elle squeals and smiles up at Ryland. "There's a *ballroom*."

"I heard, babe." He smiles broadly at her and kisses her.

I hear her mumble something about messing up her lipstick but as we venture closer to the ballroom it grows harder to hear each other so I can't be exactly sure what she said.

The ballroom is packed with people. Even though it's nearly the same crowd every year, I don't know most of them. I've always stuck close to the group I grew up with. I spot Willow and Dean sitting at one of the large round tables and make a beeline for them. Bennett calls after Elle and Ryland to follow us.

Willow wears a beautiful, blue, floor-length dress that has intricate lace detailing and her blonde hair is worn down and wavy, with extensions for added length. Seeing Willow all dolled up is a nice change. Her normal style is about as casual as it comes.

"Hey, Willow, Dean." I greet them each with a hug and take a seat. Bennett pulls out the chair beside me and Elle and Ryland take two other empty seats. "This is Elle, my roommate, and her boyfriend, Ryland. Elle and Ryland, this is my brother, Dean, and his girlfriend, Willow."

With introductions made I let them get to know each other and turn to Bennett.

"Thank you for flying them out here. It means a lot." I grab his hand beneath the table.

He leans over and brushes his lips over my cheek in a feather light caress. "Anything to make you happy."

Elle gags from across the table. "Sick. You guys make me *sick*."

Bennett chuckles and flashes her the finger before his hand vanishes under the table.

Ryland looks around, taking in the shiny marble floors, and crystal chandelier. "This place is … insane." He shakes his head like he can't quite believe it.

"It's grand." I shrug. "I guess my great-great-great … Well, however many great-grandpas it went back, really wanted to make a statement."

"Well, he definitely did." Ryland nods and tugs on the collar of his tux.

"So, what is there to do here at this party?" Elle asks, picking up a sparkling silver fork and looking it over before setting it back on the table.

"Dance," I say.

"Eat," Dean adds.

"Eat," Willow echoes.

"There will be a live band," I say and turn to Willow. "Is your dad's band playing this year?"

Willow shrugs. "Don't think so."

"Wait …" Elle looks at Willow with wide eyes. "Are you Maddox Wade's daughter?"

Willow nods with a sheepish smile. She might've grown up in the limelight but the girl hates the attention. "Yeah, that's me."

"Oh, my God," Elle breathes. "I can't believe you're Willow Wade." She shakes her head back and forth. "That is so cool. You must've seen some pretty amazing places growing up with all the traveling you guys did."

Willow shrugs. "It wasn't as exciting as you'd think. We stayed in hotels or on the tour bus most of the time."

"Oh," Elle says. "I guess that makes sense."

My mom comes breezing over, looking killer in her dress, and I introduce her to Elle and Ryland. I've talked to her about both of them, so she's thrilled to finally meet them.

"I just wanted to let you guys know the food will be here soon."

And then she's off again.

Mascen and Lylah—Willow's brother and sister—join us at our table, and Everett, Everly, Noah, Adalyn, and Mia take seats at the table next to us—they're children of two of the other members of Willow Creek.

It's nice seeing everyone since I haven't seen most of them since summer. I know I'm lucky to have grown up around so many other kids my age. We all formed a special, unbreakable, bond.

A commotion near the ballroom's entrance sends us all turning in that direction.

"Liam!" Willow cries and then she's up, dashing out of her chair. She throws herself into Liam's arms and he hugs her tightly.

Dean groans and moves his chair back to stand. "I better say hi."

I laugh. "You still don't like him?"

He shrugs and glances to where Willow stands with her

cousin and his girlfriend. "We patched things up, but ..." He trails off and shrugs like that's answer enough.

I watch him greet Liam with an outstretched hand and then Liam smiles and pulls him into a hug. Maybe things aren't as bad as Dean thinks they are.

Bennett whistles. "Fuck, you know too many people for me to keep up with all of them."

I laugh. "And you haven't even met my aunt and uncle and their kids."

"I'm going to need a drink." Bennett chuckles.

I pat his knee. "That can be arranged."

Willow and Dean return to our table and Liam pulls over two chairs for him and his girlfriend to join us. We scoot around and make room for them. It's cramped but it works.

"Hey, Liam," I greet. I last saw Liam in Hawaii over the summer when I tagged along with Dean and Willow to see him at his surfing competition. "Hello, Ari." I lean over to wave at his girlfriend.

I didn't get to know her very well while we were in Hawaii and I don't think they were dating then anyway. Who knows? Liam's always been really secretive so they could've been together and not telling anyone. She seemed nice enough, if a little wary. That wariness is even more prevalent in her vivid blue eyes now.

"Hi," she mumbles, but it's like she doesn't even notice me as her eyes flit around the large room. She looks scared, like she expects someone to jump out from behind one of the large columns that line the room and get her. Liam whispers something in her ear and she seems to relax, but only slightly.

The food is served then and we all fall into easy conversation as we eat.

When the food is gone and the plates are cleared off the table, the band finally takes the stage.

Bennett stands and offers me his hand. "May I have this dance, milady."

I laugh. "Only if you promise not to be cheesy the whole time."

"I'll do my best." He grins as I place my hand in his. He closes his over mine and my hand nearly disappears in his large grasp.

He leads me out onto the ballroom floor and we begin to dance—and not like club-grinding kind of dancing. No this is *real*, like a waltz.

"Where did you learn to dance like this?" I ask him. I can't keep the awe off my face which amuses him.

"Dance helps with skating so I took dance classes when I was younger." I snort at the visual. "What? You don't believe me?"

I shake my head. "No, I'm just trying to picture you in a leotard."

He pinches my side. "I didn't wear a leotard."

"Bummer." I laugh and he spins me around.

I hold onto his shoulders as my giggles fill the air. A few

older people give us dirty looks but I can't bring myself to care.

I hear a camera click and I look over to see the guy from our local paper photographing us. He takes a few more photos before moving on to take photos of other people.

Bennett's hand settles on my waist and I look up at him. He wears the biggest smile and my heart soars. I think it's safe to say that I've never been happier than I am in this moment.

He ducks his head and presses his lips to mine. My heels put me closer to his height and I grasp the back of his neck, holding him to me when he might otherwise break the kiss. I don't care who sees—let them all see and know that I love him and I've chosen him. We might've had the most unconventional start ever but our love is real and nothing can change that.

Nothing.

CHAPTER THIRTY-TWO

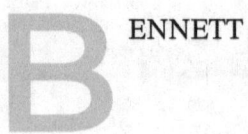ENNETT

GRACE AND I SNEAK AWAY FROM THE BALLROOM AND find a closet to fool around in. Now I really know she loves the thrill of possibly being caught. Even though there's a part of her that doesn't want to admit it, she was bad before I met her, she'd just never explored that part of herself.

It's nearly midnight and she tugs on my hand. "We need to go outside."

"Outside?" I raise a brow. "But it's freezing."

"Don't worry, they'll have heaters so we won't be cold." She pulls me toward a large set of double doors. "The fireworks go off at midnight, and I don't want to miss them."

We shove our way through the growing crowd. My wide shoulders help us move through faster, but I think Grace would be fine all on her own. The girl is a bulldozer.

We lose Elle and Ryland, as well as her brother and his girlfriend, in the crowd but Grace doesn't seem to care. She's like an eager little kid at the thought of fireworks and I'd be lying if I said I didn't like her being this happy.

We step outside into the frigid December air and onto a large ... I don't know what the fuck you'd call this. I guess it's a deck, but fuck, it's so large that *deck* hardly seems like an adequate enough description.

Grace keeps tugging on my hand until we reach the railing.

"Just wait," she breathes and her breath fogs the air. "It's amazing." She looks up at the pitch-black night sky, waiting for the show to start.

I know I should look to the sky too, but I only have eyes for her. I find myself taking a mental picture of the look on her face—the one of pure happiness and awe—so I can remember it forever. There are some moments in life that should never be forgotten; this is one of them.

The fireworks explode in the sky and still, I only look

at her. Her lips part and she gasps a soft, "Ooh," as the sparks fall through the air and disappear. Another one shrieks through the air and explodes, bathing her face in halos of red and silver. She shivers and I don't know if it's because she's so moved by the experience or because she's cold. I shrug out of my tux jacket anyway and drape it over her shoulders. She gives me a grateful smile and loops her arms into the large sleeves. She looks even smaller than normal in the jacket and I feel a tug in my gut—one saying I would do anything and everything for this girl.

She gazes up at me and a tiny smile dances across her lips. "Happy New Year, Bennett," she murmurs.

"Happy New Year, Grace."

I kiss her and hope to whatever God is out there that this year will be as fucking amazing as the last two weeks.

WHEN THINGS ARE TOO GOOD TO BE TRUE, IT'S usually because they are, and eventually the other shoe has to drop.

I sleep with my body curled around Grace's in the mansion—it was late and none of us wanted to go home—when the doors to the room come slamming open.

Both Grace and I sit up, fumbling for the covers, which is stupid since we're both clothed.

"I warned you!" Trace bellows, storming over to the bed.

I'm too stunned to move and he yanks me from the bed onto the floor.

Grace screams from somewhere in the room and I want to tell her it's all right but Trace's fist slams into my face and I taste blood in my mouth.

"Get the fuck out of my house," he yells, pointing a shaking finger at me. "And don't ever, *ever* talk to my daughter ever again."

"What the fuck is going on?" I wipe blood from my lip. "I didn't do anything."

"Don't lie." Trace's face twists with anger. "You know exactly what you did."

"I really fucking don't." I roll to my side to stand up and Trace backs a step away, his hands fisting at his sides like he's trying to hold himself back from hitting me again.

"Imagine my surprise when I wake up this morning and find *your* face on the news."

"For what?" I ask incredulously. "I didn't fucking do *anything*." My eyes dart to Olivia where she holds onto Grace. Olivia looks ... sad ... weary. Fuck, something bad is happening and I don't know what the hell it is. "Whatever it is, it has to be a lie. My coach is out to get me, he—"

"I'm sure he is out to get you," Trace spits, getting right up in my face. "I would be too if you'd raped my sixteen-year-old daughter."

Grace gasps from the other side of the room and cries out.

"He's a fucking liar," I hiss between my teeth.

I'm going to kill him. I'm really and truly going to kill my coach. All I want is to get my hands around his neck and choke him until the light disappears from his eyes.

First he took hockey away from me, the only true love I thought I had, and now that I've found Grace—the *real* meaning of love, someone that understands me and I see myself having a future with—he's going to take that away from me too.

He's fucking up my life and I won't stand for it. I'm done.

I forget about Trace and stride across the room to Grace. Olivia tightens her hold on her daughter and glares at me. "Stay away," she says coldly. "Don't you think you've done enough?"

I won't be defeated that easily, though. "Grace, baby, please talk to me. You *know* me. You know I wouldn't do that. He's lied about everything else, you know he's lying about this too. Please, baby, *please*," I beg. I've never fucking begged in my life but I *love* this girl and I need her to believe me. I would never do something like this. I've never even *met* his daughter. Okay, maybe once in a brief passing, but she never hangs around the players. She lives with her mom in another state since her parents got divorced.

Fuck, I can't believe the asshole would drag his own daughter into his beef with me.

"Grace, please, talk to me. I didn't do this. I love you."

She turns from her mother's arm, her face streaked with tears, "Just leave, Bennett. *Please*," her voice cracks.

I would have rather she yelled at me than to speak so calmly.

Anger I can handle. This resigned Grace, I can't.

"Sweetheart." I reach for her hand and she fucking *flinches*.

"Go." She flicks her head toward the door of her room.

My shoulders sag and I exhale a heavy breath—all the fight leaving me.

I don't know what to do or say, because the truth …

The truth is never enough.

CHAPTER THIRTY-THREE

GRACE

I'VE BEEN BACK ON CAMPUS FOR *TWO* WEEKS AND people still stare and whisper as I pass. Everyone's talking about the scandal with Bennett and his coach's underage daughter. I don't want to believe it's real, but the evidence seems to be irrefutable. They even arrested Bennett—seeing that image on my computer sent me into hysterics and I couldn't go to classes for a whole day—but he got out on bail a short time later.

My parents are urging me to transfer to a school back home, but I know the scandal will only follow me there. People aren't even that interested in *me* they just want to hear what I know—which is nothing.

I feel so lost and I hate that. I always thought I was strong enough to stand on my own, that I didn't need a man, and I don't, but I *want* Bennett. He made me a better person but apparently *he's* not a good person. I mean, I knew that he'd had a shady past and slept with a lot of women, but his coach's underage daughter? I *never* would've thought he'd stoop that low. I guess it goes to show you that you never really know someone.

I adjust my backpack straps and walk as fast as I can across campus without slipping on some ice.

"Excuse me? Grace?"

I ignore the voice. Lots of people call my name, hoping I'll stop and divulge some secret about Bennett.

"Grace? Hey?" A hand latches onto my arm and I'm forced to stop.

"You're awfully pushy, aren't you?" I sneer at the strawberry blond in front of me.

She wrinkles her nose and her freckles dance across it. "I'm Bennett's sister. I wanted to talk to you."

Bennett's sister?

My eyes widen in surprise. "Oh."

"Is there somewhere we could talk more privately?" She swirls her finger through the air, and sure enough there are several students, and even a professor, loitering as they try to eavesdrop on our conversation.

"Uh … there's a coffee shop around the corner."

She shakes her head. "Not private enough."

"My dorm?" I suggest half-heartedly.

She brightens at this. "Perfect."

I'm not too thrilled about this, but I lead her in the direction of my dorm.

"How did you find me?"

She shrugs. "I'm a journalist. It's what I do."

"Find people?"

She laughs. "Yes, it's part of the job. I knew if I waited around campus long enough I'd eventually spot you."

"So …" I pause. "Bennett didn't put you up to this?"

She shakes her head adamantly. "God no. He'd kill me if he knew I was here."

"Why *are* you here?"

"We'll discuss inside," she says as we start up the stairs to the building.

My heart races as I wonder what she has to say. I want to forgive Bennett so bad, to believe this isn't real, but the proof … I can't deny that, and I can't be with someone that would do something like that.

I feel like it takes forever to finally reach my room and when we do, she promptly closes the door behind us.

"First, I feel like I should introduce myself. I'm Sabrina." She holds out her hand for me to shake.

"It's nice to meet you," I tell her, "but horrible circumstances."

She winces. "Yes, horrible." She pulls out my desk chair and takes a seat without my offering. I end up sitting on the end of my bed, facing her.

"You said you're a journalist. You're not here for an interview, are you?" I ask hesitantly.

Her eyes—the same unique hazel color as Bennett's—widen in surprise. "Absolutely not."

"Then why are you here?" I echo my question from earlier.

"Because, I think you should know that Bennett didn't do this."

I try not to roll my eyes, but it's a serious effort. "But the proof—"

"Is false, just like the steroids."

I shake my head. "Yeah, I thought he was telling the truth about the steroids too, but now I think that was just a lie. I think his coach has been innocent in this whole thing and Bennett's blaming his screw-ups on the poor man."

Sabrina shakes her head. "Is that what you *really* think?"

"Yes," I say, but my voice wobbles.

"Bennett is a lot of things," Sabrina says solemnly, "and I know he doesn't have the best track record, but he's a good guy and he loves you. He's heartbroken about this, and let me tell you: I've never seen my brother torn up over a woman the way he is with you."

"He hasn't come to see me," I admit softly.

"Would you have spoken to him if he had?" she counters with a raised brow.

"Well, no," I admit.

"Exactly." She gives me a small smile. "You can believe what you want, Grace, but trust me when I say he's doing everything he can to prove his innocence." She stands and opens the door, but pauses before leaving. She levels a look at me over her shoulder. "I just hope by the time he does it isn't too late to fix things."

CHAPTER THIRTY-FOUR

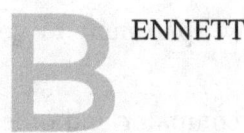ENNETT

I FEEL LIKE I'M ON *AMERICA'S MOST WANTED* AND everyone in the whole fucking United States is hunting me down. I haven't left my apartment in six days and the paparazzi are still camped outside my house. The fucking vultures. I'm tempted to throw water balloons on them but

I'm pretty sure that would make everyone hate me even more. My social media accounts have been going off non-stop with notifications, most of them from people calling me names. They're favorite name seems to be *pig*.

I'm honestly amazed by how many people will rally together to *tear* someone apart but so few build each other up.

People love drama, even if they say they don't.

I tap my fingers against the kitchen counter.

A plan. I need a plan.

My life has imploded before my eyes and I'm not going to sit idly by while the last remnants of it fly away.

A key in the door rattles, and a moment later, Sabrina steps into my apartment.

"Hey," I greet her with a half-hearted wave.

She closes and locks the door behind her and holds out a to-go bag from my favorite Chinese restaurant.

"Eat, you're losing too much weight," she scolds.

"It's not my fault I can't leave my apartment to get groceries."

She rolls her eyes. "Then use your computer and order them, Bennie."

"You can do that?" I ask, setting the bag down on the counter and pulling out the boxes.

She sets her purse down and pulls out one of the barstools. "Yes, of course. God, you're such a guy."

I grin and open one of the boxes. "Mmm, my favorite. You're the best, Bina."

"Yeah, yeah," she chimes. "You owe me, yada-yada-yada."

I chuckle and dump the serving of chicken on a plate, add noodles, and an egg roll.

Enlisting my journalist sister to help me is probably the best decision I've ever made. If there's a loose end she'll sniff it out. My parents want to help in any way they can but there's nothing for them to do. They want to be here with me in the city too, but I insisted on them staying home. The media would hound them to death here, and after my dad's stroke he doesn't need that kind of stress. I don't worry about Sabrina. She can hold her own against the vultures.

"Have you found out anything?" I ask, taking a large bite of egg roll.

"Not yet," she admits with a defeated sigh. "Give me time."

"Time," I repeat. "I don't have much left of it."

"I know," she says sadly. "I know."

CHAPTER THIRTY-FIVE

G RACE

"That's it. We're going out," Elle announces, bouncing up from her bed.

I frown from mine. "I don't want to go anywhere."

"Nuh-huh." She shakes her head. "You don't get to decide. You've been moping around for a *month* solid, and I won't stand for it any longer. You've wallowed enough. We're going out. Makenna and Celine will come too. I'll even ask Ryland if he wants to tag along as our unofficial bodyguard."

I swallow past the lump in my throat. "I doubt I'll be much fun."

"I don't care." She puts her hands on her hips. "All I want is to see you leave this god-forsaken campus and do *something*."

I can't blame her. All I've done since returning from break is go to class and come back to the dorm. I haven't even wanted coffee—and definitely not cupcakes—because it reminded me too much of Bennett.

I miss him. I miss him so much. I've picked up my phone to call him more times than I care to admit but I always set my phone back down when I think about that girl he might've raped. My heart tells me he would never do that, I *know* him, but the evidence is there and I feel wrong to support him if it's true.

Even with all that I still love him. I can't turn my feelings off like a switch. I wish I could. It would make things so much easier.

"What do you have in mind?" I place the magazine I was reading on my bed.

"A club." She grins wickedly and runs to her closet. "A sexy dress and dancing *has* to make you feel better."

I suppress my groan. I doubt either of those things will make me feel better, but I don't want to burst Elle's bubble.

She's been really sweet and there for me through this whole thing. She even confessed that she feels guilty being so happy with Ryland while I'm miserable. I told her that was silly but it still didn't erase the worry from her eyes.

Elle rifles through her closet and tosses me a black garment. I hold the dress up and my eyes widen. It's not the most scandalous thing she could've given me but it has several sections cut out with mesh, making it a lot sexier than it otherwise would be. The skirt flares out at the hips and ends above the knee area.

"Put that on," she orders. "I'm going to let Makenna and Celine know what we're up to."

I nod, feeling rather guilty at the mention of their names. They've tried to come around me in the last month and I've blown them off, afraid that they were like everyone else and only wanted to know what really happened—if the allegations are true.

I set the dress on my bed and go to work on my hair and makeup.

Elle returns and does the same.

I straighten my hair and twist it back into a slick ponytail and then do my makeup heavier than normal with lots of blacks and gray. On my lips I even use a daring black lipstick. It's definitely not my go-to style but I figure I might as well be daring and different.

Elle groans from her side of the room. "Will you help me? I'm not good at this kind of thing." She drags a brush through her hair, butchering the strands.

I run to the other side of the room and stop her. "For starters, don't do that." I take the brush from her hand and set it aside. "What did you have in mind?" I ask her, fluffing her hair around her shoulders.

She shrugs. "Could you curl it like you normally wear yours? I know my hair is naturally curly, but it's not sleek and pretty like when you curl it."

"Yeah, absolutely, I can do that." It doesn't take me long to do her hair and then she asks me to do her makeup too. I don't think she *really* wants me to do it, but she knows it'll make me feel better—*distract me*—to do it.

Once her hair and makeup is done, we both change into our dresses.

I whistle at hers. "Ryland is going to lose his mind," I tell her honestly.

She wears a long-sleeve, gray, crop-top with zig-zag cut-outs in the chest and a high-waisted pencil skirt in the same material. Only a small amount of her midriff shows, but it's enticing and sexy. Poor Ryland will have to shove the guys away from her.

She smiles at me. "You think so?"

"Yeah, of course. You're gorgeous."

Something I've learned about Elle is that she's not used to being called beautiful. I can't help but wonder what kind of home she grew up in, and if that's why she was so nasty to me when we first met. But I never ask her about it. I figure if she wants to talk about it, she will.

"You look hot too." She motions to my borrowed dress.

"Thanks." I grab a clutch and stuff my phone, ID, and some cash in it. "Let's get out of here."

She grins wickedly. "I thought you'd never say so. Let's get into some trouble."

Ryland gets suckered into being our DD so he drives the four of us to the club in his car—which is a hell of a lot nicer than Celine's.

Celine, Makenna, and I end up squished in the backseat, and by the time we make it to the club, we can't wait to get out.

Emerald is spelled out across the side of the building in an elegant script font, lit up in the same shade of green as its namesake.

As soon as the car is parked, the three of us tumble out and then spend a minute righting our dresses.

Makenna tugs on the top of hers and then nods her head appraisingly at everyone.

"We look hot as fuck," she states.

She looks killer in her dress and I find myself envious of her perky breasts. Mine seem so small in comparison.

She loops her arm through mine and says, "Let's go find you a man, Grace. Once you fuck a hot stranger you'll feel loads better."

I snort as we head toward the line. "Are you speaking from experience?"

"Of course." She giggles and flips her long hair over one shoulder.

We get in line—unlike my experience with Bennett—and slowly make our way toward the front.

The bouncer takes one look at us in our skimpy dresses and lets us in.

"Ladies, try not to get into too much trouble," Ryland warns as we make our way through the labyrinth of the club. "There's only one of me and four of you."

Celine cackles. "You worry too much, Ryland. I'm getting a drink, who's with me?"

"I am." I raise my hand like I'm in elementary school. I don't normally drink, but tonight calls for alcohol and lots of it.

Celine grabs my raised hand and starts pulling me through the club. Makenna follows and we stride up to the bar.

Celine leans across the bar top and signals the bartender. As soon as he notices her he makes his way over to us with an eager smile.

"What can I help you with today ladies?" He flips a lock of shaggy brown hair from his eyes.

Celine nods her head in my direction. "We're out celebrating my friend's new single status—and we want to get drunk. Give us your special."

He chuckles and steps back. "You got it."

I turn away from the bar and admire the club. It's nice,

surprisingly nice considering the college crowd, and the music is good so that's always a plus.

"See any contenders?" Makenna asks, raising her voice to be heard above the noise.

I shake my head. I'm not opposed to finding a guy to dance with, but I'm not looking for one to take me home.

She eyes me and says, "Don't make me choose one for you."

Luckily, I'm saved from saying anything thanks to the arrival of our drinks.

I take it from the bartender and slurp it down. I don't think it's the kind of drink you're meant to chug, but I *need* to get buzzed. I need to get out of my head and stop thinking so much. I lift my empty glass, signaling another, and slap some bills down on the bar.

"Damn, girl," Celina comments, sipping on her drink. "You're on a roll."

The bartender makes my second drink and I drink it just as fast.

I can feel myself growing more relaxed. "I'm going to dance," I announce.

I don't wait for either girl to respond before I slip into the crowd.

Now to find someone to dance *with*.

I scour the crowd, looking for a guy to dance with that doesn't look like a complete creep.

I startle when I see someone I recognize. He's dancing

with another girl, but the alcohol makes me braver than normal.

"Mind if I interrupt?" I put on my most flirtatious smile and bat my eyes.

Tanner's eyes slide toward me and he nods approvingly. "Not at all."

The girl protests feebly as he leaves her and comes to my side.

I haven't talked to Tanner much—I was embarrassed by falling on him that first day, and then when Bennett mentioned that Tanner was talking about the incident, talking about *me*, well, I decided to stay away. But I haven't been able to ignore the way he looks at me and now, tonight, he's the exact right person I need. I don't plan on taking this any further than dancing, but *he* doesn't know that, and I want to feel desired. I know Tanner will do that.

His blond hair is slightly damp with sweat, like he's been here for a while, and hangs limply in his eyes. He has a sculpted face and a nice smile, but he's not Bennett. He never has been. Maybe, if I hadn't met Bennett before Tanner, I might've actually liked the guy, but I can't bring myself to feel anything toward him.

"I'm surprised to see you here." He wraps his hands around my waist and turns my back against the front of his body. He moves to the beat of the song and my hips begin to move on their own.

I lean my head against his shoulder. "I needed to get out."

"I'd say I'm sorry about you and Bennett but I'm not," he whispers in my ear. "The guy's an asshole."

I bristle at that but try to keep the bite from my tone. "No, he's not."

He chuckles. "You obviously don't know him as well as you thought. The guy is a rapist."

I flinch at that. I don't want to believe it. I want to think that Sabrina was right—that this is just another set up, but frankly I'm confused and don't know what to believe. Everything feels like a lie.

I move to the song, trying to drown out Tanner's words, but they echo through my skull like a pinball.

I finally wrench myself from his arms and shake my head. "I'm sorry," I say, not meeting his eyes. "I can't do this. I have to go."

I push my way through the crowd and back to the bar, where I order another drink. I down it as fast as I did the others and then go in search of Ryland and Elle.

I find them on the dance floor and I yell above the noise. "I'm leaving. I'll call a cab. You guys keep having fun."

"What?" Elle's face falls. "No, you can't go. Tonight is all about you."

Tears sting my eyes. "I *can't*," my voice cracks. "I'm sorry, but I can't do this."

"Grace," she says softly, almost worriedly, and reaches for my arm.

I move out of the way and leave before she can stop me.

My cab arrives quickly and I'm relieved to get out of there.

I stare at my reflection in the glass window and I wish I could un-see the tears on my cheeks, but they're there, the physical presence of the scar on my heart.

CHAPTER THIRTY-SIX

BENNETT

"Hey, Michael." I greet the player with a handshake. I'm shocked he wanted to come all the way to Boston to see me. I figured all the college players were laughing it up that I'd finally completely fucked myself over this time.

"Hey," he says with an easy smile. "Nice place."

"Thanks." I close the door behind him. "I was surprised to hear from you," I admit. "Do you want anything to drink?" I point my thumb over my shoulder to the refrigerator.

"Nah." He shakes his head and sits on the couch. "I wanted to see you."

"Why?" I can't stop myself from asking.

He shrugs. "Call me crazy, but I don't think you did this."

I breathe out a breath I didn't know I was holding. It feels so fucking good to hear someone that's *not* family say they believe me.

"I didn't," I tell him, in case he needs to hear the words straight from me. "I've fucked a lot of women, I won't deny that, but I never touched her."

He nods like that's enough for him. "Coach doesn't think you did it, either. He yells at anyone that says anything bad about you." I smile at that. "He sent me to help you."

I snort. "Help me? I don't think anyone can do anything to help me." At this point the only person that can help me is myself and my sister—and we're working on it, day by day. I just wish it wasn't taking so fucking long.

Michael shrugs and raises his hands innocently. "Hey, I'll do what I can to help."

"Has Coach talked to Matthews?" I ask.

Michael shakes his head. "Don't think so. If he did, I

think he'd try to kill the bastard." Michael clears his throat and sobers. "I know you're getting a lot of hate right now." Understatement of the century, considering I can't leave my house without having things thrown at me and being called names. "But there are still people out there that believe in you."

I sigh and pinch the bridge of my nose.

"Bennett ..." Sabrina says softly, appearing from the guestroom. She's been staying here and working from her laptop, while also helping me in any way she can. She's a fucking saint and the best sister anyone could ask for. "Have you seen this?"

My brows furrow together. "What are you talking about?"

"Never mind." She starts to disappear back down the hall but I *know* something is up. Matthews has probably come out saying his daughter's pregnant now with my demon offspring and it's going to eat its way out of her vagina and kill her—*anything* to make people feel sorrier for him.

I jump up and hop over the back of her couch, stealing her phone from her hand.

"Hey," she protests weakly, trying to grab it.

It's too late, though. I've already seen and it's like someone stabbed a knife in my heart and twisted it. It's picture of Grace at some club and she's dancing with that douchebag Tanner.

I think I've finally found someone I hate more than Coach Matthews.

I lift the phone, ready slam it in the wall but Sabrina grabs it from my hand. "Don't even think about it," she warns. "That's *my* phone." She holds tightly to the phone in case there's any chance of me swiping it and breaking it out of spite. "There's more," she says even softer than before.

"What?" I bite out, thinking she's going to give me more bad news about Grace. My thoughts are running rampant, imagining her fucking Tanner in a closet in the club.

"Greg Paulson agreed to meet with us." All the air whooshes out of my lungs. Greg Paulson, the team captain for the Hunters, and the player I caught Matthews giving steroids to. If he has a bone to pick with Matthews the way I do then maybe, just maybe, we can take the asshat down once and for all.

"When?" I ask, daring to hope for the first time in over a month.

"Tomorrow."

I breathe out. Soon. This could all be over in the next week.

Sabrina heads back to her room, probably to do research, and Michael whistles.

"Damn, who was that? She's hot."

I stride over to the couch and smack the back of his head. "My sister."

"Fuck," he says.

"Yeah, fuck," I agree. Sitting down beside him. "I have

another guestroom. You wanna stay?" I ask him. "You can go with Bina and me to talk to Paulson."

He grins. "Sure. I'm in. Just let me know what you need me to do." He glances down the hall and I narrow my eyes on him.

"Don't even think about it," I warn.

He chuckles. "Sorry. She's hot."

"Don't make me regret letting you help," I warn him.

He chuckles. "I'll be on my best behavior."

I don't believe him, not for one second, but I can't bring myself to be bothered because he cares enough about me to be here. I've never really had friends before, but maybe now I do.

CHAPTER THIRTY-SEVEN

GRACE

IT'S BEEN THREE DAYS SINCE THE CLUB AND I CAN'T get the sticky feeling of Tanner's hands off my body. It doesn't help that there's a photo floating around of us dancing. A photo that makes it look like I was enjoying it. Ugh.

The media really knows how to skew things to make them look different than they really are.

I sit in front of my computer, *trying* to work on my paper. Trying being the keyword there. I can't seem to bring myself to care, which is bad. The last thing I need is my grades to slip because of my personal life. My parents would give me no choice on staying then and haul my ass back home.

Elle comes busting into the dorm, out of breath and red-faced.

"What happened to you?" I ask, checking her over to make sure she's not hurt.

"You have to see this." She shoves her phone at me and I take it. "Play the video," she orders and bends to clutch her knees, trying to get enough air.

"Are you okay?" I ask her.

"Fine." She waves a dismissive hand. "I just ran all the way across campus to show that to you and I'm now reminded that I'm extremely out of shape." She clutches at a stitch in her side.

"You realize you could've texted me, right?"

Her mouth falls open. "Oh. I forgot. Just play the damn video."

I shake my head, still watching her out of the corner of my eye since I'm afraid she's about to collapse, and then press play.

Bennett and another player come onto the screen and sit

behind a table. It looks like they're holding some sort of press conference.

I hold my breath and wait for them to speak.

The other player speaks first.

"I'm sure you're all shocked to see the two of us together, but we decided it was time for the truth to come out. The truth about Coach Matthews. You all see him as a legend and an amazing coach, but that's not who he really is. He's a liar and a cheater. As his star player, he forced me to use steroids to be even better. You're probably wondering how exactly he *forced* me—let's just say blackmail was involved and it involved *my* daughter. This man threatened my two-year-old daughter and I felt I had no choice but to do it. Coach Matthews is a well-respected man, and he knew how to cover his tracks, so no one would've believed me if I told." He pauses and takes a drink of water from the bottle on the table. "Until this guy accidently walked in on Matthews giving me the steroids. He didn't know what he'd walked in on, what *exactly* was happening, but Coach Matthews began messing with him too. You're probably thinking about his injury, but that was entirely an accident. But the steroid and rape allegations are all from Coach Matthews himself. He's trying to get rid of Bennett—keep him from ever playing hockey again—to save his own ass. I'm appealing to all players out there, if you've ever played for Coach Matthews and he's blackmailed you too, come forward. You're not alone. The man's a monster, and monsters need to be put down." He nods to Bennett for him to speak.

Bennett clears his throat. "I know I don't have the best track record and haven't always done the best thing, but I met someone who made me want to be better. For her and for me. In the last six weeks, I've watched my life spiral out of control and there was nothing I could do. No one believed me. It was my word against Matthews and his daughter's, and who's going to believe the guy that used to fuck everyone?" He shrugs sadly. "I understand why no one believed me, I really do, but innocent until proven guilty is nothing but a lie. I've been made to feel like the dirtiest of scum for something I didn't do." He takes a deep breath and spreads his fingers out on the table. I feel tears prick my eyes. *My Bennett.* "I don't hate anyone for treating me the way they did. Rapists should get more shit than they do, but I'm not one of them. To Matthews' daughter, I want to say I'm so sorry. I'm so sorry your father used you in a vendetta against me. That's not something a father should ever do." He licks his lips nervously. "I don't know where things will go from here. Whether anyone will believe us, but everything we've told you is the truth. Look into Matthews. He's dirty, and I'm sure you'll find proof of something he's done because I guarantee you this is the least of it." He flicks a finger between him and the other guy. "All I've ever wanted to do is play hockey and I hope that dream isn't crushed."

The video ends and a sob wracks through my body.

I read the attached article and see that in the hours

following the press conference, a journalist came forward with enough information to condemn Coach Matthews for multiple counts including slander, blackmail, distributing drugs to athletes, and even money laundering. Even though it doesn't say who the journalist was, my gut says it was Sabrina. She'd do anything for her brother and I'm sure she's been pouring all her time and energy into clearing his name. She's a better person than I am. I just abandoned him.

"I can't believe I ever thought he did it. Even for one second." I rub away the tears sticking to my face.

Elle comes and puts her arms around me. "Hey, with the information we were given, it was impossible not to believe it."

I shake my head and choke on a sob. "But I *know* him and he's a good person. I should've known he wouldn't do it." I hiccup. "I feel horrible. I should've defended him. Done *something*—like hire a PI to look into his coach. I just sat back and believed what was in front of me and deluded myself into believing everything he told me was a lie." I groan into my hands, incredibly frustrated with myself. "He probably hates me," I mumble. "And I can't even blame him."

Elle gives me a sympathetic look. "I'm sure he doesn't hate you."

"If he doesn't, then he's a better person than I am, because I would hate me." I breathe out, trying to calm the shakiness in my body. I feel untethered to the world around me, like I'm a balloon on a string about to blow away.

"What are you going to do?" Elle asks. "Are you going to go to him?"

"I don't know." I shake my head. "I want to, but what if he doesn't want to see me?"

She rolls her eyes. "Please, for the love of God, don't be one of those girls who sits back and doesn't go after what she wants because she's afraid of rejection. Just do the damn thing."

I don't know how I can laugh with how shitty I feel, but I do. "I have to make this good, though. He's been through hell and he deserves an epic apology."

She grins wickedly. "Damn straight he does.

CHAPTER THIRTY-EIGHT

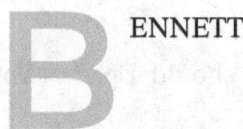ENNETT

Watching Matthews get carted away in handcuffs might be one of the greatest things I've ever seen. He yelled obscenities at everyone and even spit on one officer. I'm pretty sure I saw that officer give him a right good shove in the gut when he was getting in the car.

This feels like the best kind of retribution since only weeks before, *I* was being arrested for a crime I didn't commit.

Now, I change into my gear, about to play my first game of the season. I should've been here long ago, but I'm not going to dwell on the past. All that matters is that I'm here now, with a new coach and a team that is now banded together in a way we never were before.

Three more current players came forward after Paulson and I spoke out. Five others that played for Matthews previously also came out with grievances against him.

I wish now I would've done something sooner—*believed* in myself—but I can't undo the past and the only thing I *can* do is learn from it.

My sister ... Fuck. I owe her everything. She dug and dug and dug until she got enough proof that there'd be no doubt that Paulson and I were telling the truth once we went public. She gave Matthews no way to slander us further. I owe her everything.

Paulson claps his hand down on my shoulder pads. "You ready, James? This is your big day."

My chance to redeem myself.

"Yeah." I nod. "I'm ready."

I've learned that Greg Paulson is a decent fucking guy. Fuck, a lot of the players I never got along with before are great now. I'm learning that Matthews hatred had seeped down into all of us. A team is meant to be a family and we weren't. I think we're getting there now, though. It's just going to take more time. Something I have plenty of now that I'm not worried about losing my contract. As long as I play well until the end of the season I know I'll get a renewed contract and I have no doubts that I'm going to kick some ass. It's been too long.

Our new coach—Coach Thompson—stands on a chair and yells above the chaos to be heard. When the room quiets he finally speaks.

"I don't have much to say, but what I do have to say is important so listen up. This is our first game together, let's make each other proud." He claps his hands together and jumps from the chair.

Paulson stands beside me and nudges my shoulder with his and our pads clink together. "Let's show them what we're made of."

EVEN THE FRIGID AIR FROM THE ICE ISN'T ENOUGH to cool me down. I'm on fire and my body drips with sweat by the second period. My parents, sister, Michael, and Coach Harrison sit front and center in the stands cheering me on. It feels good to know I have a solid support system. But there is one important person missing.

Grace.

I've picked up my phone a hundred times to call her—not to mention all the times I've gotten behind the wheel of my car to go see her—but I don't know what to say. Things ended so suddenly and awkwardly between us.

All the practices with Coach Thompson haven't helped matters, either. He's been working us hard, wanting to get us into better shape and get used to his coaching style. Suffice it to say, I've been exhausted every evening when I've gotten home. It's all been worth it, though, and I know that tomorrow I'll finally figure out what to say to her. I have the whole day off so going to campus shouldn't be a big deal. I just want her back. I want her to forgive me. I understand that she might not. Even though the rape allegations were nothing but a lie, it still hurt her and she might have decided I'm not worth that kind of pain.

Paulson slings the puck into the goal and the buzzer sounds. Another point for us. The period ends and we start down the tunnel.

I'm sweaty, and tired, but riding the biggest adrenaline high of my life. We're playing like champions tonight and I think, if we keep this up, that we might make it to the finals. Maybe it's a long shot, but I'm allowed to hope.

Our break ends and we're back out on the ice.

I get in my position and focus on the opposing player I want to take out and that's when a fucking Sour Patch Kid lands in front of my skate.

I stare at it, wondering how the fuck it got there, when another one drops a few feet away.

"What the hell?" another player mutters.

My gaze is drawn to the stadium stairs to my right and that's when I see her.

"Grace," I breathe, and her name comes out sounding muffled around my mouth guard.

I don't give a fuck that we're in the middle of a game, I skate over to the bench and climb over the wall. I spit out my mouth-guard and drop my helmet on the floor along with my hockey stick before climbing to the other side to the hall. Grace saw where I was going and stands above me, the black rails keep her away from me.

"What are you doing here?" I ask.

The whole arena is silent, watching us with surprise and maybe a little fascination.

She shrugs with a wry smile. "Getting my man back."

I throw my head back and laugh. "Is that what I am? *Your man?*"

She rests her arms on the rail and leans over. Her hair tumbles over her shoulder and fuck she's the most gorgeous woman I've ever seen.

"I mean, only if you want to be. Before you say no, though, I have a list of reasons why you should say yes."

I cross my arms over my chest and fight a grin. "Is that so, Princess? What are they?"

"Number one, I'll always bring you Sour Patch Kids even if I think they're the grossest thing ever." I laugh at this. "Two," she ticks it off on her finger, "I'll learn to ice skate and maybe even learn to play hockey." I press my lips together, staving off my smile. "Three, I'll always tell you when you're wrong—which you are, a lot." I shake my head. "Four, when you start to get to cocky, I'll bring you back down to Earth." She winks, and fuck it if my stomach doesn't do a little flip because dammit that's the sexiest thing I've ever seen. "And five, I love you and that's reason enough."

"Fuck yes it is."

She bends down as far as she can and I kiss her. I kiss her with everything I have in me. All the love, and hurt, and anguish I've felt is poured into that kiss as everyone in the stadium cheers.

Grace smiles down at me and I think to myself; *Fuck, this is my girl.*

I finally got the girl.

I finally got it *all*.

EPILOGUE

Grace

I SLIDE THE ZIPPER CLOSED ON MY LAST BAG.

I made it through a whole year of college and I didn't die, so yay for small miracles.

"I'm going to miss you so much." Elle tackle hugs me.

I laugh and balance myself so we don't fall. "I'm sure I'll

see you before next year."

"But not every day." She pulls away and frowns. "I was so wrong about you when I first met you and I'm sorry for that. You've taught me not to judge a book by its cover."

"Stop saying nice things," I scold her. "You're going to make me cry and this mascara is too expensive to ruin."

She busts out laughing.

A knock raps against our open door and I look behind me to see Bennett standing there with coffees and cupcakes.

"I figured since it's your last day, you both deserved a treat."

The last few months have been beyond amazing with Bennett. We've spent as much time together as we could, but it's been hard with school and his schedule. We've made it work, though, and we're happy, so that's what matters. Even though what happened to us sucked, I think it ultimately made us stronger. I hate that I ever doubted him for one second. I know it wasn't my fault—I mean, with the evidence presented in front of me, there was only one way for me to think—but I *know* Bennett. I know his heart and soul and those things count more than anything else.

"Thank you." I smile at him.

"Thanks, Bennett." Elle takes a coffee. "Well—" she turns to me "—I have to get to the airport before I miss my flight."

Emotion tugs at my heart. "I'm going to miss you." I hug her again. "Call, text, send a carrier pigeon—just don't lose touch."

"I won't," she promises and picks up her bag. "Ryland's outside waiting."

"Tell him goodbye from me, please?" I ask her.

She nods. "I will."

As soon as she's gone, Bennett picks me up and tosses me on the bed before jumping on beside me. My laughter fills the air as we bounce up and down.

He props his head on his hand and gazes down at me, tracing his fingers lazily over my bare stomach where my shirt has ridden up.

"Are you *sure* you want to live with me?"

When he asked me to move in with him for the summer, I was ecstatic. The thought of going home and being away from him for all that time *sucked*. My parents weren't thrilled with the idea, but they didn't hate Bennett—they were just struggling with letting go.

I bite my lip but my laughter still escapes. "Yes."

"Even if I snore?"

"If you snore, I'll just smother you with a pillow." I shrug.

His laughter booms and I grin.

This is *us*.

We smile.

We laugh.

We fight.

We make up.

But most importantly we always love.

Because love … it's everything.

ACKNOWLEDGMENTS

I can't believe we're here again. The end of another book. Thank you so much to everyone who made this happen.

Regina Wamba, you have once again rocked another cover. I can't handle the cuteness.

Mackenzy and Jeff, thank you so much for bringing Bennett and Grace alive.

Thank you to my beta readers, Haley, Raquel, Genesis, Stefanie, and Becca for helping shape The Game That Breaks Us into the book that is. I value all of your opinions so much.

Wendi, you rock my socks off.

To the girls and guys in my Micalea's Minions group, I love you all so much. You have no idea. Whenever I go into my group I feel like I'm heading into my safe place where I get to hang out with my best friends.

Regina Bartley, you are such a huge part of every book I write. I don't know what I'd do without you. Probably die of boredom.

To my family, I don't say it enough, but thank you. Thank you for believing in my dreams when at times I didn't. Because you I am where I'm at and I'll always be thankful for that.

And to my readers, without you I couldn't do this. Whether you've been here from my very first book or you're just discovering me with this one, I love you very much.

www.ingramcontent.com/pod-product-compliance
Lightning Source LLC
LaVergne TN
LVHW031608060526
838201LV00065B/4777